Further Praise for *The*

"*The Emissary* is a uniquely exciting adventu.
soul of the reader."

— Beau Bridges

"I am a giant fan of creativity that takes us out of our daily thinking. Patricia Cori has penned just such a tale. A broad fantasy adventure that speaks to those who want to think differently and challenge the daily onslaught against nature and our own future."

— Pen Densham, Oscar-nominated screenwriter, director, producer, author, and artist

"Simply Brilliant!"

— Tanya Roberts, actor and animal activist

"Best-selling author Patricia Cori has found a profound and captivating way to wake us up to the necessity of honoring Nature's life in the seas. There is a direct correlation between the creatures of the deep and us as human beings. The creatures of the deep are our sacred teachers; they show us that in order to transform where we are we must be willing to go to the depths of ourselves. They not only model this necessity—they are crying for it. Our lives as well as theirs are counting on us to answer. Thank you, Patricia, for reaching out and making the first call with *The Emissary*."

— Temple Hayes, spiritual leader, author, and founder of Life Rights

"The whales and dolphins of this planet need our help—and Patricia Cori is their Emissary!"

— Elisabeth Röhm, actor, author, activist, and mother

"Phenomenal! Her extraordinary vision and the way she communicates her truth to her readers will make Patricia Cori a staple in every library."

— Donald Newsom, president, BBS Radio Network, Inc.

"Patricia Cori has done a great service to us all, and I believe the majestic creatures of the sea as well, by turning her skill, passion, and intelligence toward understanding and protecting them, and simultaneously illuminating a path for human transformation."

— *New Consciousness Review*

THE EMISSARY

PATRICIA CORI

North Atlantic Books
Berkeley, California

Published by
North Atlantic Books
P.O. Box 12327
Berkeley, California 94712

Cover art by Malcolm Horton, malcolmhorton.co.uk
Cover and book design by Brad Greene
Printed in the United States of America

The Emissary is sponsored by the Society for the Study of Native Arts and Sciences, a nonprofit educational corporation whose goals are to develop an educational and cross-cultural perspective linking various scientific, social, and artistic fields; to nurture a holistic view of arts, sciences, humanities, and healing; and to publish and distribute literature on the relationship of mind, body, and nature.

North Atlantic Books' publications are available through most bookstores. For further information, visit our website at www.northatlanticbooks.com or call 800-733-3000.

Library of Congress Cataloging-in-Publication Data

Cori, Patricia.
   The emissary / Patricia Cori.
      pages cm
   Summary: "This powerful and captivating novel will appeal to readers who enjoy fantasy, science fiction, adventure, and the supernatural as well as those who believe in the afterlife, animal communication, and saving the whales and other endangered species from extinction"— Provided by publisher.
   ISBN 978-1-58394-706-7
   1. Missionaries—Fiction. 2. Psychics—Fiction. 3. Telepathy—Fiction. I. Title.
   PS3603.O736E45 2013
   813'.6—dc23
                                                                    2013013612

1 2 3 4 5 6 7 8 9   VERSA   19 18 17 16 15 14
Printed on recycled paper

To Chicca, my beloved four-legged companion
who just crossed over the rainbow bridge,
another bright star in the heavens

Acknowledgments

So many people help an author find the creative space to work in, like an understanding partner who misses a lot of nights out and special dinners, or a friend who provides encouragement and love—even a faithful dog who sits patiently on her pillow, knowing food follows the inspired moments! I am blessed to have some wonderful people and animal companions holding that space for me, and I thank you all for your patience and understanding when I'm typing away into the wee hours of the morning, in the magic of the creative process.

Many editions later, I still celebrate the bond I enjoy with all the people at North Atlantic Books, who have continued to support me with almost blind faith over the years. The team changes a bit as time moves us all forward, but the commitment remains steadfast. Special thanks to Richard Grossinger, who knows how the stars shine; to Doug Reil, for his commitment to the Earth and for the support he has shown me over the years; to Janet Levin, who believed in *The Emissary* from its beginnings and has stood behind me all the way.

Much gratitude to my crackerjack editor, Emily Boyd, who really knows how to put things together and does so with great eloquence; and to my dedicated copy editor, Adrienne Armstrong, for perfecting the words, never losing the voice. There are many others behind the scenes at North Atlantic Books, so please feel my gratitude for all you do to guide my books out to the world.

I'm excited to be working with my new publicist, Dea Shandera, a true visionary, and with acclaimed film producer Dan Sherkow, who is determined to bring *The Emissary* to the big screen. Thank you, Vitaly Safarov, for opening those doors with your undying enthusiasm, inspiration, and loyalty through this process. Thanks, too, to Captain Graeme Stoner, for telling me how ships work.

Oh! To the mighty whales and gracious dolphins, you are my inspiration, my hope, and the dream of the Earth.

And last but never least—to my beautiful mother, Sara, who speaks to me from beyond the veil; to Franco, my beloved soul mate; to Bobbo, for his ongoing feedback; to my family of four-legged beings who love and have loved unconditionally; and to the light beings who guide my path, through this lifetime... and no doubt, many others.

Contents

1

Earth Under Siege

Nathan Beals punched out from work at precisely 6:00 p.m., smack in the middle of Los Angeles rush hour. After the most ballistic holiday shopping mania he had ever seen in his twenty-odd years working security at the mall, he finally had an entire weekend off.

Exhausted, he dragged himself out to the employee parking lot, only to find that his faithful old Chevy sedan, "Miss Jezebel," had been vandalized. The side mirror was smashed up against the window, and glass covered the asphalt—shattered reflections of what Nathan always referred to as "the broken society." Examining the few remaining splinters wedged inside the frame, he could see it was no accident, and that someone had whacked the mirror deliberately— another anonymous punk with a baseball bat in his fists and a big, huge chip on his shoulder. He checked the passenger's side and, sure enough, the attacker had also keyed three feet of the front fender and both doors: through the paint—right down to the steel.

"Aw-w-w man!" he shouted, though no one was there to hear. "Look at this, now!" Nathan ran his fingers over the unforgiving scar on Jezebel's smooth, clean body, feeling the pain of it just as sharply as if it had been carved into his own flesh. "It never ends," he said, shaking his head. "Good god almighty, it just never, ever ends."

A senior guard for so many years at the mall, he thought he'd seen just about everything—shoplifters, gangbangers, lost kids, vandals, stalkers—but never had he experienced anything like what he'd lived through the last year. This was the year of years in bizarre world and he could feel the tension rising, as if the whole planet were in a giant pressure cooker that was just about to blow its lid off, along with the whole human race, right out of Earth's orbit.

He clutched his phone from his shirt pocket and dialed the first three numbers of the local police station—he certainly knew everybody there—but then, he thought it over for a moment, and hung up. With everything that was going on out there, on the streets of Los Angeles, they weren't about to investigate petty vandalism—not even as a favor to him. And of course he wasn't insured for anything like this anyway—so, what was the point?

Nathan grabbed a plastic bag out of the trunk and carefully picked up the shards of glass, piece by piece, so that he could discard them somewhere safer, far away from the mall, before anyone else got the idea to do any more damage with them . . . and just maybe sparing someone a flat tire. Shaking his head in frustration, he wondered if this malicious little gift might be payback for having intervened in a brawl earlier that day, knowing it was unlikely and that it was probably just him being overly paranoid—but thinking it, just the same. Violence, these days, didn't need a reason or a cause. As a security guard with authority, though, he was good enough "reason" for any number of vengeful punks and petty criminals that he had to deal with—every single day.

Nathan always started his mornings with coffee at his favorite café in the mall. But that day, he never even got to taste it. Just as the clerk was handing him his latte, he got called to the south end, where trouble was brewing at Electronics Warehouse. The store clerk who called it in reported that there were two men fighting—he thought they were gangbangers—so Nathan was warned to use extreme caution approaching. When he got there, they were one minute away from killing each other, over what each had claimed as his own territory—the one remaining "super sale" stereo in the store. One pulled a switchblade on the other, and he was about to use it, fired up and ready to kill.

Nathan managed to calm the kid and take the knife away, without him or anyone else getting hurt, preventing what very nearly could have resulted in another in a long list of urban L.A. killings. If security hadn't gotten there in time—if he had stopped to stir a packet of sugar into his coffee—they would for sure have found the boy lying dead in a pool of his own blood... over a fifty-dollar discount on a damned car stereo that probably wasn't even worth twenty bucks in the first place.

Because the situation involved a concealed weapon, Nathan was duty bound to call the incident in to the police immediately, which resulted in the knife-wielding youth being arrested on the spot and taken down to the station in handcuffs, while the other, not-so-innocent delinquent, just as responsible, was let go.

The thought of that kid pulling a knife on the other, for something as trivial as a stereo, was unconscionable to a simple, peace-loving man like Nathan, who grew up in a time when people still talked to each other... when there was still a dialogue going on. Sure, there had always been violence, he didn't deny that, but it was the exception when he was growing up, compared to the new "normal" of today: this constant threat, all the time, everywhere... around every corner. The world was seething now, bubbling over in a cauldron of rage. From the looks of things that he saw come down on a daily basis, in that microcosmic corner of a crazy new world, the Mall, reason was all but gone. The human dialogue was over, and what had replaced it was irrational, unyielding disregard for everyone and everything. It had given way to the animal instinct: take what you want; kill or be killed.

That was how Nathan had come to perceive the world in which he was growing old... and he did not like what he saw.

Was a human life really worth nothing more than fifty bucks to the youth of today? He knew that answer. Kids were killing each other out there for far less than that—even just for the fun of it. And where the hell were these kids' parents, he wondered, dragging them, like a couple of snarling pack dogs, back to the security office, by the scruffs of their necks. Where, for the love of god, were the parents?

Meanwhile, while this drama was unfolding, at the north end, a frantic young mother came running out of Macy's, screaming hysterically, moments after her little girl disappeared, in seconds, from her sight. The security team of more than one hundred guards—in uniform and plainclothed—executed emergency procedures throughout the mall, controlling all the exits, questioning anybody who looked suspicious and everybody with small children. They scrutinized every inch of the stores and the parking grounds via the network of surveillance equipment, but the girl was gone without a trace. Nothing showed up on the monitors; nobody had seen a child fitting her description; not a soul had noticed anything out of the ordinary.

It was as if she had simply evaporated into thin air.

Shoplifting throughout the mall's seventy-eight stores was rampant—security arrested thirty-four people in one day alone, and more than two hundred in a week. Each time they had had to call in the police, and these people were booked, handcuffed, and taken away in squad cars. Why had this national pastime become so predominant in the youth culture of the day? Did they have any idea what it meant to spend even one night in a jail cell? Nathan just couldn't get his mind around what people were thinking anymore; he was admittedly out of step with the times. He didn't understand what motivated the youth, if anything even could, or where society was headed, and he just generally felt out of place and out of touch with the twenty-first century, altogether.

By the end of his shift, he couldn't even feel his feet anymore. His back hurt, his head was throbbing, and it was just adrenaline, he knew, that kept him from collapsing. He wondered if he really could wait out another whole year, until the glory days of retirement—the minute he turned sixty-five. Then, at long last, between Social Security and his pension, he would finally be able to live out his old age with dignity: enjoying the grandkids; going fishing like he used to do; leaving the mall and the world at large to work themselves and all the drama out without him.

He opened the door of his wounded Chevy, placing the bag of splintered glass carefully on the floor in the back, and fell into the driver's seat, so worn out he could barely turn the key. "Take Daddy home, Jezebel," he said out loud, caressing the steering wheel. "Poppa's all out of gas."

Nathan sighed wearily at the thought that on top of his ten-hour workday, he still had to face two hours of stop-and-go traffic before he could finally kick off his shoes and dive onto the sofa, next to an ice-cold beer . . . with nothing he had to do, and nobody he had to think about for the next forty-eight hours. The only thing on his mind was "chilling out," like the rest of America, with the NFL playoffs in his face, pizza in one hand, and beer in the other.

After being trapped in Ventura Highway's infernal freeway gridlock for more than two excruciating hours, he finally reached the exit that led to his neighborhood, where, but for kids playing loudly on the streets and a few barking dogs, life was relatively quiet . . . and still reasonably sane. He'd lived there twenty years. It was a small, tightly knit community, where everyone knew and watched out for each other, and where trouble rarely found its way in: as safe a hamlet as one could find in suburban L.A., where "normal folk" (as he referred to himself and his neighbors) still lived.

He smacked his lips in anticipation of a frothy cold brew, knowing how close he was to being finally able to escape, away from people, into the sanctity of his own four walls.

Turning onto his street, he honked and waved at his neighbor, who was outside watering the lawn. "Yo, Willie boy!" he shouted, rolling down the window. "You have got to have the greenest lawn in the country, dude!"

"Mister Beals!" Will called back, approaching the sidewalk. "How about this heat—in January? Wild, huh?"

Nathan slowed the car to a complete stop in the middle of the street. "We just took down the tinsel at work and it's ninety degrees out here. The world is some kind of upside down, man."

"It is indeed! Are you finally off duty?"

"I am! Not a minute too soon, neither," Nathan answered, wiping the sweat from his brow, with the crisply ironed handkerchief he carried in his shirt pocket.

Will took a long slurp from the water hose. "And you're sure I can't convince you to come over tomorrow? We're throwing some mighty fine lookin' sirloins on the grill!"

"Thanks. You know I'd love to join you guys, but I am too wiped out even for Will's mean-ass barbeque." He didn't have the heart to tell his good friend that the only human activity he wanted to see for the next two days was a bunch of helmets running the ball down the field on his thirty-six-inch screen, and the pizza delivery guy from Guido's knocking at the door.

"The Jets and the Patriots . . . gonna be one hell of a game!"

"I hear that," said Nathan, tempted.

"Thelma and the girls—they'll be going out to spend the day with her mother, so it's just us dudes, plenty of brew . . . barbeque . . . and some kick-ass football, man."

"I thank you, I do," said Nathan, "but I have just got to lay low this weekend. And as tired as this ol' body is right now? I am just as likely to sleep right through the whole thing anyway."

"Hey, man, you know the invite's always open, if you change your mind. After a good night's sleep, I bet you'll be knocking on my door!"

Just as Nathan waved goodbye, his foot about to step back on the gas, two small blackbirds dropped, simultaneously, out of the sky—right in the middle of the street, between the two men. Before either even had a chance to react, hell unleashed its fury. In one terrifying moment, hundreds of red-winged blackbirds plummeted to the ground, all at once, blanketing the pavement, as if something had zapped them right out of the sky. Not one of them moved. No flutter of wings. It appeared they had been hit by a force so fierce it had killed them instantaneously—in flight.

"Damn!" Will shouted, having been pummeled on the head and shoulders several times, as the tiny corpses hailed down from the sky and crashed down around him. He stared out at Nathan, dumbfounded. "What the hell?"

"You get yourself into the house and stay there, until we find out what just happened!"

Will dropped the hose and walked hurriedly back towards the porch, stepping over dead birds everywhere around him. He felt a strange, gripping fear—a sense of foreboding—rising in the back of his throat. As he turned off the faucet, he looked back over his shoulder at Nathan, mystified, before going inside, and then he slammed the door closed and locked it with the dead bolt. Both of them were incredulous, sensing that something sinister—something ominous and unprecedented—was literally coming down all around them.

As in a scene reminiscent of Hitchcock's film *The Birds,* Nathan drove in a slow crawl to the driveway, trying to avoid the fragile little bodies, but there were hundreds, maybe thousands, of dead birds strewn in every direction. They lined the pavement for as far as he could see down the road ahead of him. Their bodies were smashed against the windshield and the hood of the car and, looking through the rearview mirror, he saw the same black blanket of death, covering the street behind him. He cringed as his wheels crunched over each little bump, praying that the little creatures had died instantly, knowing no pain.

As he guided the car slowly onto his driveway, he asked himself if Judgment Day had finally arrived, just like the Reverend had warned them—only days before, in congregation. When the automatic door of his garage opened, he pulled the car in, closed the door back down, and went straight inside, through the kitchen. Once in the house, he threw the dead bolt—knowing that whatever had killed those birds wasn't going to be deterred by locks or closed doors if it wanted in, but somehow it felt like the right thing to do.

In a quiet little resort town in Maine that same day, Judy Levine prepared a nutritious picnic basket for her and the children, after home-teaching them all morning. Outdoors, the whipping wind snapped with the chilling sting of winter, but she had them bundled up in their down jackets and, besides, the rugged beach and the fresh air beckoned. It was a welcome break having lunch outside, at the water's edge—no matter how challenging Maine's winter weather proved to be. Judy always marveled at how invigorating it was to breathe in the crisp sea air and to listen to the roar of waves breaking, mighty and commanding, over the jutting cliffs nearby.

Situated directly in front of their beachfront property was a rocky cove, which served as a natural barrier to the winter winds that rolled over the coast. She and the children called it their "secret fort." There, the kids would entertain themselves for hours, making sculptures in the moist sand, and Judy would kick back and relax, watching the blue water crabs climbing sideways, up and around in rocks of the tide pools: one of Mother Nature's oddities that so enriched the palette of her artistic creation.

Spending time together out by the water was always a great way to break up the tedium of the day's lessons, and it was a vital part of her work with the children, teaching them to honor and always celebrate the wonders of Earth's own garden, while enjoying the magic of play. That day, however, when they stepped out through the backyard gate and approached the shore, she was horrified to discover a strange, silvery patina covering the sand that, on closer inspection, turned out to be an enormous mass of dead fish. Their suffocating bodies littered the entire beachfront, all the way down the coast. She stared in disbelief, gazing as far down the shore as she could, estimating that there were tens of thousands of them, heaped up over each other, their gills expanding and contracting, as they lay dying in the open air.

Whatever had caused this horrific catastrophe had to have struck so suddenly that it still had not been picked up by the local media. No mention was made of it on the morning news that she and her husband had watched at breakfast, only a few hours earlier. There was no stench of death, that putrid odor of rotting fish, in the wind. No, this was fresh—many of them were still alive, so it had to have only just happened. She was quite possibly the first person to discover the disaster: massive and instantaneous—and probably highly toxic.

Panicked, she dropped the basket and grabbed her children, almost dragging them back to the house. Pouting and carrying on, they wanted to stay outside, and they couldn't understand why their mother had done an immediate turnaround. Trying not to frighten them, she rushed the children through the gate and back into the house, closing all the windows and doors, and locking them all inside—until she could find out what dangers lurked outdoors. Who knew what new environmental catastrophe had taken place out off the coast, enough to cause such a massive fish kill? With the way things were going in the world—the poisoning of the skies, the earth, and the sea—she knew anything was possible. She most certainly wasn't going to let the children or herself get any more exposure to whatever had killed those fish than they had already. God only knew what toxin was being released into the air, or what chemical was laced within the ocean's spray, seeping deep into the sand.

Just hours later, halfway around the globe, on the South Island of New Zealand, locals woke up to the horrifying news that fifty humpback whales and more than a hundred bottlenose dolphins had beached themselves during the night. According to the first morning news reports, it was a scene of "devastating proportions." Almost all were dead when the first observers discovered their lifeless bodies, lined up along the beach, like ships thrown out of the sea, in a hurricane. A gruesome, heartbreaking scene, it made no sense at all. Why were such unfathomable numbers of whales and dolphins washing up along the beaches of the world in such catastrophic scenes as these? What was driving them from the deep waters to meet their death on Earth's shores?

Hundreds of animal conservationists and volunteers poured onto the beach to help, but with low tide sucking the waves back out to sea, there was no way to save the immobilized prisoners from their fate. To the despair of those who worked tirelessly throughout the day, the few remaining mammals still alive were dying now, and it was clear that not even a shift in the tide could save them. It was too late. Captives of the scorching summer sands, they struggled to breathe their last breaths, their eyes fixed on the humans who were there for them, in their final hours.

Desperate people worked unrelentingly to free them, but it was all for naught. Slowly, torturously, the mighty whales and their cousins, the dolphin beings, succumbed, leaving an immense void in their passing.

All anyone could do was to try to comfort them.

To be utterly impotent before the mass death of such magnificent beings was to lose a piece of oneself forever. No one present that day would ever be free of that memory. The heartache would linger forever in the deep, deep waters of the subconscious, from where such sadness would ripple and wave, always asking, "What could have been done differently?" Who amongst them could not be struggling to accept the inevitability of such a cruel, tragic death? Such painful memories would never be erased from the hearts and souls of the people who had watched, helpless to alter the course of the events that day, and it was only right that they not be forgotten.

While the determined still scrambled to haul buckets of seawater from the receding tide, a few stopped dead in their tracks, looking up... becoming aware that they were now almost shrouded in an eerie, fog-like haze. It was oddly unnatural, as if low clouds had been scooped up in a gigantic atmospheric vacuum cleaner and then released, adhering to what appeared to be some sort of man-made, perfectly perpendicular matrix. There was a palpable electrical charge to the air so intense that many of the volunteers could feel their hair literally standing on end, and, after a short time, they began suffering from debilitating headaches, nausea, and difficulty breathing. Most of them were well aware that whatever was causing the acute physical symptoms and the stranding and deaths of the whales and dolphins was sourced in that strange electrical grid that hovered, low and menacing, overhead.

No one knew what in the world could be causing it, but they did know, without question, that something highly abnormal had most definitely taken place on that isolated beach off the Southern Coast.

While all three of these bizarre, seemingly unconnected events were unfolding, only a few hours apart at different locations across the planet, from the icy fields of a remote top-security military station in Alaska, a covert network of complex antennae, covering ten city blocks, emitted destructive, extremely low frequency (ELF) energy waves around the Earth, across the oceans, and out into the atmosphere. Free from any kind of scrutiny, the facility buzzed with the sizzling sounds of high-voltage bolts of electrical lightning that shot like crackling whips from tower to tower, surging with enough electrical energy to light up the entire West Coast of the North American continent.

What no one was ready to hear, much less talk about, was that these same ELF energy waves were also being beamed into the cloud layers, and then bounced back down at the secret government's military targets of choice—all around the globe: anywhere and everywhere their evil little hearts desired. Anyone paying the least bit of attention would have recognized that these events—the blackbirds in Los Angeles, the fish carnage in Maine, and the whale and dolphin beaching in New Zealand—were indeed connected, and that the emergency on Planet Earth was about to explode in an all-out and, perhaps, irreversible global disaster.

Unbeknownst to most of its dormant and otherwise distracted inhabitants, one beautiful tiny blue sphere, spinning through the dark cloak of galactic space, was clearly under siege.

2
Jamie Hastings

Among the rescue workers on the beach that terrifying day in New Zealand was a woman whose life was dramatically affected by the unfathomable death of the whales and dolphins. For Jamie Hastings, it was a mystery that would chart the course of the rest of her days, seeking an answer she might never find. Those long hours of their struggle would forever be inscribed on her heart and soul, like a nightmare that haunts from the deep and murky waters of the subconscious—repeating and repeating—until finally it leaves its imprint on the conscious mind with a fierceness so great it can never again be released back into the shadows ... nor forgotten.

Immortalized in her memory forever would remain the moment she sat eye to eye with a dying giant and, there, up so close, she was able to gaze into the whale's very soul. What an ironic twist of fate that such an extraordinary opportunity—coming face to face with a great whale—should manifest in so cruel a circumstance.

So immense was the love and compassion pouring out of her, she felt as if she had completely merged with the being, and she knew the whale felt it. It was love that flowed from a place so deep within, in one sense, and from so far beyond in another that, for that moment, she was ready to leave with her, to swim alongside the pod as one of them, and journey with her ancient family—through the veils—to another world.

Experiencing the immensity of that love and the longing to leave with them was the most transcendental experience of her entire life. She and the great whale were in the flow of infinite love, from Source: a love like nothing she had ever known before; a love she doubted she could ever know again. In that moment of blissful union, soul-to-soul, she no longer knew where the whale ended and she began—where that point of separation could be defined, on any level.

The swollen female Humpback was so pregnant—she seemed just hours away from delivering her calf. Sadly, this helpless mother would never live to know that ecstatic moment of birthing her infant, or teaching her baby the joy of swimming in the open sea with her: weaving the music of the waters, nestled in the safety of their pod. There would be no song, no light from the sun for these transiting souls as they passed from life, entwined and connected forever…at least not until they reached the other side. Here, in this massive grave with their kin, shrouded in this strange electric cloud, there was only sadness and suffering: a time of farewells; a time of silenced songs that might have been.

Jamie peered deeply into the mother's eyes, asking permission to connect with her baby: to touch her soul. With that, the whale let fall a tear. It dropped to the sand and dissolved into fading traces of ocean foam, while for Jamie, that one tear was so deep she felt she could drown within it—immense as the greatest ocean, and timeless as the waves.

The mighty whale looked back into Jamie's eyes with that same sense of knowing, and a light sparked between them—a flicker of recognition between two ancient souls—and then, the gentle giant, a mother-to-be who never would, blew the last precious bit of air out her blowhole.

She and her unborn baby died in that instant—within that last breath, with Jamie's love around them.

As unbearable as it was to cope with the immensity of emotions surging within her, Jamie saw the others through their pain and the dying, until the suffering ended, at last, and every soul had made its passage. They deserved at least that. She knew how to hold the light for the dying, assisting in their transition to another plane, where they would be free to swim in clear, sacred waters once again. It was the pure essence of her shamanic work, conducting souls through the transition from physical reality back to spirit, and she considered herself blessed to have been of service to such noble beings in their hour of going.

After all the teams of exhausted volunteers packed up and went home, and the sunless sky turned cold and gloomier still in the blackness of that senseless night, Jamie stayed, a grieving guardian in the darkness, alone but for the graveyard of dead corpses lined up on the shore. Morning would bring crews of cleanup teams, with all the necessary equipment. Theirs would be the horrific, utterly unthinkable job of disposing of the bodies, to protect against the obvious threat to public health, and to assure that the beach could be reopened for their summer tourist season—in full swing. But, for that sacred moment, hers was the only human presence there, and she stayed through until dawn, knowing how very profound it was to her and to the transitioning souls of one hundred fifty whales and dolphins, who, for some mysterious reason, had chosen to die.

Hopefully, thought Jamie, as the great beings crossed over to the other side, they would remember that someone—some human being—had known and cared enough to stay through the night, to see them across the rainbow bridge.

In that difficult time of great sadness and loss, Jamie felt each laborious breath of every whale and dolphin strip her of her own life force—a psychic pain so intense she could barely breathe. For a fleeting moment, she was able to escape the sadness, focusing her eye within the spirit realm, where she could see them swimming out of the tunnel of darkness and into the brilliance of illuminated waters. They were on their way, back out to the cosmic sea, where they would be free again.

That was her consolation.

She knew her lifework had changed forever that day. She was being called to use her gift to help prevent a tragedy such as this from ever happening again. And she knew, without question, that the whales and dolphins would reach out to her again, from the other side of night... and she would be there.

By the love of god, she would be there... forever.

According to her mother's many stories, Jamie Hastings was born with her eyes wide open—right through the sacred birth canal and into the world. Herself a psychic of noteworthy ability, Amanda Hastings often talked about how Jamie spoke to her before she was conceived, announcing, in a dream, that she was coming, and to "get ready" for a remarkable reunion. Amanda loved to tell the story of how her daughter came through her, in a nearly painless birth process, with the amniotic sac still fully intact.

When the midwife cut her out of the caul, her very first sound was not the usual cry of a newborn at the slap of the doctor but, rather, baby laughter. That was why her mother used to call Jamie her "Buddha baby," and it was a name that stuck throughout her life. And that is how she knew Jamie would always be protected, surrounded in her love, no matter what life would throw at her— from either side of the veil.

Suffice to say that any kid with an entry into the world like that was born to be an interesting soul, at the very least, from the onset.

From the early days of her childhood, Jamie exhibited exceptional abilities that her mother noted and encouraged, without reservation. There were none of the distractions of the day back then: no computers, electronic games, cell phones, and other gadgets that have hijacked the minds of computer-age children, and programmed them not to see beyond the illusions of their electronic devices. Children of her time were creators . . . freethinkers . . . and the pictures they drew came from their vivid imaginations, not copied and pasted from computer screens.

Jamie had real vision. She was connected from birth with the spirit world, and she spent time with beings and teachers from other realms: light beings from other dimensions. She would spend hours on end alone, in her room, rather than playing with the other children in the neighborhood, as she never exhibited an affinity for playing make-believe, when her own experience was so real.

Occasionally, she would burst out of her bedroom to report some extraordinary new revelation that spoke with such intricacy and knowledge that Amanda knew it could be only of worlds other than theirs, even if she herself could not conceptualize what her little daughter could see so clearly. Sometimes, she grew concerned that the child was becoming too attached to the spirit world, and that she was disconnecting from the earthly realm altogether. Jamie always knew when her mother was becoming worried about those times. She would sit Amanda down and explain, patiently, that she had to spend time with the faeries, and the spirits, or they would disappear. It made sense to both of them, and only them, so they managed to keep it their carefully guarded secret, and no one, not even her father, was in on it.

At the young age of four, she began drawing articulate, complex pictures of other galaxies and star systems, through which she constantly tried to explain her own galactic voyages in other lifetimes. It became almost a fixation. As she grew older, these visions became more frequent, rather than fading away, and Jamie would recount vivid memories and quite elaborate descriptions of herself living in and being from another galaxy, which she always described as being "parallel" to the Milky Way.

So precise were the images and information her daughter brought through that Amanda was quite convinced they were sourced in some other dimension, in which Jamie was somehow consciously involved and to which she was still very clearly connected. She had plenty of reason to believe that her daughter's encounters with the spirit world and her memory of other lifetimes were more than mere fantasies of childhood, and that they were actual perceptions of a parallel lifetime in some extraordinary simultaneous reality.

Her daughter appeared to walk in and between two worlds. Amanda dreamed of knowing that other world, too, but she didn't have Jamie's same gifts. Her visions of what lay beyond were mostly gleaned through her daughter's precise descriptions, and an ongoing narrative of Jamie's passage through a "space tunnel" into her womb.

She knew, without a doubt, that her baby was a soul that had reincarnated from a very distant world. Amanda believed in immortality, so it was not a far stretch for her to consider how very ancient a soul she was, nor how far she had come to live her life, this time around, as her beloved daughter.

As the years passed, the two of them, mother and child, held this magical secret private, far from the skeptical "doubting Thomases," who could never have understood what perceptions are truly accessible to certain human beings—nor would they have been willing to even consider the possibilities. Then again, back in the sixties, the realms of the invisible were far less approachable than they are now, at a time when an undeniable global awakening is stirring people out of their convictions, and opening minds.

The Buddha baby was just a little ahead of her time.

Amanda was careful to protect her daughter, as best she could, allowing her all the space she needed to investigate her parallel worlds and interact with them, without the censorship of a society in denial, attempting to shut her down to those experiences.

Through all of it, Jamie remained a beautiful, sunny child, who seemed to glow almost all of the time. In fact, people often commented that she had an otherworldly quality about her. As she grew, so did her beauty, both inside and out. This was a person who definitely had some kind of guiding star over her—a light that grew only brighter with time. It was a lifetime of extraordinary gifts she had earned, her mother was certain, from the good she had done in many others: pure good karma.

She grew up in San Francisco, *the* place to be "different" in the seventies—her college years. People used to say that everything crazy—every new wave—began there and then spread to the rest of America, before splashing over the rest of the world. It was no wonder that Silicon Valley sprang up nearby; this was one of the most likely places in all of America, maybe the world, for innovation and change.

Yes, indeed. San Francisco was the perfect place for a walker between worlds like Jamie Hastings to grow up in. Her soul had chosen wisely before coming in, born to a visionary mother like Amanda, and situated in one of sunny California's most beautiful landscapes.

Her gifts became more acute with the onset of her twenties, and they did not go unnoticed. In fact, Jamie's uncanny accuracy as a medium paid for her college education, since the New Age phenomenon seemed to have exploded there—right in her own backyard. She eventually got hired on at the Stanford Psychic Institute, where she was involved in extensive testing and experiments in all things paranormal, and there she established herself as one of the leading psychic visionaries in the country. Without even planning for it, Jamie's career and her life's work revolved around that ability to connect with worlds beyond the veil, pulling images and information out of the ethers, and helping others see things they could not see—on levels many of them thought could not possibly exist.

After twenty years of working off and on at the Institute, and consulting privately—usually with people in distress—she went on to work with the Los Angeles Police Department. Over a five-year period, she solved numerous crimes, providing detectives with precise information that she picked up in visions—invisible details that were so accurate they would almost always lead the police straight to the criminal's front door. After many years helping out the police and one too many gruesome murders, however, she grew tired of the work and had to leave. The violence weighed on her spirit, and the darkness of it all began to interfere with her personal life and her overall state of mind. When a television show was designed around her actual involvement as the Police Department's psychic investigator, and she was able to see her clouded reflection in the portrayal made of her by the leading character, she realized it was time to move on.

As knowledge of her uncanny successes spread into the corporate world, people called upon Jamie to dowse for water and underground oil wells, and other commercial uses of her extraordinary gift. She traveled the world helping her clients locate the hidden, expose crime and corruption, and invoke the spirit realms for needed information—and she was good at it. In fact, she was the very best in her field.

It was that one day in New Zealand, however, that showed her what she had really come to do in this lifetime: her true purpose for being alive. Beyond a shadow of a doubt, the death of the whales and dolphins had helped her finally realize who she was, and what she had come to Earth to do.

She knew her mission would lead her back to them.

She knew she was an Emissary.

3

USOIL

By January 2012, USOIL stock had tumbled for the tenth week in a row, despite the chokehold the oil companies held over the economy, and the power they wielded over the global political scene. The constant downward slide was inexplicable. All the other oil giants were showing billion-dollar quarterly profits, but Houston's own, USOIL, was apparently taking more gas than it was pumping, while draining the corporate tank through outrageous overspending and mismanagement. After year-end closing figures confirmed the tenth quarter of losses in a row, the CEO, Mat Anderson, had all but run out of time to pull a rabbit out of his corporate cowboy hat.

At sixty-four, he still carried himself like a Marine. He was in remarkable shape and was every bit as commanding now as he had been back in what he always referred to as "the glory days" of service. His suits had to be tailor-made to fit his muscular torso and trim waist, while his executives, a few of whom were twenty years his junior, were already folding over the belt line, from what Mat called the "soft" life. He was a man's man: an expert on the golf course, a force to be dealt with in business, and a Texan through and through—and proud of it. He could drink any man under the table, ride faster and farther than anyone he knew, and outrun people half his age out on the track. Above all, he was an unrelenting businessman—always working deals with big money players.

And when he wanted to be, he was quite the lady's man as well: a regular J. R. Ewing.

You just didn't want to cross him: man or woman, friend or foe.

Gray now, he still wore his hair shaved to less than a half inch; he ran five miles every morning; he worked out in the gym for hours each day—but suffered, despite all his physical prowess, from high blood pressure and an almost chronic state of acid reflux.

This day, the acid had climbed all the way up into his throat. Along with the official financials from headquarters had come orders for him to report to the top brass in New York the next morning: no prep time; no guidelines. Just show up. He knew that meant one of two things: either USOIL, one small, but important cog on a huge multinational wheel, was about to be sold … or the "powers that be" were bringing him in to negotiate what it would take to get him out.

In the ten years he had served as chief executive officer for the company, he consolidated a formidable network of power players like himself—people who had their own reasons to want him to hold his position at the top of the corporation. "Interested" people. At that level, the strings of corruption become so entangled and the people who dangle them so entwined in each other's affairs that unraveling them—enough to extract one person from the web— becomes downright messy, if not impossible.

He knew who he had behind him, and he also knew all kinds of secrets and dirty deals that had to "stay in Vegas," as he loved to say. If they wanted him to go quietly into the night, they were going to have to make the parting nice and sweet … way too sweet to refuse.

There were still three years left to his mandate, which he was sure were turnaround years for the company—and he knew what he had to do. And then, he had his people in high places, pulling on those strings. He needed just a little more time to get the job done, so that he could step out of the corporate world and into retirement a hero—or at the very least, a winner. He wasn't about to go out in a trough, after a career of surfing the high waves.

That just was not his style.

He left for New York with these thoughts racing through his head, swinging like a pendulum . . . left to right and back again. He couldn't seem to stop his mind from jumping back and forth, between the trepidation of being thrown into a pit of Wall Street vipers, and a certain self-assured complacency, knowing that he still had three years to reverse the spiral, before his mandate ran out.

It didn't help the balance sheets that Mat had a consummate ability to spend the corporation's money, even though he was, in his own right, a multimillionaire. His flamboyant spending was driving USOIL into debt about as fast as the White House was draining the wealth of the country: only the best for him and his overpaid executive staff; only the most sophisticated technology for exploration and refineries; only the classiest corporate work environment in Houston.

He flew by private jet and stayed in the most expensive hotels, even thought he hated them. They were cold and indifferent. No matter how upscale they were—nothing was like his own bed, in his sprawling eight-hundred-acre property outside Houston: Sundown Ranch. Every minute he could spend away from work, he spent there, shared with three hundred wild horses and a staff of ranch hands who took care of the business of running the place.

He loved that freedom, and the privacy of a world that made sense: a place to go home to, when the other side of real got too crazy for him.

Manhattan was just that kind of crazy to Mat. The noise was unbearable, the women were too aggressive, and life moved too damned fast. So many people, it was a blur in the streets—all the empty faces and too many bodies walking around every which way, like they were all on some giant urban conveyor belt, going everywhere and nowhere at the same time.

When push came to shove, Mat liked to think of himself as a southern gentleman, even though a lot of people thought of him more as a ruthless manipulator, and he could be both—depending on what the situation called for.

He loved those "down home" comforts, and the way people just generally behaved in the South, more than anywhere else he had ever been in the world. Things were far more civilized in Texas; people smiled at each other on the street corners—even strangers. New York? It made him feel like a mouse in a cement jungle, scurrying along the side of the road, trying to find his way out of the gutter and back to Central Park.

It was late, by the time he got into the city that night and checked into his hotel suite. He ordered room service and settled in, going over the profit/loss statement, and preparing a strategy for questions he might have to field in the meeting. Mat was determined to turn in early, to be prepared for the next morning, but he could not relax enough to fall asleep—it just refused to happen. He turned on the television, set to CNN. There was nothing new about the news— nothing but the same footage, repeating over and over again, and the inane, insignificant banter between a few pretend journalists that had little or nothing to do with the real story unfolding on the planet—the story he knew from the inside. He surfed all the channels, about to give up, when he landed in the middle of *Katie Lee Live!*—a popular late-night talk show.

It was a rerun of an earlier show entitled "Psychics and the World of Spirits," featuring three self-proclaimed visionaries of note: one of whom was a woman named Jamie Hastings—a very beautiful, very intriguing woman who caught Mat's eye and sparked his interest immediately. At the point when he came in on the program, Katie was asking her specifically about her work with the Los Angeles Police Department, which served, she told her audience, as the inspiration for one of the leading TV dramas of success. Jamie

Hastings condensed into a few minutes an entire five-year story of her work for the LAPD, with fifty-three cases officially solved, through her contribution.

Katie was taken aback when she heard the figure. "Did you hear that, ladies and gentlemen? Fifty-three crimes solved—and that's on the police record for you doubters out there—thanks to the psychic investigation of this one woman." She addressed Jamie alone, ignoring the other two guests seated next to her. "How many years are we talking about here?"

"It was over a five-year span," Jamie replied, matter-of-factly.

"Is that unbelievable?" Katie asked of her audience, and when the camera scanned the theater, they all were nodding, in amazement. "That works out to be ten violent crimes a year, solved thanks to this lady, right here," she said to the camera. "I'd like to see how the skeptics can refute those statistics." She paused, preparing for another commercial break. "When we return ... we'll be hearing about Jamie's successful work—dowsing for water in the Down Under ... stay with us," said Katie, and then they cut to the commercial.

Mat couldn't believe it. How was it he had never heard of this woman before then? He was impressed with how natural she was—it came right through the screen. No pretense. No drama. He got up quickly and poured himself a drink from the bar, while ten or more annoying commercials, smashed together into a three-minute pause, ran their course, and then he sat back down, transfixed by Jamie Hastings.

He was drawn in by Jamie's good looks, her poise, and her unassuming personality, considering what she clearly had proven herself capable of doing with her incredible powers. He had always laughed off the idea that psychics were anything more than a bunch of con artists in turbans, playing people's weaknesses, and selling flimflam to fools. Yet, here was this highly credible woman, with a list of undeniable successes and accomplishments, making him reexamine that prejudice. There wasn't anything phony about her: she was solid as a rock, down to earth, and humble. She had nothing to prove—her successes preceded her. That was an irrefutable matter of record—a police record, at that.

He decided to verify it directly with LAPD, once he was through with the meeting. "Hell," he thought, "if this is even half as true as it sounds, I may have just found my magic wand."

When they returned, Katie engaged her in a discussion about dowsing, curious to know how in the world she had managed to locate an extensive underground river, flowing a half mile below the arid surface of a desert region on the western coast of Australia.

"When you are seeing," Jamie replied, "...or shall I say 'experiencing' from a higher level of awareness than that which we achieve through our sensate experience, Katie, you're tuning in your antennae to reach the vibrational frequency of the target. You reach resonance with it...and it appears on your mind's screen. It's not much different from the way a TV antenna pulls the image onto your TV screen."

"Makes sense," Katie said.

"Or, the opposite can hold true. A spirit or a conscious essence tunes in to you and it reaches you—and appears in the material realm. Sometimes I just get flashes, but others—as in the case of dowsing below the earth—involve focusing my mind's eye on the desired frequency, and then attuning my body to it."

"Wow! How does it feel to attune to a flowing underground river?"

"Huge," Jamie replied, unpretentiously.

Katie looked into her camera. "You getting that, people?"

"Once you learn how to use the gift of vision that way, it's really that simple. You focus on the objective, tune in to its vibrational essence, and then you make the connection."

"You find a river down deep in the earth—water that can change the lives of millions of people—and you call that simple?" Again, Katie looked into the camera, playing her audience, stirring excitement.

"Well, I suppose 'simple' is not the right word. Let's say it is 'doable,'" Jamie replied.

"And you are certainly walking proof of that. Jamie Hastings, ladies and gentleman, and our guests, Miranda Symons and Robert Holloway: Psychics and the World of Spirits." The audience applauded and Mat watched for as long as the credits ran, studying Jamie Hastings, a most intriguing personality, until the commercials came back on, and the show was officially over. Then, he switched off the TV and lay back in bed, promising himself that when he got back to Houston he would find a way to meet her—as soon as possible.

The very last thought in his mind, before he finally closed his eyes and fell asleep, was, "If this woman can find water underground, what's to say she can't find what we're lookin' for, at the bottom of the ocean?"

He woke up early, to be sure to get in his morning run in the park, and then came back energized—ready to take on the world. He thought about what Jamie Hastings had said. *"Just tune in your antennae to reach the vibrational frequency of the target,"* and that was precisely what he did. And it worked. Things went far better than he had even expected: he said what he had to say, providing projections for the next three years, and told the big boys what they wanted to hear. He secured their approval—provided USOIL could keep the conglomerate's "pocket politicians" appeased enough that they would continue bending the rules in the right direction, which meant their direction.

By three that afternoon, he was already back in Houston. Mat decided he had to meet Jamie Hastings—a matter of first order. A man of infinite means and inimitable style, he managed to pull a few strings with a political ally, the governor of California, to get the man she had worked for, the current chief of police in the Los Angeles Police Department, to open the door with Jamie. He told the governor that he wanted to be sure his was a request, not an order, to keep everything, in his words, "friendly like."

Once Mat got the green light from the governor, he immediately telephoned the police chief, Martin Kaszlow, and tried to engage him in conversation about her. He was dying to know more about her investigative work for the force, and what it was like having worked with her, from an insider's point of view. He piled on the questions, but Martin was generally tight-mouthed and cautiously uncooperative, especially when it came to Jamie. Too many people had tried to get to her through him, and he was extremely protective.

Then again, the governor demanded that he cooperate....

"So when was it, exactly, that she was in your employ?" Mat asked, probing.

Martin hesitated, choosing his words carefully, determined to reveal as little as possible. "Ms. Hastings was never employed by the Police Department. She was a consultant."

"Right. And when was that?"

"That was from somewhere around the middle of 2003 through 2008—give or take a few months."

"Is it true that she helped solve fifty-three cases in that time?"

"She did more than help—she actually led us to the criminals."

"Wowee. Fifty-three times?"

"Yes, in a manner of speaking. That's correct."

"That is damned amazing. Do you happen to know where she's been working the last five years?"

Martin was increasingly uncomfortable and he didn't take kindly to being cross-examined, which was how he felt the whole time he was on the line with Mat. He was used to being on the other side of an interrogation, in control. "I know she's been overseas a lot," he said, "but, to be honest, I don't keep track of her."

"Look, Chief, I am really not trying to put any pressure on you, here. I just really need to meet this woman," Mat said, trying not to alienate him. "Now, I'm thinking it would be very helpful if you would be kind enough to introduce us, at least make a little phone call, so she knows who I am when that phone rings—now how about that?"

He told Mat that, the last he'd heard, she had gone on an extended winter retreat in New Zealand, where she was vacationing and hiding out from the long list of people and organizations who were lined up, hoping to consult with her. At last count, Kaszlow said, she had a two-year waiting list. What he didn't tell Mat was that prior to that, Jamie had been working in Pakistan, locating oil wells—but then again, he figured that was information Mat already had, and that it was his reason for seeking Jamie out in the first place. Still, just in case, Martin figured it was best left unsaid.

Mat pressed him. "So I'm wondering... why did she leave you and where can I find her?"

According to Martin Kaszlow, Jamie had signed off because she didn't *want* to be found. She knew she was being called to serve in other capacities, and that using her vision for corporate and criminal investigations simply didn't fit the bigger picture. Everybody wanted her, but she basically had a case of burnout, and she just could not do the work any longer. "I had to respect her wishes, and let her go," Martin said, pointedly.

That she would refuse notoriety and god knows how many more business opportunities, where all she had to do was to turn on her lightbulb now and then, intrigued Mat even more. That kind of personal integrity didn't fit into any formula he had ever encountered in his business or personal life—it just wasn't American!

"I heard her tell Katie Lee that she was dowsing out there—where was it again?"

Martin knew Mat was trying to trap him, but still ... he didn't have much of a choice but to answer his questions. It was political. "She was in Pakistan last."

"Dowsing for water out there, in the desert?"

"No, Mr. Anderson—she was dowsing for oil." He figured Mat already knew, and that holding back information would only get back to the governor. He didn't need the pressure.

Mat, great actor that he was, hid his shock at Martin's disclosure, but, inside, his heart was pounding with the excitement that his hunch was right on the money. The woman dowsed for oil! "Right, right, plenty of oil over there, that's for sure."

Eager to avoid any further questions, Martin mustered up all the diplomacy he could manage, to get Mat off the line. He did his best to convince him that Jamie was recovering, and that she had made it more than clear she didn't want to be disturbed—under any circumstances.

He was uncomfortable getting into the Lahore situation with Mat—that was Jamie's own business to discuss, if she felt like it. He emphasized that, as far as he was concerned, with what he'd seen her go through with the LAPD work alone, she had more than earned "time for Jamie"—however and wherever she wanted to spend that time, without interruption.

Having learned that Jamie had actually dowsed for oil in Pakistan, Mat couldn't wait to get his team to run a full profile on her—but he still had to have that introduction from Martin. He pushed him to make the call, looking for that wedge that only Martin Kaszlow could provide—just a "friendly-like" way into the life of Jamie Hastings.

Under pressure from the governor's office, Martin had little choice but to accommodate the man. They hung up, agreeing that Martin would get back to Mat after he'd made contact.

In the meantime, Mat cleared his desk completely to focus on her and the mysterious world she moved in—the paranormal realm. Who was this woman, really, and how did she see these visions so clearly that she was capable of overriding every tool available to the police, leading them to solve case after case of unsolvable crimes? How did she dowse for oil in the middle of the desert in Pakistan—and for whom? How outrageous was that—or rather, how perfect?

Jamie Hastings's experience surpassed by far anything that could have been dismissed as "coincidence." The L.A. police record certainly attested to that, with fifty-three cases solved in a framework of five years, thanks to her intervention. All things considered, from what Mat had gleaned so far, Jamie Hastings had managed to qualify and position psychic investigation as a tested and credible resource, to explore and bring into the foreground.

He knew the government had people training in "remote viewing," but she could see and talk to dead people and all kinds of spirits; she could locate underground water and, holy mackerel, she could find oil, too. He was waiting to hear about her success with the Pakistanis, but he was convinced she'd managed to produce for them, too.

Considering the world Mat had always walked in, these were feats that made her a phenomenon he wanted to learn more about and, quite naturally, to exploit as best possible. He just couldn't believe she was out there in the world, walking around, free—even if she was hiding out for a while, on the other side of the planet. With what she knew and what she could do, she was fortunate that most of the world would dismiss and discredit her. He laughed at the irony of how, rather than putting her at a disadvantage, other people's negative perceptions of her were most likely the perfect shield to keep her out of harm's way.

Now that was some kind of divine protection.

He ordered some of his most reliable staff members to do a complete workup on her and to have it on his desk before the end of the day. These were people he could count on for discretion; they were people who were dedicated to him and him alone—his "intelligence" gatherers. He wanted specific information about where she had been the last five years, and everything they could dig up on her time in Lahore.

What they gathered about her work reconfirmed that she was an exceptional psychic, with an unbelievable track record, as he already knew. She was the real deal: they found indisputable proof. She had pinpointed three sites in the middle of the desert, in less than a year, which became three successful oil wells for the Pakistanis. Jamie Hastings's keen vision was like an arrow and she had a remarkable record of hitting the bull's-eye. In her world, the unknowable was the known, and the scientific, analytic world of reason was the unknown: shady and inconclusive.

No one else he had ever heard of had been better able to validate the credibility of superconsciousness, which she used to pluck answers out of the void, leaving the empirical process of science scratching its head, in the dust.

This was a person Mat wanted on his team, without question, at any cost. There was just one small detail to contend with. Martin had driven home the fact that she had had enough of police work and enough of corporate, and had gone into hiding, to escape the whole business of using her psychic acuity to serve other people's needs. For all intents and purposes, Jamie Hastings was no longer available for any of it. She was out of service—and not planning to return.

Mat's favorite expression was "everybody has his price," and he was determined to find Jamie's. He learned that she had been paid a fortune in Pakistan and that she was also up to her neck in extraordinary high yield stock options as part of the deal—so money was not going to be the bait that would lure her. She had no husband he could pull strings for; no children to put through college; no debt he could pay off. She had no legal problems that he could make go away. No matter how deep they dug, the team came up with absolutely nothing on Jamie Hastings.

She was a perfectly clean slate—a total enigma.

4

Reeling in the Buddha Baby

After her long vigil that terrible night, with the passing of the whales and dolphins, Jamie was ready to return to San Francisco. She knew it was time to come out of hiding and get to work, doing whatever she could to help assure that scenes like the one she had just lived through never happen again. She trusted that she would get guidance to help her turn her gifts over to the imperiled whale communities—those interdependent pods of amazing, loving beings, who were clearly calling out for help. And she was absolutely clear that there needed to be a massive shift in human awareness, if the whales were to survive the ecological blight that was rapidly overtaking the oceans, or whatever else it was that was causing them to die, in mass graves, around the world.

When Martin Kaszlow's call came, she was almost in the right frame of mind to listen, since she was over her retreat from society, packing up her suitcases, and heading home. Jamie was pleased to hear from him on the one hand, but wary on the other, knowing he never called without a motive. He always sought her out when another grisly murder had occurred—usually a serial killer was on the loose—when no one else, and no police forensics investigation, could provide even a clue where to look, before the killer struck again. How much terror had she had to witness and work through? How much darkness and suffering? She was absolutely unwilling to return to it.

His face flashed into her mind before the phone even rang.

"I don't need bad news right now, Marty," she said, folding her jacket into the suitcase, the phone wedged up between her shoulder and her ear. She always knew when Martin was going to call, sometimes even before he knew, himself. For Jamie, "caller identification" pre-dated cell phones by decades. She called it an "elementary psychic exercise," which she had mastered since childhood.

Martin searched for the right way to start the conversation. He was always asking her for a favor or for help, and, as always, he was awkward about how to approach her. "We miss you out here in crazy world," he said, attempting sentimentality, but failing, as usual.

"I don't want to know," she replied, tersely.

Martin felt embarrassed at having been forced to invade her privacy, and that awkwardness came through in his voice. "It's been a long time, James—what have you been up to, down there in the Down Under?"

Knowing how uncomfortable it made him to deal with anything remotely resembling what he called her "emotional issues," she did her best to conceal them, but she knew that neither one of them was interested in, nor good at, small talk. Their relationship was about real life, fast and furious, all the time. Ironic it was, too, that, in a district of toughened street cops and violent crime, feminine sentiment was simply too frightening for the Big Chief to cope with.

"I just said goodbye to about a hundred and fifty whales and dolphins, who, for whatever reason, decided to beach themselves on the coast here," she said. Jamie tried to keep her voice from breaking, but she couldn't hold back. "I watched them die—it was a mass suicide." The tears welled up in her eyes and her profound sadness poured through, her voice cracking as she tried to hold it all within . . . for Martin's sake.

"That's bad news," he replied, solemnly. Martin was not a man of words. He was coarse, rough police material. No room for sentimentalism over a bunch of whales, with what he saw unfolding every day on the streets of America.

Jamie sighed. "Yes … yes, it is bad news, Marty—extremely bad news."

As always, Martin sidestepped Jamie's feelings and got right to the point of his call. "Yeah, look James, I have someone who needs your help—a guy by the name of Mat Anderson, out in Houston." Martin started shuffling some papers on his desk, preferring to be doing anything else than having to ask Jamie for this favor. "He's the CEO of USOIL—a friend of the governor," Martin said, clearing his throat, "and he wants to talk to you."

"Not interested."

"I'm in a kind of spot here, Jamie … it's pressure from the top."

"Still not interested," Jamie snapped.

Martin expected a cool reception—it was no surprise that Jamie would be annoyed. She had let him know, in no uncertain terms, not to look for her while she was regrouping in New Zealand: not for serial killings or other unsolved murders, nor any other horrors he would want to call her in on. Certainly not this. He knew she would be incensed that he was willing to break his commitment to her—governor or no governor.

"I thought I was really clear about this, Marty."

"You always tell me everything happens for a reason, right?" he replied. "The governor says this big-shot oil guy is looking for 'environmentally friendly' ways to find drill sites out there in the Pacific Northwest. That's all he told me. Who knows? Apparently he thinks you can help. Maybe it's important, James. If it is for real. I mean, if this guy is legit, maybe helping him out will be good for the whales too, right?" He leaned back in his chair and stretched his feet out on the desk.

"Jesus, Martin. Drilling in those waters? That's one of our last relatively intact ecosystems, for god sakes." She poured a cup of coffee from the room service tray. "And there is no 'environmentally friendly' way to suck oil out of the earth—who are we kidding here?"

"Hey—don't shoot the messenger. Talk to this guy—he's a really big player."

Jamie thought about it a moment and figured it couldn't hurt to at least listen to what USOIL was really up to, and how exactly this Anderson character wanted to use her to do it.

"Can I give him your number?"

"Sure," she said, and hung up. She figured that if Oil Man had pull with the governor of California, he most likely already had the number anyway, and that he was going to call, regardless.

Martin called Mat back as soon as he hung up with Jamie, recounting the conversation and passing on her number. He advised Mat to move quickly, since Jamie was packing to return home. "Go easy on Jamie Hastings, Anderson," Martin said, authoritatively. "She's a real lady and a precious commodity for us all."

Mat bristled at the chief's tone of voice. Not too many people got away with talking to him like that. "Yeah, sure thing, Marty boy," he said, condescendingly, controlling the impulse to cut Martin down to size. "And thanks, my friend, I will definitely put in a good word for you with the gov, next time we're out playing a few rounds," Mat said, throwing his weight out in Martin's face, and then he hung up, abruptly. He smiled at himself in the mirror, straightening his tie. "Way to go, Mattie boy! Ecology, man! You found the hook and you have cast the bait. Let's reel in Jamie Hastings."

Jamie was in the middle of battling with the airline to get a flight back to San Francisco when his call came in. Juggling between the hotel phone and her mobile, she was not feeling her most receptive when he rang, at a point of sheer exasperation with the airline. She couldn't seem to make him understand that she was on another line, trying to get a flight home, and that she wasn't free to talk. She tried hanging up as politely as possible, but he insisted.

"Look, how about you let me solve that little problem for you, in exchange for you coming out here to Houston for a friendly business dinner?"

Jamie couldn't believe the audacity of the man. She held the phone away from her ear and just stared at it, incredulous.

Mat's secretary, Louise, walked in on the conversation, carrying a stack of payroll checks that needed to be signed. A former Miss Texas, she was the classic trophy secretary: she wore too much makeup, her pearl pink fingernails matched her clingy cashmere dress, and not one strand of her lacquered blonde hair was out of place.

He snapped his fingers at her dismissively, and ordered her to go get him a cup of coffee. She did her best to eavesdrop as she closed the door behind her, lingering just a moment more than she needed to, in the hallway outside his office, listening in on Mat's side of the conversation.

Jamie said, "I don't mean to be rude, Mr. Anderson, but I can't even get a flight to Sydney at the moment, much less Houston. Not sure you're getting my drift, here. I seem to be stuck down here for the time being."

"I sure am. But I think you're missing my drift. I don't fly commercial myself, can't be bothered," he replied. "I can have the company jet on its way within hours. Painless. You'll have the whole plane and crew to yourself, VIP all the way. All I'm asking from you is a chance to talk to you about a little business proposal I have in mind. Now how in the world can you say 'no' to that, Miss Jamie? How can you say 'no' to that?"

Jamie just stood there, speechless.

He waited for a reply. "Miss Hastings, I am not a man who gives up easily."

As she listened to the tempting offer from the Oil Man on one ear, on the other she was still being bombarded by the irritating, repeating recording, which kept drumming home the automaton message that no human being was available to help her get on a flight home. How hard a choice was this to make: praying to get squeezed into a seat on some oversold transpacific flight back home, or flying home on a luxurious private corporate jet, like royalty, with a quick detour through Texas? She rested the phone connected to the airline on the end table. The voice of the recording kept repeating the message, *"Your call will be answered by the next available agent,"* but it never was.

"Let me guess," she told Mat, "you heard of my work in Lahore, right?"

"Yes, yes, I have. It's clearly something I find extraordinarily interesting; I won't be tryin' to hide that for a minute. But it's a whole lot more than that, I assure you. I just need a chance to talk to you in person. That's what I'm asking for. That's all I'm asking you for at this moment."

"Mr. Anderson, I have got to be in San Francisco by Wednesday. Can you make that happen?"

Mat grinned. "Can I? Miss Jamie, all I need is just a few hours of your time and then I'll fly you anywhere you need to go—door-to-door—first class all the way. You sure as hell do have my word on that."

Jamie took the other phone to her other ear for a last time—still the recording droned on. She slammed it down in frustration. "Okay, Mat Anderson, your offer is gratefully accepted." How could she refuse? Jamie figured if he was willing to spend the kind of money it would take to get the company's plane all the way down to New Zealand to pick her up, surely she could at least give him a few hours of her time, and do dinner.

"Now that is the answer I was hoping for! That is right friendly of you, Miss Jamie. I am putting things into motion as we speak. You just lie back and wait for my secretary to call you, in the next hour or so, with all the details. Have a drink on me in the meantime," he said, "and when you wake up tomorrow, we will be there."

Louise came in with his coffee, and Mat instructed her to get his flight captain on the line—pronto.

"Alrighty—I've got a plane to get moving, so I'm signing off for now," he said. "And please—call me Mat. I like to be on a first-name basis with my business partners."

"Whoa, Mat. I'm not agreeing to anything more than your very generous flight home and dinner," she said, cautiously. "But, I will admit… you've certainly got my curiosity. I'll be there, with an open mind," Jamie replied, and then she fell back onto the bed, tired but relieved, letting herself be taken to this appointment with destiny, in style, and knowing, at the very core level, that it was going to be important.

"That's all I'm asking," Mat said, his voice trailing off with orders for his secretary, as he cut the call.

After she hung up with Mat, she asked for clarity about what he was all about and what he really wanted from her. In her mind's eye, all she could see was whales swimming everywhere around her—singing their haunting melodies and calling out, like sirens to ancient mariners, for help. It was clear that whatever was unfolding had to do with them, and that her new mission, which seemed to be managed from a higher plane, had some reason to detour through Dixieland on her way home.

While packing up the last of the last of her vacation, Jamie heard from Mat's secretary, who confirmed all the coordinates of her journey. The limousine would be there for her at 1:00 p.m. the next day. She would be driven to the airport in Christchurch, a short ride from the resort, where she would board at a private terminal. Upon arrival in Houston, she would be escorted to the company's presidential suite at the Four Seasons Hotel, where she would be met by Mr. Anderson for dinner at 7:00 p.m., and then flown by private jet to San Francisco the following morning.

"Mr. Anderson's personal chef will be serving you on board," Louise said. "Do you have any special food preferences?"

Jamie grinned. This had to be some kind of proposal to be getting such red carpet treatment: something really huge. "I'm a vegetarian," she replied.

"I will convey that to our chef, thank you," Louise replied, officiously, adding, "We look forward to hosting you in Houston."

Louise hung up with Jamie and then sent a text message to the chef to prepare a strictly vegetarian menu aboard the flight. "What's with San Francisco?" Louise pondered, "…all those burned-out hippies. Damned vegetarian do-gooders…they think they're gonna fix the world by not eatin' a hamburger?" She pulled an emery board out of the desk drawer and retouched one of her pearl pink lacquered nails, filing the chipped edge. "Good Lordy! Who the hell is this bimbo, anyway, and what has that man got in mind now?"

Jamie luxuriated in the presidential cabin aboard USOIL's extraordinary private jet like a diva—loving every minute of it, but wondering where the strings were attached. She was well aware of the chimera of wealth, and how easily one could become lost in pursuit of castles in the sky, and here she was…soaring over the Pacific Ocean in one. Sipping a glass of vintage Dom Pérignon, she giggled at the thought of it, reminding herself to keep a clear head, stay objective, and exercise caution when she touched ground. She had only committed to hearing Mat Anderson's proposal—nothing more, nothing less—and then she was heading home to get to work for the whales and dolphins.

She took another sip of champagne and then lay back drowsily into the plush pillows, dozing off—thoughts of them guiding her way into the dreamtime. Deep in slumber—flying above and away from the tragic hour of their death—she dreamed her way back to the beach, where she was lying up close to the great mother whale. They were so close, she could feel her heart beating, pulsing through Jamie's sleeping body, and then, slowly failing, like the last ticking of a clock, unwound.

As she and the whale gazed into each other's eyes anew, a voice spoke out, ringing clear and powerful through the dreamscape. "Help us," the whale was saying, "before we leave you."

And then, there was silence—cold and lifeless, like long, icy shadows cast of the hollow light of winter—calling her back from the dream.

Jamie awoke with a lingering sense of grief and emotion that bridged the sleeping brain to her conscious mind, pervading the waking process, but from it she gleaned a clear idea of what she had to do. She was going home to set up a foundation for psychic investigation into what was causing the Cetaceans to die in mass suicides, like the one she had just lived through.

How could Earth, the great mother to all living beings here, be so cruel as to trick her mightiest into beaching themselves on her shores, where certain death awaited them? Why would the all-powerful, living oceans cast their gentle giants out and then pull back their great tides, empty-handed, unwilling to carry the mighty whales safely home, into the womb of the deep? What other forces were at play? Where was the disconnect?

How could there be Divine Order in such a travesty of nature?

These were the questions that tormented Jamie's soul, and yet they served as clear pathways to answers she needed to find. Somehow, she reckoned, Mat Anderson and his big project had to figure, on the way to that truth. Big Oil, ocean ecology, and whale protection—what an unlikely trinity. How possibly could either one of them make that improbable combination work to fit the interests of the whole? She was intrigued at the thought there might be a way, but deep down inside, at the gut level, she knew that there was something truly "bad news" about this Mat character: something deep and dark and ugly, hidden behind the facade.

5

Oil and Water

The presidential suite at the hotel was luxury in overdrive—pure, understated elegance. Mat Anderson clearly knew how to make a statement, about this Jamie had no doubt whatsoever. He was proving himself to be the king of Southern hospitality, and he definitely lived up to his promise of pure VIP treatment, door-to-door. She was duly impressed.

A most exquisite bouquet of her favorite flowers—irises, baby pink roses, and daffodils—filled the dining room table with her colors: the colors of Spring. How he could have known these were her absolutely favorite flowers she didn't know... but she was sure it was no accident.

The refined decor smacked of old money and had a distinctive male feel to it, with its dark leather couches and high-end rustic antique furniture. Everything was exquisite—and expensive. A subtle scent of sweet tobacco permeated the lounge—no doubt emanating from the suite's own cigar room, off the living room. All things considered, the men of the world were still, primarily, the ones holding the big money strings. Surely a few sheiks and their entourages had been hosted there before her. She knew that opulence was all part of the OPEC theater, and laying it on was part of the deal-making game, in which all the key players were constantly trying to outdo each other. The stakes were too high not to. She was not the least bit interested in getting caught up in it, but it was undeniably pleasant enjoying a taste of it—Texas style.

Within minutes of being escorted to the suite, the phone rang. It was Louise, calling to formalize Jamie's arrival at the hotel and officially welcoming her, on the part of her boss.

Jamie thanked her, as she fumbled with her purse, trying to tip the bellman. He refused, politely, and closed the door behind him. Tips, extras, flowers: USOIL saw to all the details.

"You've got the whole day to enjoy the spa if you like ... everything is already signed to the room, so you just enjoy yourself. It's all been arranged for you." It was clear that Louise managed all the VIP hospitality details for Mat. "I took the liberty of scheduling you in for a hot stone massage at noon. The spa is always booked up in advance."

Jamie was a bit overwhelmed, having not even had a chance to set her bag down. "Oh, okay, thanks," she replied. "I think I can make that!"

"It's just a miracle to get someone in at the last minute, but you just let them know if y'all are not up for it."

Jamie thanked Louise for the gesture and assured her she would definitely not cancel.

"Mr. Anderson will be there for you at seven this evening to escort you to dinner. Enjoy your day!" Louise said, attempting to sound cheery and efficient, but the sharpness of her resentment and a touch of pure female jealousy clipped her words just enough for Jamie to know she was not that welcome at all.

At 7:00 p.m. sharp, Jamie stepped out of the elevator, looking poised and relaxed, after a day of self-indulgent spa treatments at Houston's finest. She cut such a striking figure, her unpretentious beauty radiating light around her—a rare and indefinable essence that

simply commanded attention whenever she entered a room. More than her physical beauty was this mystical quality about her, as if she were aglow from the inside out. Her eyes, warm and embracing, were like lighthouses, in a sea of vacuous faces passing in the night. Her presence was disarming and she had this very magical quality about her. Everywhere she went, people noticed—both men and women alike.

Even though she'd never before set eyes on him, Jamie walked right up to Mat, who was at the front desk, on the house phone. He had his back to her, yet she intuitively knew it was he. He could feel a presence from across the room but, when he turned to see who was approaching, he was amazed to see Jamie walking straight towards him. It was not that often that someone could catch him off guard. In fact, it was just about next to impossible.

"Mat Anderson?" she asked, stretching her hand out to greet him.

Mat was visibly taken aback. "Well now, that is impressive, I have to say." They shook hands. "I mean, wowee. I guess there aren't too many women who can walk up to strange men in hotels like you can." He bit his lip, knowing how the comment could easily have been interpreted as a real insult and he hadn't meant it to be. "What I mean is, it must be nice bein' able to just cut through formalities and all that."

"It is," Jamie said, feeling quietly pleased that she had managed to catch him with his guard down, and fumbling. It was a great way to begin the evening's negotiations, which were bound to be forthcoming, sometime closer to cocktails than dinner.

"Well, then, let's have a drink to no formalities between us," he said, motioning towards the restaurant. "I actually reserved dinner here tonight—it's one of my favorite places ... best Italian food in town, and I know the chef personally." He placed his hand gently on Jamie's back and guided her towards the restaurant entrance, where the maitre d' welcomed him by name and immediately escorted them to a private dining room.

As they were being seated, Mat said, "I hope you don't mind, but I don't ever talk business in a crowded room. The walls have ears . . . I'm sure you know what I'm talking about."

Jamie was thinking, "Oh, honey, if only you knew!"

He waved over the waiter. "A bottle of your finest." He then turned his attention to Jamie. "I want to thank you for accepting my invitation, for starters."

Jamie thanked him back. In all fairness, he was the one jumping through all the hoops to make the meeting happen. All she'd done was to accept his more than gracious hospitality.

The waiter returned with a bottle of vintage Cristal, popped the cork, and poured. Mat tasted the champagne, and nodded his approval, before the waiter poured for Jamie. He set the bottle in the ice bucket, and walked away, discreetly.

Mat proposed a toast to their "mutually beneficial union," and the conversation was off and running.

"I hope my crew took good care of you on the way over."

"I almost didn't want to get off the plane," she replied. "Thank you, Mat. That was a very generous thing to do."

"That's fine. My pleasure. We aim to please." He took his cell phone from his pocket, opened the back casing, and removed the battery before placing it on the table in front of him. "So I guess by now you have fully understood that I have something very important I need to discuss with you."

"I guess!" Jamie answered, sipping the world's finest champagne from a beautiful Waterford cut crystal flute. One thing was certain—whatever he planned to talk about, he definitely did not want anyone else in on it.

"I'm not good at small talk, so excuse me if I cut right to it here. I have got to tell you, Miss Jamie, I have never in my life heard of anything like what you did for them Pakis, out there in the desert. I could barely believe it when I first heard about it—when I was, shall we say, investigating y'all."

Jamie sat back in her chair, placing her glass back down on the table, feeling suddenly defensive. "And to what do I owe the honor of being investigated by the CEO of USOIL, Mr. Mat?"

"Hell's bells, lady... finding three wells out there in the desert—that makes you an extremely valuable commodity. Extremely valuable. I can't understand at all how you did it, and I can't even understand how you managed to walk away from it!" Mat raised his glass. "Here's to you, Jamie Hastings! You have got to be some kind of remarkable."

Jamie raised a glass back. "Cheers to you, my curious and generous host." Inside, she was thinking, "Good god. Oil, oil, oil. Where will it all end?"

"You just have the most remarkable track record—it's some story to a guy like me," he said. "Why, you have actually made me a believer, and that is no easy feat, let me tell you."

Guarded, Jamie simply said, "Thank you." Listening to Mat and watching his body language, she couldn't help comparing him to the bumbling George Bush Jr., reminding herself that under the clownish veneer that he presented to the world, Bush was a ruthless oil man himself—all of them members of the same "club elite." Maybe some giant machine just cut and pasted them all out of the same mold.

"But wow... three wells out there in Pakistan. That is just this side of unbelievable! How in the hell did you manage to get out of there, once you struck gold for those greedy bastards?"

Jamie was becoming annoyed with Mat's probing and the emerging racist edge to his talk. "After locating that first site, I was asked to stay and, to my client's utter amazement, I found another two."

"Just like that?"

"Just like that."

"And they just let you go?"

"What a strange question—of course they 'let' me go. I finished what I had gone to do and left. Why would that surprise you?"

Mat realized he was pushing, and that she already had her back up. "Sorry—I do have experience with my colleagues over there. I just find it surprising that they let you slip out of their hands like that."

She felt uncomfortable at the idea that he would even think she could be held against her will. "Well, for starters, the psychic faculty can't be forced. They knew that I was tapped out, after finding those sites, and I can tell you that they were more than satisfied with what they got."

"Well, they sure as hell should have been, with three brand-new wells to pump—man oh man! That is utterly out of this world."

The waiter appeared, just to refill their glasses, and then disappeared immediately. It wasn't the first time he had served Mat Anderson in the private dining room. The staff knew that the CEO of USOIL didn't want anyone around until he wanted someone around, and whoever waited on him had to know how to dance to that rhythm.

"And now, you have brought me all the way here because you want me to go out and find you some oil, is that right?"

Mat felt Jamie tightening up and a "no, thank you" forthcoming.

"Well, yes, I guess I'm pretty obvious about what I'm looking for, here. We're out searching for oil in the Pacific, up there in the north—well, actually, we've been moving north after two years off the California coast."

"Brilliant," she said sarcastically, interrupting. "You're in one of the richest ocean ecosystems of the planet. Rumor has it, for us mere mortals, that this ocean region is protected against drilling. Are you telling me that is not the case, and that we've been duped, yet again?"

"Well, yes, Miss Jamie," he replied, ignoring her comment, "and I'd like you to listen up, because I am very aware of the ecological danger that poses. You see, I am in no mood for another big oil disaster out there, especially one with our name on it. That would finish us off, proper."

"Not to mention what it would mean for the ocean, of course," she retorted.

"Well, of course . . . that goes without sayin'."

"I'd like to think so. . . ."

He tossed some almonds into his mouth and washed them down with a big gulp of champagne, as if he were drinking a glass of soda, rather than the most expensive champagne in the world. "I mean, I live on this planet, too, and I've got grandkids. I want them to be able to swim out in the big, beautiful ocean, and I want their kids, after them, out there too—but they're going to have to find a way to get there from here. That's going to take fuel, ma'am. That is our dilemma, right there."

Jamie listened attentively—trying to read him on all levels. "There won't be any ocean worth driving to if the maniacal, unquenchable thirst for oil keeps leeching the life out of the seas and the rest of the Earth. Your industry is pushing the Earth to its limits, do any of you realize that? It's insane what you're doing to the planet."

"Well, I know that, ma'am. That is why y'all are here. I want to see that another disaster does not happen."

"Well then, why don't you call your boys off and get, as they say, 'out of the water'?"

"Now, you know that isn't gonna happen. I mean, the world runs on oil and we need more and more to keep things going out here and . . ."

Jamie interrupted before he could finish. ". . . And alternative energy, clearly, is not on the table, because there's not enough money in it for all the fat cats to build more obscene wealth, right?"

Mat fumbled with his cocktail napkin, folding the edges, nervously. "We're workin' on it," he replied, knowing, as the words came out of his mouth, that Jamie could see right through them.

"Why am I here?" she asked, abruptly. "There's no point us talking about the justifications for drilling for oil. You're an oil man, period. Tell me what it is you think I can do for you."

He knew he was clearly losing ground with her and didn't know how to get the conversation back on track. "Miss Jamie, I have a five-year agreement with the U.S. and Canadian governments, giving me rights to explore out there, before anybody else gets a shot at it. Two are gone—wasted. I've got three more years: I get things done the right way, we get our platform set up out there, and nobody else can move in. We have a clean track record—no accidents directly attributed to our corporation. I do not want anything to happen to the environment. No ma'am. But I have to make the brass in New York and the politicians in Washington happy. I have to find the crude. And I need help."

"I can't believe Martin Kaszlow forgot to tell you that I am done with this work, Mat. I am still coming back from being present during a massive whale death in New Zealand, and helping prevent any more of them is where I am putting my energy now."

"Well, I can certainly appreciate that," he said.

"So, helping you and your boys dig up the ocean floor just doesn't flow at all—you're a very big part of the problem. I'm sorry. Within days now I will be filing for my foundation, to help fight for the whales and dolphins, and you will be part of what I'll be fighting against."

"You can't win against the oil industry, Miss Jamie," he said, flatly.

"Watch me."

Mat was keen and alert, looking for a way to win her over, and get the momentum back. "Yes, and I appreciate that, I do. It's a very honorable thing to do and it's a 'feel good' thing, I can feel that. Y'all are going to need funding, though, I'm sure—a lot of it too. And, well ... we can help you."

"Funding from an oil company—to save the oceans? Now that is rich."

"Yes, ma'am. An 'ecologically friendly' oil company. That's what has to happen now. USOIL is that company."

Jamie sighed.

"But if you really want to help the whales, Miss Jamie, you are going to need a whole lot more than money. You're going to need connections upstairs: decision makers; friends in high places. My kind of friends."

Jamie studied Mat, watching him shift around, working his angle. There was something hidden, inaccessible, something skillfully buried that she just couldn't read.

"So please now, just hear me out, before you turn me down. My main research vessel goes out in a few weeks' time, just as soon as the rough weather passes, and we're moving up the coast, off Vancouver Island, right out there in the Pacific Ocean. I'm asking if you are willing to go out with my crew for a few weeks and use your powers, or however you want to call it, to look down on the ocean floor and help us find what we're lookin' for out there. A few weeks of your life is all I'm asking, Miss Jamie—and you can be sure you'll be well rewarded for your time, just like you were out there with the Pakistanis. And meanwhile, you have my word of honor ... you will have a chance to get to the power players, and we'll see what we can do to get the military to ease up on those big ol' whales."

"What about the whale communities that live in those waters? You're talking about some of the most important migratory routes for the whales on the whole planet! How can you ask me to help you destroy the ecosystem, by helping you find what you need to start dredging up the ocean floor? It's out of the question."

Mat took a deep breath, trying to keep cool. "If you don't help me—and I remind you, I'm a guy who is determined to protect the environment—then some other group is going to come in there and tear the place to hell. Look here, Miss Jamie—I'm the CEO of one of the leading oil corporations of the world, and here I am, turning to a psychic for help. I'm going completely on trust, not asking for anything more than you just giving it a try. Now that must surely tell you I'm an alternative, out-of-the-box kind of thinker, doesn't it? You see what happened in the Gulf of Mexico? You don't want that kind of mindless disaster to happen again. I just know you do not want that."

Jamie reflected. She couldn't help but feel there was more to it than what Mat was asking for, and she knew that his purpose for bringing her in had nothing to do with "saving the ecosystem." It was a ruse that he knew would resonate with her—she knew it. No, there was something more: something hidden.

"I want you to go out on our ship for a four-week study, and see what you can find out there. You'll be out on one of the most sophisticated, high-tech vessels, with a fully supportive crew, and my crazy-ass captain, Jimbo, who can out-navigate anything and anybody on the water. And we will steer clear of the whales—you have my word on that. As for terms, I'll have a contract written up for you before you leave in the morning. I hate to talk money over dinner, and with a fascinating woman like you to boot! But I assure you, we will do way better for you than your friends overseas, all around. It'll be a significant consulting fee for going out and, of course, a monumental one if you bring back the prize."

"And if I don't 'bring back the prize,' as you say?"

"Well, then, I will be able to put my mind at ease, knowing I was willing to try thinking outside the box of convention, Miss J." He reached into his jacket pocket and retrieved his checkbook. "Meanwhile, this here is just a little token of my esteem and support for what y'all are doing for the whales," he said. "Just to help you get your foundation off the ground. There will be more."

Jamie watched in disbelief as he wrote her out a check for $100,000. He tore the check out and handed it to her. Jamie looked at the amount and asked herself, "Is this a bribe?" She had the impulse to stand up and walk out, but where was she going to go? As she sat there, the heat flooding her cheeks, she heard Martin's words running through her head like neon lights in Times Square.

"Maybe helping him out will be good for the whales."

She struggled, but managed to resist the knee-jerk reaction to walk out, grab her suitcases, and catch the next flight back to San Francisco.

Mat studied her reactions, and she studied his. Looking back at him, she was reminded of the expression *"The devil that you know is better than the angel you don't."* She thought about the monumental task that lay before her: the battles she would have to face; the resistance she would come up against from private interest groups, politicians, the military. She decided, right then and there, that having Mat Anderson as an ally would be, by far, the better alternative to having him as an enemy.

"There will be a backlash in the community if I take donations from an oil company—you know that." She slid the check back across the table. "It may be easy for you to buy souls, Mat Anderson, but this one's not up for sale. Be sure you get that right—from the start."

Mat picked up the check from the table, and put it in his lapel pocket. He looked embarrassed and out of his depth. In his world, nobody walked away from easy money.

"But I will go out on your ship and see what I can do to help prevent you from ripping the ocean floor apart, like they've done in the Gulf."

Mat never expected her to agree, especially after she handed back $100,000. Jamie was like no one else he had ever met. She had ethics; she had moral integrity. She was clearly not corruptible, at least not for money—that test was over. These were uncharted waters for a guy like him, because he always found a person's "price." Always.

"One month is all I can give you."

"One month is all I've asked you for."

"You'll help me talk to the right commissioners and subcommittees in Washington?"

"I can do better than that. I can promise you that they will listen—but I can't promise that they will hear you."

"No matter what happens out there?"

"No matter what. I know there are no guarantees, and it would be ridiculous to set it up that way. Then again," he said, wryly, "let's not forget Pakistan."

She said yes. They shook hands and made their deal, and it was more generous than she could have imagined, just as he promised. Whether she liked it or not, Jamie was stepping up into the big leagues, back into the oil world, about to take her work to the next level. She would fly home the next morning, put her house in order, and get the lawyers to work on her PICC Foundation—the Psychic Institute for Cetacean Communications—so that she would be sailing out on the ocean with that intention clearly in place when Mat Anderson's call to action came in.

6

Political Maneuvers

Just two weeks after the command performance in New York, Mat was summoned to Washington, DC, where he had been "invited" by a White House insider to dine with some of the corporation's favored congressmen and -women, and a few of the company's most important investors.

The employees knew that, if the CEO of the company was being called to Washington, it meant a shake-up was likely to come when he got back. Everybody wondered what he would be serving up after his return to Houston, particularly his team of executive directors, who had all received an official memo, advising them to make themselves available for a top-level management meeting at eleven o'clock that Monday morning. Rumors flew, fueled by Mat's secretary, Louise, and her gossip network in the secretarial pool. The word was to keep an extremely low profile while everyone waited for the boss to return. Then, they would have to ride out the storm until after the meeting, where, no doubt, the proverbial shit was going to be hitting the big, giant fan.

In Washington, biting cold pierced the darkness, entombing the capital in a shroud of wintery gloom. Obstructed by ice and snow, the city streets were in mayhem, with traffic in a virtual gridlock. Mat was late. His limousine pulled into the driveway of the private dinner club on the Hill at 7:00 p.m., past the cocktail hour. He was running low on antacid tablets, and the evening hadn't even begun.

Already, the temperature had fallen to ten below. Weather forecasts predicted that the light snowfall that had dusted the trees and the lawns of the city earlier that afternoon was just a teaser for what was moving in from the coast. News of the imminent storm had grown more and more alarming throughout the day, with travel warnings issued for Sunday morning, just when Mat would be flying back. It was all the more incentive for him to spend as little time as necessary playing politics, and to leave Washington as early in the morning as possible, ahead of the storm. He would do dinner, take care of business, and then get out of town fast, before his plane got grounded or he simply froze to death, stuck to a sidewalk somewhere on Icicle Hill.

As he stepped out of the car, Mat told the driver to be back for him at 11:00 p.m. sharp. Four hours would cover what needed to be said and done, and still get him to bed early enough to give him a head start on his way back to Houston—back to his comfort zone. Here, he was out of his element completely . . . and he knew it.

He hated the fat cats in Washington. They all placed themselves above the law they supposedly upheld, while meanwhile their palms were out, under the table, waiting to be greased—or up in the air, pointing fingers at everybody else. He always referred to them as "highfalutin politicians and bottom-feeding lobbyists," and they all came with an agenda . . . and an extremely high price tag.

Bracing for an evening of backhanded deals and political maneuvering, Mat tipped the coat check clerk, straightened his tie, and made his entrance. He glanced around the room, gazing at faces he already knew all too well, thinking, "At least hookers are honest about what they do for a living: 'This is my price; this is what you get; show me the money.'"

Whenever he reflected on who was really running the show on the Hill, he would inevitably make that analogy, reminding himself that he actually respected and trusted prostitutes far and beyond the whores in Washington. Worse yet, he was well aware that that night, there would be guns pointed at his boots and he was going to have to dance for them all, buying time for the corporation and votes in Congress.

The club's private dining room was stiflingly overheated, so much so that walking from the freezing night air into the room was like going from a freezer straight into the oven. In the company of people who seemed to suck whatever oxygen there was from the very air itself, Mat could feel his heart pumping overtime... his blood pressure rising. The passage of time was excruciating: the minutes seemed like hours—slow and tedious. Longing for the moment when he could escape into the crisp evening air—to breathe again—he became fixated on the time, like a nervous football coach trying to run down the clock and get off the field, victorious.

He spent the evening dodging bullets and putting on a show for the power players—divulging nothing and promising everything. He so resented having to be "politically correct" and play their game, a game over which he had little or no control. It was high-stakes poker: you had to know when to bluff, when to call, and when to throw in a good hand, because even if you were holding all the aces, the guy across the table still *had* to win.

After hours of laborious conversation, when Mat was all played out, he said his goodnights, grabbed his coat, and burst out into the freezing night air, where the limo, parked and waiting across the road, immediately pulled into the drive to pick him up.

"Back to the hotel," he told the chauffeur, gruffly, and then he loosened his tie, poured himself a drink, and finally relaxed into the seat, grateful to have another command performance behind him.

Circumventing the primary roads on the Hill, where the Secret

Service had set up roadblocks, the driver had to divert at Pennsylvania Avenue, no longer open to traffic. That great bastion of democracy, the White House, was now barricaded and hiding from its own people. He felt a pang of conscience, knowing he was part of the corruption that was helping eat away at the foundations of a dream.

America, and all it had once stood for—all he had fought for— was dying . . . on life support, and counting.

Images of the killing fields of Vietnam, the blood of women and children, flooded his river of memories, as they always did whenever he came to Washington. Something here triggered the haunting; those tiny ghosts still managed to enter and exit through a locked door in his soul. Doing his best to shake them off, Mat promised himself that these visits to the capital were somehow going to have to come to an end.

Before turning in for the night, he sent two strategic text messages, alerting his team to be prepared to fly him out, at the first available runway slot. He set his alarm for 4:00 a.m., knowing he would have to get out of town first thing in the morning, or be stuck for days in Georgetown, which was not an option, for more reasons than he cared to even think about.

While the city slept into the pre-dawn hours, the snow intensified, pushed into the region by the massive storm front that had already dumped mountains of snow across the entire Eastern Seaboard. Snow flurries played cat and mouse with the plows, their drivers working through the night to free up the most important districts, and all the main roads, before morning. As they groaned their way through the city streets, breaking the muffled silence of blanketing snowfall, they engaged in a futile game with nature: the powder falling stealthily behind them, instantly covering the pavement just as quickly as they got it cleared. It was as if Mother Nature, with all her graceful artistry and mighty determination, had decided to override the business of man, and to remind those who dared attempt to control her that she was—and would always be—the ultimate authority.

Weather was never a deterrent to Mat's daily workout regime of running five miles every morning; his motto was "Once a Marine, always a Marine." In fact, he usually enjoyed the cold and found running in it stimulating—within reason, which subzero temperatures were not. Still, he awoke before his alarm and got suited up and out the door by 4:30, jogging in the freezing black night: just him, clearing his head from the night before, and the plows, clearing the roads. It was his surefire way to release the adrenaline overload of all that he had to do to keep the big boys happy, to keep the hungry wolves at bay, and to hold on to his seat of power.

He got back to his suite as day was breaking. A hot shower, a bit of breakfast, and he would be on his way to the airport by 7:00. With the driver waiting outside the lobby, and his pilot on standby at the airport, he called Jamie, enlisting her into active service. Just two weeks after their encounter, he had to call her back to Houston and get her cleared with his management team before sending her out to search for buried treasure. Even though it was only a formality, it was still important.

What Mat did not need now was a Judas from the inside.

On the other side of the continent, there could not have been a more picture-perfect San Francisco morning. Jamie lounged around in her flannel pajamas, gazing out at the sun, as it broke through the cloud banks: the fog curling slowly back out over the ocean and gulls, diving the waves. From her precious bay-view bedroom window, she looked out over Fisherman's Wharf and the incredible vista that extended beyond, as far out as the Golden Gate Bridge: a view most people only dreamed about.

A third-generation San Franciscan, she was convinced that there was nowhere on Earth more breathtakingly beautiful than this magical place: the City by the Bay. Drinking in the natural beauty and the warmth of the sun's golden rays, Jamie snuggled up lazily under her down comforter, savoring the moment—deciding how she wanted to spend the day: hanging out down at Fisherman's Wharf, playing tourist, or driving with her mother up the coast for a stroll . . . maybe a picnic . . . amongst the great sequoias in Muir Woods.

Unfortunately, Mat's call interrupted her sun-filled morning reverie, breaking and entering—as out of place as a burglar in a candy shop. He apologized for calling on a Sunday, explaining how things were moving faster than he had anticipated, and that they were pushing the sail date up by a few weeks. He wanted her on the first flight out, so that she could be in Houston that same night and available the next morning for an 11:00 a.m. executive management meeting at the office. Louise would handle all the details—she merely had to confirm her availability, and all her travel arrangements would be managed from their end. He planned to introduce her to his executive directors, get her back to San Francisco the next day, and then fly her to Vancouver as quickly as possible, just as soon as the weather would permit, to join the crew of USOIL's ship *The Deepwater*—before anybody had any time to throw a wrench into his plans.

Jamie couldn't understand the purpose of or the sense in losing two days flying all the way out to Houston and back, just for a meeting, and she needed time to get her house in order before leaving for a whole month. She tried to persuade Mat that they could just as easily do a conference call, saving time and money for him, and a lot more wear and tear on her, especially since Vancouver was on the West Coast, just a couple hours' flying time away.

In a tone of voice that she had not yet heard from him, a voice far more direct and authoritative than the playful Texan drawl with which he had wooed her, he simply said, "Jamie, I need everybody on board here." He let her know that bringing her into the project meant that he was going way out on a limb, risking his position and his credibility, and that he owed his executive directors at least an official introduction. He was consensus building, counting on Jamie's presence and keen abilities to win over his twelve-member team of die-hard cynics and naysayers. The last thing Mat needed was someone turning traitor on him while he was sailing out into the unknown, uncharted territory, in every sense, with Jamie Hastings.

She agreed, and by 3:00 p.m. she was on a flight to Houston, more than ready to go through the motions for the white-collar boys at USOIL.

The twelve executive directors arrived early Monday morning, greeted with the usual fare of gourmet coffees and elaborate French pastries, freshly baked every morning by the company's executive chef. USOIL spared no luxuries for its management team, and they were, admittedly, spoiled. The privilege afforded them by the company contributed to their feeling more than confident about their own job security. Every one of them had served in the company for as long as or longer than Mat himself—a company that had soared for so long under their management, until the recent slide.

But they weren't so confident this day. They knew trouble was in the air and feared cuts could actually be on the table, mandated from the stir at the top levels of the multinational, where Mat had been dealing for weeks. That was the buzz between them, as they waited around anxiously for the meeting to begin, and for Mat to bring in the news from DC. If heads were going to fly, it was anybody's guess as to whose was going to end up on the chopping block that day.

The men sat nervously awaiting Mat Anderson, anticipating bad news. Today the boardroom, with its huge mahogany table and the twelve chairs the men filled, felt cold as steel. Everything about the room was Mat Anderson to the finest detail: sleek, modern, and edgy enough to be just slightly intimidating when he wanted it to be, or warm and inviting when it was deserved.

And that was the way Mat liked it.

He marched through the doorway at 11:00 a.m. sharp, with military precision, looking somber and resolute. The men stood in deference. Mat walked to his seat at the head of the table and nodded to them to sit down.

"Gentlemen." He reached ceremoniously into the lapel pocket of his jacket and placed his two cell phones, a laser pen, and two packs of Rolaids squarely on the table in front of him, and then they all sat down. His face was red hot with emotion, threatening but never exploding, yet dangerous—like a volcano ready to blow. "As you all can imagine, this here is not going to be a good news get-together," he announced, in his decisive Texan drawl.

Louise swayed into the room carrying a stack of reports, whereupon she circled the table, distributing one to each of the participants. Her formfitting dress and the way she knew how to move in it were almost enough to distract the men, but they knew better. She was Mat's "personal" assistant, and everyone knew what that meant. Don't look twice—and don't even think about touching.

He knew how to use her for strategic impact, among other things.

Mat rolled his director's chair up closer to the table's edge. "Let me cut right to the chase. We are in deep shit, here, gentlemen. Lost our asses out there in the Gulf, and we won't even talk about the BP disaster—and what that has cost us all in image, in resources, and in long- and short-term profitability." Dry-mouthed, he filled his glass from the crystal water pitcher in front of him, and took a drink. "Hell's bells—we've been out there tearing up the Pacific for more than two years now and we have got shit to show for it."

Slowly Mat's gaze moved around the table, squaring off with each of the men to see which of them had enough presence to look back at him, head-on. Most of them never locked eyes with him—it was too uncomfortable looking into those icy blue spheres. "We know the gold's out there," he said, "but for all our high-tech equipment, we are no closer to daylight on this than a hair on a possum's ass."

A few of the men around the table smiled, but the unmistakable lack of laughter only served to accentuate their breathless silence.

"I just don't think y'all have any idea of the kind of pressure I got bearin' down on my 'special place.'" He unwrapped a packet of the antacid tablets, popped one into his mouth, and then another immediately after. Clearly agitated, he loosened his tie, sweating around the collar. "I've got these clowns on the Hill with their greasy palms all over my behind, and all I can tell them is 'We're getting close.' Now how do y'all think that goes over with our, shall we call them, 'constituents'?"

Somebody's phone rang. Mat looked around the table, but whoever possessed the phone had managed to switch it off immediately.

"This big-shot congressman from New York says I've been playing horseshoes for too long, and everybody thinks that's real funny . . . real funny. See, that's what you call 'Mat the Texas cowboy' humor." He slapped his fist on the table. "I am getting it from all sides. Corporate screaming about media pressure, and public interest groups making waves about the goddamn whales. Let's face it, the Navy *is* out there blasting their big ol' brains out. We got crazy natives and all them do-gooder environmental freaks making a lot of noise. They should know what a mess we got out there. Hell, they're still screaming about the *Valdez*!" He stood and pointed at one of the men, seated nearly across the table. "And face it, John, PR is doing a piss-poor job of cleaning up the mess in the meantime. I think you know what I'm saying here."

John Galloway, the vice president of public relations, was about to respond, but Mat cut him off.

"I am telling you all loud and clear: my boys here just cannot be squeezed any further." He sat down again. Taking time to calm himself, Mat removed his glasses and a cleaning cloth from the case and vigorously wiped the lenses before putting them on. He opened the cover of the report, peering strategically over his glasses at the men. "Let's take a look at these figures—shall we? See page five. Pharmaceutical, General Foods, Agriculture all closing with healthy gains, and then there's us—way down there at the bottom: USOIL—the big loser for another quarter."

Mat Anderson, former Marine commander, didn't do "loser."

"We have overspent and underproduced more than any other division, and I shouldn't have to remind you that y'all are the highest-paid, most-pampered executives in the whole damned corporation. Gentlemen, what I'm telling you all is that USOIL is seen as an extremely ineffective and costly branch of this big ol' oak— and there are some very important people wanting to just chop it off, before it rots out the whole damn tree."

He pushed the document away from him on the table. "I hope you get my metaphorical drift, as they say. This dog won't hunt, my friends," he said, shaking his head, "…this dog just will not hunt."

The phone buzzed. It was Louise, announcing that Jamie Hastings had arrived. Mat told her to entertain her for a few more minutes until he called back. "Now, while all of you nice folk are sleeping, comfortable-like, at night, playing golf at the country club and shit like that, ol' Mattie here is thinking overtime. 'How the hell am I going to pull this one out?' And I'm sitting there at two in the morning, watching TV in that hellhole, New York City, and on comes this psychic woman from San Francisco—lady by the name of 'Jamie Hastings.'" He fiddled with his pen, avoiding eye contact now, rather than seeking it. "Katie Lee was interviewing her about her work down in L.A. with the police department. Now you all know that this LAPD squad—they aren't exactly lightweights, and yet, in many situations, they had to go and turn to a psychic for help. Seems this Jamie Hastings woman solved a bunch of unsolved crimes down there just being able to tune in and see it happening, or talking to spirits and shit . . . all through the 'mind's eye.'"

He stood up again, and walked over to the buffet, where he poured himself a cup of coffee, stirring in three teaspoons of sugar, slowly and methodically, keeping his back to the room. "Now that impressed me. That impressed the hell out of me. I can tell you that." Without turning around, he added, "And here's the good part." He turned back to the men, staging his body language, and sat back down, sipping his coffee as he spoke. "When I finally tracked her down, which was not easy—let me tell you—this woman told me she had been traveling on and off for more than three years, working on several projects, and I got curious real fast. So I did a little sleuthing on my own, and what did I find out? It turns out she was hired by the Pakistanis to locate wells out there in the freakin' desert, using her 'third eye' to find the black gold, for our friends over there. Can you dig that?"

One of the men laughed out loud.

"I'm glad you find that so funny, Jimmy. This little woman finds three wells in the middle of the desert—in uncharted territory, mind you—with just a 'sense' of it all, through her mind's eye. No sonar, no radar, no high-tech instruments, no fracking . . . no outrageous costs, no shit. She just 'sees' it. Not one mistake, no false starts. She sees it and now they've got three wells pumping crude. Now I am dying to know what is so funny about that, yes I am."

"She must have gotten real lucky," said one of the men. "Sorry, Mat, that's all I have to say."

Mat leaned back in his chair, his hands clasped behind his head. "Well, thank you, Parnell, for that astute contribution to my humble little dialogue over here. Now why didn't I think of that? 'She just got lucky.' Three brand-new wells gushing crude in less than a year. That's lucky times three. If that is luck, gentlemen, then it appears I have been lookin' for it in all the wrong places." He sat back upright in his chair, annoyed. "I guess I don't have that kind of 'luck,' as you call it, 'cuz if I did, I sure as hell wouldn't be sitting here with you all today, looking at your clueless faces, let me tell you. I wouldn't be fighting to save your asses out here, y'all can bank on that. No way, my friends ... and I wouldn't be line dancing for everybody in Washington, DC, neither."

The execs looked at each other, having a hard time believing they were really hearing these words come out of Mat's mouth. Mat Anderson, a die-hard, cynical conservative Texan, espousing the virtues of a left-wing, New Age psychic? They kept expecting the punch line of a joke that never came.

"Let me reiterate this for y'all, in language your fun-lovin' little minds can understand. Jamie Hastings worked for the LAPD for five years. In that time, she helped them put away over fifty child rapers and murderers, after the cops themselves admitted the trails had gone cold. Fifty-three, to be exact. That is not luck, my friends. There is something much more powerful at play here, whether you want to understand it or not. An OPEC guy finds out about her and the very next thing you know, they're flying her good-lookin' American ass out to Pakistan. How did we let that happen? Really? How did America let that happen? Don't you think somebody here should have recognized she was a real live national asset, and kept her home? Of course not. It's too much of a joke, right? Well, boys, I am that guy. I don't understand it, but I have her track record to go on: this little woman gets these 'visions' or whatever and bam! Slimeballs go to jail. New water wells are bringing vital water to the surface. The crude starts gushing. That's what I know: I can count on it. And that's all I need to know." He pushed aside the report in a dismissive gesture. "It's amazing she got out of there alive. I know I sure as hell would have held on to her, y'all know what I'm saying? This woman finds three drill sites in a year... and here we are, with all our technological superiority, storming around the Pacific Ocean with nothing to show for it but one giant mess on the ocean floor and a bunch of mean, nasty barnacles growing all over our man parts. I hope y'all see the irony in that."

He leaned forward with his elbows braced on the table, his right hand in a fist, cupped tightly in his left. "Gentlemen, I've got Jamie Hastings outside. I have made her the proverbial offer she could not refuse, and she has agreed to come and give us a hand. Oh ... and that'll be coming out of your developmental research budgets for the next two quarters, if y'all are still around by then, so don't choke on your French roast when you get that memo in the morning." Mat forced a smile. "We got ourselves a first-class psychic gonna help us out before we tear up the whole damn Pacific Ocean, like some crazy-ass gophers out there on the golf green—and I am feeling good about it. Yessir, I am feeling really good about it, I can tell you that right now."

His vice president of marketing, Ben Ackerman, finally spoke out. "This is some kind of a joke, right?"

"Is that what you think?" Mat stood up and buttoned his jacket. "You think I'm in a jokin' mood?" He buzzed Louise and told her to show Jamie in. "I want you nice Southern gentlemen to show Miss Hastings the maximum cordiality and respect, as we all are fixin' to welcome her to our team—y'all hear Mattie boy, talking loud and clear?" As he walked over to the door to show Jamie in, he looked back over his shoulder at them all.

"Get ready for the New Age, my friends."

7

All Aboard

Jamie walked into the executive boardroom looking as radiant as ever. She was the personification of confidence and grace— not at all what they had most likely envisioned: surely something more akin to Guinevere or the Good Witch from Oz. Dressed in an elegant, cream-colored cashmere suit, offset by her golden New Zealand tan, she was the picture of natural beauty. She wore her thick, wavy auburn hair tied loosely in a French knot, with no other adornment but a pair of gold earrings and a Hermès scarf draped across her shoulders.

Her masterful presence threw them. Very few women ever entered the hallowed halls of the corporate boardroom as equals, if at all. This was Texas, after all—the white boys' club. A woman of power in the boardroom? They didn't like it, they didn't like her, and they weren't going to make the pretense of making her feel at all welcome. Mat had already presented her as a "done deal," however, so they knew they were not there to engage in discussion. This was a *fait accompli*—an executive order. They were there to observe. Period.

Mat escorted Jamie to the seat next to his. "It is my pleasure to introduce our consultant for the *Deepwater* operation, Ms. Jamie Hastings. I know y'all are gonna join me in welcoming her to our happy little family here today." Mat had this amazing gift of being able to weave sarcasm through his thick Texan drawl like needlepoint.

No, they were not. A few of the men nodded stiffly—others could not even fake it.

Mat was visibly annoyed with the rude behavior. He was, after all was said and done, a Texas gentleman, and he expected the same from his team. "I have already filled you in on Ms. Hastings's remarkable feats and track record," he announced sternly. "I have assured her that my decision to fly her in from San Francisco, just to meet with y'all, has nothing to do with her needing to seek anybody's endorsement here today."

Relaxed, knowing there was nothing she needed to prove, Jamie sat back comfortably in her chair, observing the men and their collective body language. She knew she was anything but welcome, and found it almost amusing how men inevitably showed their weakness by being aggressive and resistant to women in positions of authority.

Didn't they realize how transparent they were?

After working with macho cops at LAPD, and the Pakistanis, she knew all about what she affectionately referred to as the "testosterone dilemma." Hence, they didn't faze her at all. She was there because the chairman of the board had begged for her help, and she assumed that the executive directors were just going to have to get their heads around it. From what she could discern from Mat's behavior, he would have liked them to be okay with it, but it was going to be their problem if they were not.

Mat leaned back, pointing the laser at a large navigational map of the Pacific Northwest. "*The Deepwater* is in port in Vancouver, and we begin our explorations very soon now: here, farther north than we've been until now, covering new ground. We have carte blanche from the Canadians to open this new area, and we're going farther out, significantly distancing ourselves from the coast."

As Jamie observed and listened, she was struck by the fact that Mat was pointing to a place on the map where the words ORCA SANCTUARY were written in ink. Breaking protocol completely, she interrupted Mat at the onset of his presentation, right in the middle of his speech.

"Excuse me, Mat," she blurted out, "but you've got an Orca sanctuary in the middle of your target zone? Am I seeing that right?"

Jamie Hastings had just interrupted the chief executive officer of USOIL, in the middle of an executive directors' meeting. Mat was not amused. No one else had ever dared to do that: it was simply unthinkable. Jamie challenging Mat in front of these men, in the inner sanctum of the boardroom, was emasculating. It was a question she certainly could have asked him in private, rather than blasting him in front of his colleagues.

One of the executive directors, Jeb Richardson, almost laughed out loud. He was the most conservative of them all, and the least cooperative. He put his hand over his mouth to conceal a snide remark to the man seated next to him. "Like I always say, a woman's got to be a bitch in bed and a slave in the kitchen." He coughed, concealing a laugh, but he projected exactly what he was thinking to everyone in the room.

He was the most unapologetic sexist in Texas.

Mat bristled, sharing enough of Jeb's views on women to imagine what he thought of Jamie. He didn't need this antagonism from her, breaking down what he was trying to establish in her favor. Where was her "heightened sensitivity," now?

"Yes," he answered, dismissively, "there are a few stretches where the whales have the right-of-way, but that won't be a problem."

"No? How do you figure?" Jamie demanded. Terms had been clearly defined just days prior, when he was courting her into the deal, and she was not going to let it go, regardless of how this Jeb character or any of the others dismissed her.

Mat tried not to lose his patience, but, at the same time, he had to maintain his posture in front of the men. "Well, now, Ms. Hastings, I mean we can avoid it."

Jamie would not be dissuaded. "I need to be real clear with you and everyone here present that, if you want me out there, we're going to have to stay far away from any whale migration routes and this sanctuary."

In that moment, Mat realized he had set himself into a trap: how to keep Jamie on board while holding his position of authority? All eyes were on Mat, waiting to see how he was going to handle this woman who they had heard, through Louise's grapevine, was a "pain-in-the-ass, liberal female from San Francisco." She had stepped right into the stereotype.

"Yes," Mat said, tightly, "we will be careful to avoid any collateral damage."

"Collateral damage? Where have we heard that term before? Sorry, Mat—either the whales have your full protection, and this Orca sanctuary and all whale migratory routes remain off-limits completely, or I can't do this. I will have to back out."

Mat looked around the room. He felt he was being usurped, his credibility waning. The meeting was a disaster—Jamie was not playing ball with him at all, making him look small in front of his peers. "I assure you we will stay clear of the whale sanctuary," he said, through clenched teeth. "Now do you mind if we move on?"

Jamie continued to press him. "I have your word on that?"

Mat clenched down so hard you could see the muscles in his jaw contracting. "Yes, you have my word."

They all sat waiting for Mat to put Jamie in her place, as he would have done to any one of them, but to their amazement, he held back. That never happened in Mat Anderson's boardroom.

"I tell you what . . . if you gentlemen will accompany our guest to the dining room, I think a few drinks are in order. Let's lighten things up a little, and then we can continue this over lunch."

He motioned to them to leave the room. Jamie looked at him, quizzically.

"I'll be right with you, Ms. Jamie—I've got a few urgent matters to clear off my desk before lunch. You just tell the boys all about your time down in L.A. Let them in on the kind of work you did for the police," he said, winking.

Everyone stood and started for the door. It was a welcome reprieve from the highly charged environment of the meeting room. After the last executive closed the door behind him, Louise came in with a stack of memos that had to go out that morning. She put the pen in his hand and stood next to him while he signed each one. Despite the pressures of the moment, these were documents that could not wait until after lunch.

Once she was out the door, Mat picked up his cell phone and speed dialed the number 2. He held it close to his mouth, almost whispering into the phone. "I want you to keep a very, very close eye on Jamie Hastings," he said, furtively. "And tell that boy Sam to be cool or I'll yank him, even if we need his daddy's pull up there on the Hill." He hung up immediately, and went off to join the others, hopeful that a few drinks and a little Texas-style hospitality would be enough to break the ice wall that had formed around Jamie.

To his amazement, by the time he entered the dining room, Jamie had managed, like magic, to turn things around. The men were captivated, engaging her. She was recounting the story of the famous serial killer, Willie Hynes, who had terrorized four states on the West Coast and brutally murdered seventeen young women, before the Los Angeles Police Department finally turned to Jamie for help, and officially hired her as a psychic investigator for the department.

Hynes remained one of the most elusive serial killers in history. A girl would go missing without a trace and then, days later, the police would get a call, directing them to the body. He never left a trace of evidence at the crime scene. He was meticulous: no blood, no prints, nothing. Police forces from L.A. all the way up as far as Seattle were absolutely stumped. After seventeen murders, covering four states, no one had come up with a single clue or lead to follow. Empty-handed, with nothing at all with which to appease the good citizens of the entire West Coast, they had had to admit that the trail for all the murders had gone absolutely cold.

Jamie stopped talking when Mat walked up to the table, deferring to him, but he insisted she continue, seating himself at the head of the table. The only man without a drink in his hand was Jeb. By now, he was so openly annoyed with what he perceived as psychic fairyland that he just could not contain himself any further. He wanted to dismiss Jamie completely and cut the floor out from under her.

"Let me guess," he said, condescendingly, "you're saying *you* solved that case?"

"Yes, that's right."

"Little ol' you, up against the police power of four different states?"

"Well…I was not 'up against' them. We worked together; LAPD headed up the investigation, since most of the murders happened in their jurisdiction."

"And you worked for LAPD?"

"That's right," she replied, getting back to her story. "The only evidence they had on him was what we call 'the signature.' Serials always leave one for the police—it's part of the power trip behind the killing. That's all the police had. Sixteen dead girls, their bodies thrown into the woods or on a beach, and each time they would find a little white plastic chess piece next to the body." Jamie continued, enthralled in her own story. "After the last murder, the sixteenth, Martin Kaszlow—he's the chief of LAPD—received a one-word letter from the killer. It simply said, 'checkmate.' The killer knew the police had nothing. They believed that he felt he had won the game and . . . this 'checkmate' . . . they hoped it meant he was done—that the game was over. In fact, six months passed with no further incidents—at least none that fit Hynes's pattern. Then, out of the blue, another young girl—she had been missing for forty-eight hours—was found with her throat cut, in the Hollywood Hills. This time," Jamie said, "they found a black chess piece—the king—jammed into the gash across her throat. He was back. And now he wanted more attention, so he upped the stakes—more gore, more violence."

Mat belted back his drink. "Ugly business," he said, grimacing.

"As you know, gentlemen, there are sixteen white pieces and another sixteen black pieces in the game. He was letting the police know that he was going to murder another fifteen girls: daring them to stop him . . . playing this game serials love to play with their minds."

The waiter interrupted with a tray of hors d'oeuvres and started to hand out menus, but Mat stopped him, and told him to bring another round of drinks.

"Go on," he said.

"Well, that's when I first got called in for consultation. Marty heard about some of my work at the Stanford Psychic Institute and he asked me to come down and give them a hand—sort of like Mat has done."

"Bingo," thought Mat. *"One major PR point scored for Jamie."*

"That was sort of it, really. Once I held that black king in my hand, I saw the tattoo—The Black King, written across the killer's chest—just as clear as day. That's how we identified him. I saw the house, too, and . . . well . . . I just managed to lead the police right to him." She took a drink, looking as if she wanted to forget the pictures that had surfaced in her mind, looking back at her from the bottom of her glass. "There, they found all the grisly evidence they needed to convict him and put him away for life."

"Give us a break," Jeb said, openly defying her. "You can't seriously be telling us that, after years of these unsolved murders, all you had to do was hold this piece of plastic in your hand and the murders were solved!"

"I am *dead* serious," she replied, dramatically.

With all her other talents, Mat was discovering, Jamie was a master storyteller. She had the track record and the proof to back up everything she was saying, and she clearly did not feel she had to impress anyone. She spoke her truth, from the gut, and that truth was compelling and real. He didn't speak or try to intervene. He knew that no matter how impossible it was to understand how or why, Jamie had these extraordinary abilities and such an incredible truth about her that even the most determined skeptics amongst them could not help but consider the possibility that she was for real.

They had at least fifty-three reasons to believe her.

The more his colleagues became absorbed in her story, the more belligerent Jeb became. He was in complete denial. Despite the facts, which, knowing Mat, had obviously been verified, Jeb refused to believe a word of anything she had to say. He did everything he could to deflect attention away from her and to disrupt her stories of specters and psychic visions.

For some reason, he saw Jamie as his adversary. "So, the next thing we know, y'all are gonna start reading everybody's palm or something, is that right?" He was smug and condescending, doing his best to discredit her.

"I'm not a fortune teller," she said.

"Ah, you mean you're not going to read my horoscope?"

"No, but what I can do is to give you a chance to speak to Billy. He's here." Suddenly, she jolted. Jamie's body became quite rigid. She sat bolt upright in her chair. Looking straight into his eyes, she reiterated, "Billy is here."

Jeb looked like he had been hit by lightning. He turned ghostly white, almost as if he were in shock. His only son, Billy, the only thing that had ever made sense in his life, had died in a car crash when he was only twelve years old. Jeb was behind the wheel, two sheets to the wind after too many Jack Daniels he'd downed at the bar before picking the boy up from basketball practice.

Not a day went by that he didn't think of that moment of impact, and when he watched, helplessly, as his son died in his arms. For all intents and purposes, he died too. Jeb Richardson sealed his heart that day; he closed his mind. He cursed god, gave up on his dreams, and turned away from love altogether.

Enraged, he leaped out of his chair, staring at Mat. "What the hell kind of game is this?" he screamed. "My boy is dead and buried."

Mat just said, "You know me better than that, Jeb." He, too, was having a hard time getting his head around what had just happened.

"How the hell do you know about my Billy?" he yelled accusingly at Jamie.

The men sat there, in disbelief, trying to understand what was happening, and waiting for what Jamie would say next. They could feel the cold of the paranormal encounter—they were in it, all of them, along with her.

"Please, sit down. I need everyone to just stay calm. He's here. Billy is here for you. Help me bring him through."

Visibly shaken, angry, and confused, Jeb sat down.

Jamie was gentle: her voice was so soft, it was just more than a whisper. "He is begging you to please stop beating yourself up over the accident. He's alive, he's happy where he is … except for your suffering—he can't bear to see you in the dark." Suddenly, her voice changed into the voice of a child. *"Please forgive yourself, Daddy-o. I'm here, I'm always close to you … you just can't see me. I love you, Champ."*

Upon hearing those words, his son's voice coming from Jamie's own mouth, Jeb lost it completely: all his walls came crashing down and, with them, the prison doors of his shame and guilt swung open. In front of all his peers, his boss ... in front of the woman he was afraid could indeed reach him, he put his head into his hands and sobbed like a baby. It was a scene no one could have remotely imagined—never in a thousand Texan years.

If ever there had been a doubt for any of them that the soul survives death, or that some people can reach through the veil and connect the living with those who have passed over, then surely Jamie had dispelled it all. All their resistance was out the window.

Jamie Hastings was "in."

She got up from her chair and went to Jeb to comfort him. Like a loving mother, she put her arms around his shoulders, holding him, silent, allowing all those years of pain to finally flow freely—allowing Billy to put his arms around his dad, one last time. In that intimate moment, it was as if nothing else mattered and no one else was in the room.

Overwrought with so much emotion—the guilt and his unbearable sorrow—Jeb scrambled clumsily to extract his wallet from his jacket pocket. From it, he pulled out a photo of the beautiful little boy Jamie had just seen sitting next to him, his hand shaking almost out of control. He held it up to her.

It was signed: *I love you, Champ.*

8

The Deepwater

Jamie would have very little time in San Francisco before she would have to leave again, embarking on her big adventure out at sea. She had only just returned from New Zealand, after so long away, and already she was being pulled from home again. How she had missed hanging out with her mother, going to shows together... socializing with friends. She wanted to fit back in, as much as she ever had or could, and have a personal life. Yet, as much as she longed to set down those roots, with time to dedicate to a number of important projects, including the whale foundation, she seemed to be in some way destined to a life of endless travel. She was forever being called to duty on levels she herself did not fully understand, living out of mismatched suitcases she had never learned to pack efficiently. She sighed at the thought of another flight, another journey, and more time away from the home she so loved, but never managed to enjoy—at least not for any significant stretch of time. And yet, deep down inside, she was thrilled at the prospect of being on a ship out in the Pacific, knowing something important was going to happen out there.

Something was already stirring beneath the waves.

Her mother used to say Jamie had "wanderlust" and that she would never settle down and, indeed, she never really had. The very idea of "settling" in any way, shape, or form held no appeal whatsoever. Some great relationships had come and gone, winding and bending like the path she walked, until they could no longer bend far enough to flow in the direction of her life—and then they would snap. Inevitably, the men she met and fell in love with were never able to handle the intensity of the life she needed to live, and so she walked away—time and time again—until finally she realized that her mother was right. There could be no "settling."

All she knew was that she had to follow her heart, trust her gut, and reach for the stars, and that is how Jamie Hastings lived her life, from as far back as she could remember.

Children never came—not that she didn't try. Like unfinished tattoos, three tragic miscarriages were etched in black on her heart, and complications with the last one had closed the doors to the possibility of motherhood and family. It took time, but she eventually resigned herself to it, knowing that she was destined for other things, and yielding to the wisdom of forces beyond her control. Oh, but how she would have loved to share her life with a child ... a daughter she could have showered with love, as she had always known from her own mother.

It just wasn't meant to be. Those were long ago sand castles that had been snatched by the waves and tossed back into the sea.

Jamie forced her mind to shift from the weightiness of thoughts of the past to the excitement of what lay ahead. To be out on the ocean for any reason always thrilled her, but now—working to protect the whales from the oilers? This was one of the greatest challenges she had ever faced and yet, it held within its potential one of the greatest opportunities. Her true motivation for taking this on was what it could mean for the whales, the dolphins, and all the ocean beings. She promised herself that she would give Mat Anderson and his oil-hungry conglomerate enough to work with, so that, hopefully, they could take what they wanted from the ocean floor without destroying everything in their wake.

In exchange for that effort, what she would bring back with her, Mat's promise, would be the strength of his political influence, which would enable her to speak with a far greater voice for the whales and all the rightful citizens of Planet Ocean. PICC would serve as the vessel for finding that voice, and making sure the message was heard.

Jamie promised herself that, after this trip, her travel years were coming to an end, so that she could dedicate more of herself to the foundation, and really make a difference. Even if it absolutely killed her, she would learn how to say "no," and spend more time at home, maybe even sneaking in some fun between causes—maybe *even* falling in love again.

The call to duty came later than expected—precisely Tuesday, March 12—when finally the worst of winter had passed, and *The Deepwater* could sail. Mat called personally to ask that she be ready to depart that Thursday to sail the day after, as the ship was in port, being readied for their expedition.

"That's the Ides of March," she told Mat. "Interesting sail date."

"The what?"

"*'Beware the Ides of March'*—Shakespeare wrote it into the play *Julius Caesar*. He was referring to March 15th, when Caesar was betrayed and murdered in the Senate."

"Sorry, Miss Jamie, but I am unfamiliar with that little piece of culture. Is it supposed to mean something to me?"

"Only if you're superstitious," she said, making light of it. She sensed Mat's embarrassment over his inability to reference the greatest literary master in all of history.

Louise tapped on the door and walked into Mat's office. "I have everything set up and ready to go," she said, handing him Jamie's itinerary. He winked. She really took care of business for him and he forgot, sometimes, to take care of her back. He placed his hand over the mouthpiece on the phone. "Why don't you free yourself up for lunch?" he said, lasciviously.

"Can do," she replied, feeling Mat's eyes caressing her backside when she exited.

"Sorry, Jamie...I had Louise here with all your transportation information. She'll be sending it to you now in an email. We'll have a private plane for you out there—timing's all spelled out in detail for you. My staff and crew have been briefed. You just need to be ready."

She thanked Mat and told him she was all set to go.

"Anything you need out there—anything at all—you just let me know," he said, and hung up, feeling very satisfied with himself.

The limousine arrived that Thursday morning to escort Jamie to the airport. How generous of Mat, she thought, to arrange to fly her by private jet, in the style to which all the corporate hierarchy had become accustomed. It surely was overspend, considering it was only about a two-hour flight, but she wasn't complaining.

The driver was a big, cheerful man who looked more like a bodyguard than a chauffeur. He came up to the apartment, carried Jamie's bags down to the car without even losing his breath, and settled her into the passenger's seat with a glass of fresh-squeezed orange juice, served chilled, from the bar. He drove her right onto the tarmac, to the door of the plane, where she was greeted like nobility by a private airport security official and the crew, and accommodated in style. No pain, no strain, no security harassment...and no long, empty hours at the airport.

Ever since she had been dealing with the oil industry, Jamie had experienced the ease with which the rich and privileged live their lives, a world to which mere mortals are not entitled. To an outsider looking in, or even to the occasional visitor, tasting it now and then as she did, it is a lifestyle one can only imagine—if even that. But it comes with a high price for the planet, and it eats away at the soul of man, and Jamie felt uncomfortable with it. She decided then and there that it would be the last time she accepted such material enticements from Mat Anderson or anyone else, as they were all manifestations of a polarized, greedy world that needed to change.

After a gourmet vegetarian lunch in flight, they landed in Vancouver—ahead of schedule—and once again, the car was waiting for her right there, as she exited the plane. Forty minutes later, she arrived at the entrance to the main harbor, where *The Deepwater,* USOIL's magnificent ship, was moored. Jamie hadn't really given much thought to the ship itself and really didn't know what to expect, but what little her mind had conjured up was certainly nothing like this. In utter disbelief, she stared out the limousine window at the incredibly sleek mega yacht, wondering if the driver had taken a wrong turn. This was no research vessel. It looked more like a luxury liner—one unimaginably expensive man toy—designed for the likes of some eccentric billionaire, like the sultan of Brunei . . . not for scouring the ocean floor.

The guards waved them past the security gate and into the VIP parking area, close up to the ship. Sunlight bounced off the letters, written in gold on the stern: *The Deepwater.* As the chauffeur was opening the door for Jamie, a couple walked up the path from the ship, approaching her. They looked as if they had just stepped off the cover of *Vogue:* he, a too-tanned rich boy in khakis and Louis Vuitton designer sunglasses; she, a statuesque, leggy blonde with the scrubbed, innocent beauty of a college co-ed. Jamie found them oddly out of character for what she had visualized as "crew members" on a research ship, trawling for oil in the deep ocean. Then again, here she was—a psychic trying to glean coordinates for a drill site, twenty thousand leagues under the sea. Surely, she was no less out of place than they.

As the driver helped Jamie out of the passenger's seat and then proceeded to get the bags from the trunk, the young man came right up to her.

"Miss Hastings," he said, crisply, "my name is Sam Kemmeries, chief technician of *The Deepwater,* and this is Liz Bartholomew, our new intern from the London office. We're your official greeters."

Liz reached her hand out to Jamie and, in a perfect Oxford English accent, said, "It is such a pleasure to welcome you! We are so delighted to have you."

Jamie looked them both deep in the eyes before shaking hands. This fellow, Sam, looked anything but delighted to be welcoming Jamie aboard. Her gut reaction had already been triggered: something didn't feel quite right about the two of them. Mat had promised her a top-notch crew, but here she was, standing before a couple of beautiful people who looked more like Ken and Barbie dolls than they did technical engineers.

Sam ordered the driver to bring the bags down to the ship, and Jamie noted the tension between the two men. He was aggressive and superior, and she took an instant dislike to him. This was the chief technician? She hoped that meant he would be holed up in a room somewhere for the next month, where she would have as little exposure to him as possible.

Jamie had been around all sorts of people, even nobility, and none of them fazed her. This Sam Kemmeries person, though ... he had a smugness about him that was completely off-putting. He had more than "rich kid" written all over him—he had some kind of power trip on steroids going on, and he wanted the world to know it. Jamie always trusted her visceral, gut-level reactions, but still, she promised herself to give him a chance and stay away from judgment—for the time being.

As the driver walked down the walkway, dragging Jamie's luggage, the three of them stood for a moment gazing at the ship.

"I didn't expect anything as monumental as this," Jamie uttered, facing Liz. "This is how they're designing research ships these days?"

Liz leaned closer to Jamie. "The company bought it from the sultan of Brunei."

Jamie laughed out loud, but they weren't privy to her psychic moment. It was a little cosmic present for her to savor on her own: a private joke.

"Ladies?" Sam gestured towards the ship and they made their way down to the pier. "USOIL adapted the ship to include the most sophisticated technology available," he said, pointing to the upper deck. "You can see we've got elaborate sonar and radar equipment. She's fitted with the ultimate intruder-detection alarm network and, just in case, we are also equipped with an advanced missile defense system."

Jamie's jaw literally dropped when she heard that. "My word!" she retorted. "Sounds like I'm boarding a warship!"

"We're prepared for any inconvenience. You never know who we're carrying aboard."

How odd this all was. Jamie had never imagined she would be signing up for weeks out at sea on a high-security luxury yacht—fitted for a war zone. As they got up close, Jamie saw there was not one but two heliports, a small submarine in its own launch platform, and endless portholes, which she thought were most likely staterooms—in which case the ship was big enough to house a whole football team.

"Big ship," Jamie uttered, under her breath.

"Wait until you see inside. It's just beautiful," Liz remarked. "There are eleven staterooms, some of them are just luscious suites, and over six thousand square feet of public living space."

"That's big."

"And that's not including crew, of course. There's another whole layer down below."

As they approached the ramp onto the ship, Jamie gazed uncomfortably at the ship's complex radar equipment, with all its strange and unrecognizable antennae, and several huge satellite disks. Granted, she was no technician, but it seemed so utterly foreign to her, as if the world had leaped ahead thirty years and no one had remembered to tell her.

The driver walked past them, on his way back up to the car. Jamie reached out to tip him, but here again, it was politely refused. She thanked him. He tipped his hat, and walked on.

Sam smirked. "We don't tip staff," he said, snidely. He had a condescending edge to every word he spoke and he grated on her, like fingernails on a chalkboard. He walked ahead of them onto the ramp and extended a hand out to Jamie, only out of a sense of duty, to help her, and then Liz, aboard. "I'll show you to your stateroom."

For whatever reason he had decided to dislike her, Mat's choice as *The Deepwater*'s official greeter was doing his very best to make sure Jamie felt as if she were crashing a party to which she would never have been invited, had it been up to him.

Liz looked awkward, and almost apologetic for Sam's behavior. "I'll be right back," she whispered, and then she disappeared through a main door.

They walked down the long corridor to the very end, where Jamie's cabin was situated. It was the master suite—she'd seen it as they were boarding: this big room opening on to a private pool on the main deck. Sam opened the unlocked door and instantly the hallway was flooded with light, pouring in from three porthole windows in the dining room area of the luxury cabin.

Jamie stepped into the room, so impressed with its impeccable design and style, and amazed at the sheer size of the suite—it was bigger than her own living room back home. "Nice digs," she uttered.

Once again, as in Houston, there to greet her was a bouquet of her favorite spring flowers: irises, baby pink roses, and daffodils. She pulled out the card she found nestled in the bouquet. In that inimitable style that she had come to know as Mat's, it read: *"Welcome to the Dream Team."* Jamie smiled, genuinely pleased, and tucked the card back in between the roses, wondering when the "dream" part of the team was going to arrive.

Sam didn't enter the room. He stood at the doorway, preparing a quick exit. "Liz will be down in a second—you can ask her to walk you through all the gadgets and answer any questions for you."

Jamie's patience was wearing thin. Sam's rudeness and unfriendliness were at the very best inappropriate and she had done nothing to merit it. Soon, she would have to pull rank on him and establish some boundaries that he would not be allowed to cross. "I'd like my bags, please," she said.

He rapped his fingers against the wall, draping himself against the doorframe like a poor imitation of James Dean. "I'll get one of the guys to bring your bags down later."

"How about sooner?"

"Yeah, well . . . I'm not sure who's around right now. There's a lot of ship to take care of."

"Where's the captain?" She couldn't believe Mat would have left such a gap between the royal treatment he had always shown her and this offensive little man. Who was he, anyway?

"Jimbo? Last time I saw him he was up at the Crow's Nest."

Jamie bristled, and stepped into her authority. "Okay, here's where we start over. You go get the captain, wherever you have to go to find him, and tell him that I've boarded the ship. It's role reversal time, Mr. Kemmeries. I want a meeting with the staff and the captain in an hour."

In a gesture of total disregard, Sam turned and started walking away back down the hall. "Sure thing," he said, his voice trailing behind him. *Nobody* told the captain what to do or when to report to his own ship. It would be interesting to see his reaction when he got wind of her command.

Jamie closed the door firmly. "And don't worry about the bags, you little preppy bastard. I'll get them myself." It was so unlike her to get so angry and aggressive—completely out of character. She reminded herself to keep her emotional reactions in check, and not let this first obstacle disrupt what she had come to do.

With Sam's negative energy out of her space, she relaxed into appreciation of the amazing stateroom where she would be spending the next month out at sea. It was spacious, so beautifully furnished, and filled with light. To the right, off the entry, was a full dining room and bar, fully stocked of course; to the left, down a hallway, was the master bedroom and a presidential bathroom area with a floor-to-ceiling window that looked straight out on the ocean. Pure luxury. She pulled open the sliding doors that led out to the private swimming pool, complete with Jacuzzi on the far end, and there she found another doorway, which opened upon a Swedish rock sauna and a fully fitted gym. Everything was designed with elegance, flair, and the utmost attention to detail. Most likely, she realized, this actually had been the sultan's personal suite.

Jamie fell down onto the rich, creamy-white leather sofa and kicked off her shoes. She was suddenly overcome with a fit of the giggles, recalling her commitment, just hours before, to never again be enticed by the trappings of Mat Anderson's world and deciding that, just this one last time, she would let herself be. Why not enjoy it? After all is said and done, it isn't every day that a girl finds herself aboard the former yacht of a sultan, right?

There was a knock at the door. "It's me, Liz."

Jamie called out to her to come in. She stood up and slipped her shoes back on.

"You like?"

"I like!" Jamie replied, emphatically.

Liz dragged one of Jamie's bags into the room, after struggling to get it over the safety frame of the doorway. "I'm sorry about Sam—he's got a bit of an attitude sometimes," she said. "Don't mind him."

"A 'bit' of an attitude? You're generous." Jamie walked over and helped Liz lift the bag into the room.

"His father's a bigwig in Congress. He's a Republican, for what that's worth."

Jamie smiled. So that's what the power trip was about. "Not sure what that's worth these days, to be honest, but I'm not bound to be impressed anytime soon."

Liz brought the room key to the suite, which she placed on the entry table.

"Nice of you to drag this here for me."

"No problem at all. I chose the lighter of the two."

"I never learned how to travel light." Jamie's wetsuit alone filled half of one of the suitcases, along with her fins and underwater mask.

"As for Sam—he really is a sweetie, once you get to know him."

"Sweetie? That's an interesting way to describe him."

"When you get to *know* him."

"Yes, well, I guess that is something I have to look forward to, then."

"He definitely knows he's gorgeous," Liz added, as an afterthought. Jamie noticed the little gleam in her eye on that one.

"Yes, there is that," Jamie thought to herself. The congressman's son was a perfect combination of Hollywood good looks: he was a tall, blue-eyed blond, thirty-something, with a great physique and plenty of style—and very white teeth. Obviously moneyed. If you could get past the obnoxious personality, he could very well be considered a good catch for a girl like Liz. That is, *if* you could get past the attitude.

Jamie reached into her purse, scavenging to find her luggage keys. She unlocked the case and unzipped it.

"The big suitcase and some freshly brewed coffee are on the way," said Liz.

"Coffee? Ah, yes! That is just what the doctor ordered. Coffee and…" Jamie pulled a fancy cookie tin out of her suitcase. "I hold before you a box containing one of life's greatest pleasures: Max's chocolate chip macadamia nut specials. Right off Pier 39 in San Francisco."

She opened the precious tin and extended it to Liz, who held it up close to her face and breathed in deeply before reaching for one of the irresistible cookies. "*I shouldn't,* says she, as she undoes two weeks of salads!" Liz broke the cookie in half and left the rest.

Jamie took the other half and bit into it, almost moaning with pleasure. "Into every life a little sin must fall."

They heard the squeaky wheels of Jamie's second suitcase rolling down the hall towards them.

"Here comes Bobby!" Liz said.

The scent of strong coffee wafted through the hallway. A man balancing a tray with one hand and pulling Jamie's case with the other appeared at the door. He propped the case up against the wall and then carefully set the tray down on the entry table. Before Liz could introduce him, he extended a hand to Jamie and said, "I'm Bobby. Pleasure to meet you." Unlike Sam, he was unpretentious and welcoming.

"The pleasure's mine," Jamie said.

"Bobby's the second in command on the ship," Liz added.

By the looks of him, in his faded jeans and a Grateful Dead T-shirt, Jamie thought he was an off-duty deckhand. So far, the cast of characters on *The Deepwater* was just about the antithesis of her idea of a "tightly run ship."

"I'm more like the jack-of-all-trades around here, but yeah—I'm the senior officer. Tomorrow I'll even look like one." He turned back to the suitcase in the hall and lifted it across the entrance. "Service staff doesn't come in until morning."

"Well, I'm sorry you were bothered with having to carry my bag, but thanks, Bobby. I do appreciate it."

"No problem at all, ma'am." He lifted Jamie's case onto the luggage stand, clearing the space in front of the door.

She reached for the tin and offered it up to him. "I was just tempting Liz with some San Francisco sweets—please help yourself."

He reached in and grabbed three of Jamie's precious cookies. "Ouch! Don't mind if I do," he said, and then heading back out the door, he excused himself. "Duty calls," he said, munching on a cookie as he disappeared into the hallway.

Liz and Jamie looked at each other and broke into hysterics.

"And they say chivalry is dead," said Liz. She lifted the coffee tray and brought it over to the coffee table. "May I pour for two?"

"Of course!" Jamie carried the tin over to the table and they both sat down as Liz poured for them both.

"I hope you don't mind my inviting myself, but I'm just so excited to meet you. I couldn't wait, really—I heard all about you and checked you out on the web. You're amazing!"

Jamie smiled, but said nothing.

"I just love the paranormal. Actually, my mum is quite psychic. They say it skips a generation." She handed a cup to Jamie, and then placed the creamer and sugar bowl in front of her.

"Not necessarily," said Jamie.

Liz rattled on. "My father is an aerospace engineer and my mum says I took after him more than her. I've always been passionate about science, since I was a little girl." She poured herself a cup. Jamie observed, silent. Something about this girl . . .

". . . but I am so fascinated at how some people have the gift, like you. I mean, it's definitely not something you can learn, I know that. You either have it or you don't, right?"

A subtle shadow—like a black Venetian mask—passed over Liz's face. It took Jamie aback for a second, and she felt a sudden vulnerability.

"Well, I'm not so sure about that," she said, guardedly. "People can develop it like anything else, with the right training and intention."

"Mum says you're born with it," Liz replied, matter-of-factly. "Weren't you?"

"Well, yes . . . I was."

"And you can turn it off and on?"

Jamie set her cup down on the table and walked over to her bag, where she reached for her cell phone. She suddenly felt as if she were being interviewed, as she had been so many thousands of times, and she was ready for the conversation to end. "Sorry, excuse me just a minute—I do need to call Mat."

Liz got the message. "Oh, forgive me, chatting your ear off and you still haven't even had a chance to unpack. Shall I go round up the guys in the meantime?"

"Sounds good," Jamie replied. "Is there a meeting room? The Good Samaritan was in such a rush to get rid of me, all I saw of the ship was a blur."

"Well, there are a few. There's the executive dining room—that's where we take our meals, with the captain. Then the mess, for the crew, but we only meet there when the crew is involved. Nice recreation area/living room space—we spend a lot of time there. It's just down this corridor and to the right. There is an executive boardroom up on the next deck, but we never use it. Basically, any kind of space you need—the ship's got it."

"You've been here how long?"

"They flew me in ten days ago, when the ship came back into port."

"You seem to really know your way around, already."

Liz reacted, somewhat defensively. "Well, yes, I came out early to do some training with Sam. It's really state-of-the-art equipment and I've so much to learn—just out of university, you know."

"I see," Jamie replied, not wanting to trigger another conversation. "I do think I'd like to lie back and just close my eyes for a few minutes—will you excuse me?"

"Oh, yes, of course, sorry. May I call you Jamie?"

Jamie nodded.

As she turned to leave, Liz looked back at her and said, "... and thanks for the thousand calories."

"Five hundred. You left half," Jamie replied, accompanying Liz to the door and locking it after Liz disappeared into the hallway.

With Liz gone, Jamie methodically unpacked both suitcases, hanging her clothes in the bedroom closet and then placing her gear in the storage area, next to the entrance door. Tucked in between her sweaters was a pure quartz crystal carved skull, which she placed on the night table next to the bed. She never went anywhere without it. Jamie believed it opened a window in the space-time continuum. She sat down a minute, and then leaned back into the soft down pillows, realizing how tired she felt after the day's events. With an hour to go before the meeting, she decided she could indeed use a short rest to refuel.

She slipped into the velour bathrobe she found hanging in the closet, and set the digital alarm on the nightstand for 6:00, thinking she didn't really need it, because she had an automatic alarm in her head. Still, it was a backup, just in case. She undressed, crawled naked into the crisp linen sheets, and then, with things relatively in place, she dozed off.

Jamie awoke suddenly, as if the caffeine had taken hold in that moment and the adrenaline rush was buzzing her back to reality.

She looked at the clock: 5:59. Then, as she sat up, the alarm went off at 6:00. She leaped out of bed, ran into the bathroom to freshen up, and then threw on her clothes in a hurry. By 6:15 she was out the door, making her way down the hall and into the main public area of the ship—late for a meeting she herself had called.

There, sitting on the sofas, were Sam, Liz, Bobby, and a few others she had yet to meet. A more incongruous group of people she could never have imagined. Sam had a bottle of beer in his hand—he was just twisting the top off when Jamie walked in.

"Ah! Here she is," he said, with just the right inflection to let the others know she was late. To her surprise, though, he did stand up—at least he had some manners. "Come on in, Miss Hastings—don't be shy. The gang is almost all here." He pointed to Bobby, who was standing at the bar in the corner of the room. "I hear you've already met Bobby, our senior officer—and bellboy in his spare time. The grumpy little guy with the crew cut next to him is Brady, the junior officer."

Jamie already felt uncomfortable in the strange environment but, thanks to Sam's sarcasm, she felt all the more the outsider.

"Doc," he said, pointing to the man sitting across from him in the lounge. Doc was every bit the sailor stereotype with his white beard, a ruddy Irish complexion, and weathered skin, what little one could see of it behind all the hair. "He's the medic on board, when he's not keeping the captain out of trouble."

Doc didn't even bother to stand up for Jamie. He nodded, rigidly, as if he had already formed an opinion about her. Jamie could feel his disapproval. So much for Mat's promise of a full support staff on board. She felt like she did the first time she walked into the police station of the LAPD, with a whole squadron of tough-guy, macho cops against her.

For some reason, part of Jamie's mission in life was to help these archetypal men—cops, sheiks, sailors—understand and recognize that there was, indeed, a realm they couldn't penetrate and dominate. They couldn't reverse engineer it, build it and tear it down again. They could not dissect or restructure it. Her world, the quantum field, was the state of consciousness where one recognized how all is interconnected and accessible. It was a world where new perceptions were constantly replacing old structures—one in which "feeling" prevailed over "thinking." It simply didn't conform to their model of reality, which they clung to, despite all odds, like medieval scholars who held, unyieldingly, to their conviction that the Earth, the center of the universe, was flat.

Jamie represented sailing to the edge and falling off the world. She simply scared the hell out of them.

The door from behind the bar swung open and in walked a swarthy, good-looking Italian man, in shirt and tie—the first to resemble a professional crew member. Count on the Italians to always leave everyone else in the dust when it comes to style. He carried a tray of appetizers into the room for the meeting. When he saw Jamie, he put the tray down and walked over to her, shook her hand, and greeted her.

"Benvenuta a bordo."

Jamie was thinking how refreshing it was to find a little class and charm on the ship, and charming he was, for certain. She inadvertently looked over at Liz, a little woman-to-woman acknowledgment, and Liz winked at her.

"That's Alberto," Sam announced. "He's Italian, in case you couldn't guess. God blessed us with an Italian chef. How did that joke go? In a perfect world, the mechanics are German, the French are the lovers, and the Italians are the chefs? Somebody help me out here."

"Actually," Alberto said, looking right into Jamie's eyes, but responding to Sam, "it goes that the French are the chefs and the Italians are the lovers ..."

She felt the blood rush to her cheeks. "Oh my god," Jamie thought to herself, "I'm blushing? When was the last time that happened?"

Alberto picked the tray back up and, starting with Jamie, offered hors d'oeuvres to each.

"Where's Philippe?" Sam asked Liz. "Our marine biologist is missing."

Liz jumped up. "He went to find the captain." That was a job Jamie had told Sam to do. Clearly, he wasn't about to take orders from her. "They're on their way."

Sam took a swig of beer, looking superior and self-satisfied: in charge... on top. "Then there's Mike, the chief engineer—you may never even see him; Spyros and his band of mechanics—them neither. They live in the below. Let's see ... ah yes, Mr. D, the machine man, and the steward, Domenico. He boards in the morning. Is that everybody?"

Philippe's big, robust frame filled the doorway.

"Here he is. Philippe, representing the Marine Authority." He was there to assure that no violations were perpetrated in Canadian waters, and also to conduct studies on the marine life, so Jamie figured they were bound to hit it off.

Philippe approached Jamie, shook hands, and apologized for being late. She felt a connection with him immediately: it was in his eyes, his voice, and the strength in his hands—a kindred spirit.

Sam spoke again. "As you can see, it's a pretty international team we've got here."

"Well, it's great to meet you all, thank you. Hopefully the captain will be here soon, so I can just give you a quick briefing and get out of your hair."

Outside the door, the sound of a dog's collar jingling alerted the staff that the captain had arrived. The dog, a golden Labrador retriever, pushed the swinging door open and entered the room. Jamie was delighted to see there was a dog on board. That meant for sure there would be at least a little unconditional love on the trip.

"Ah, here we go!" said Sam. "Allow me to present the amazing Fin…Captain's alter ego."

Fin walked straight over to Jamie, as if no one else were in the room. That was always the way with Jamie and animals. They gravitated to her, no matter where she went. It seemed as if he had read her mind, as animals do, and that he wanted to show her that unconditional love immediately. She put her hands out to him, letting him sniff and investigate her, and within seconds he started licking her fingers. He bonded with Jamie like he'd known her all his life, fully trusting and receptive. Within moments of sitting near her, getting familiar with her energy, he lay down right by her side, placing his big front paw over her feet, letting her and everyone else present know she was safe.

And then, in walked Jimbo.

If ever a solitary word could epitomize someone's essence, then "presence" was surely that word for Captain Jim. His was such a big energy, he filled the room before he even entered it. When the door swung open and Jimbo walked through, his huge personality was five steps ahead of him, projecting itself through the space like a floodlight in darkness. Here was a proud African American, the ship's master, with a style all his own. He wore a faded brown leather hat crushed down low over his left eye, faded jeans, and a sky-blue plush parka, unzipped halfway down his chest to reveal one really big shark's tooth, hanging from a leather cord around his neck. His skin was weathered from the sea, his gray hair peeked out over his ears, and you could see, just reading the road map of the wrinkles in his face, that this was a man who had definitely lived a big life. His eyes told her so much of his story— eyes that had seen way more than they had ever wanted to.

He was surprised when Fin did not run to greet him. That was a first. "Well, well, Miss Jamie Hastings." Speaking to her from just inside the entrance, he said, "I see you have met my staff."

Fin got up and walked over to his master, and sat by him, obediently.

"And my main man, Fin, here. It looks like we're all here."

Jamie felt the edge in Jimbo's voice, and she realized that demanding a staff meeting before even meeting the ship's captain was overstepping her bounds...she regretted it now. She had reacted—to Sam, and in the end she had come across like a bulldozer. And, of course, the captain was going to have to put her in her place, with a little cold-shoulder overture.

Jimbo walked to the refrigerator, grabbed a beer, and crossed the room to his armchair: the captain's official armchair. Fin followed, and lay down in front of him. He twisted off the bottle cap, threw his legs over the coffee table, and took a nice long swig from the bottle. "I would have liked to introduce you properly, but you have beat me to it."

Jamie looked around at the eclectic cast of characters before her, feeling unusually uneasy, as if the curtain had just gone up, she was on stage all alone, and she had forgotten her lines. "Okay, well... I'll be very brief. Mat Anderson told me you've all been instructed as to why I'm here for these next few weeks, and I can understand that you may not be comfortable with the whole idea of a psychic oil hunter, but nonetheless, here I am."

Fin got up, unexpectedly, and walked across the room to be near Jamie. It came as a surprise to everyone that he would do that. He was attached to his master like iron to a magnet, and he was rarely more than a few steps out of reach.

Jamie scratched him behind the ears, as she spoke. "I work with subtle energy. That means that how we all interact energetically is so very important. A lot depends on how things flow on every level, and I need a positive exchange with each of you from the start, like I've had with Sam, for example."

Liz lowered her head, rubbing her fingers over her forehead as if she had a headache, when in reality she was shielding her reaction to Jamie's barb at Sam.

"I know it's not easy to find yourselves in this situation, not that it is easy for me either, I assure you. You've got to be wondering what it is I do and why I'm here. I do get that."

Philippe appeared to be genuinely interested in what Jamie had to say, while the others merely accommodated her, because they knew they had to.

"In fact, before I located those three drill sites in Pakistan . . . I'm sure you know about that?" she said, pointedly, ". . . I wondered if the locals were going to grab me from my bed some night and drag me into the public square, to burn me at the stake, like some sorceress infidel Western whore."

Philippe and Liz laughed out loud. They hadn't expected that one.

"But they came around when all that sweet crude started bubbling up out of the deep sand."

One by one, the attitudes in the room seemed to shift, with the exception of Sam's, and Jamie knew she had their attention. "I guess what I'm saying is, even if you don't understand what I do—even if you think it's ridiculous—your boss does not. I had no intention to ever do this again, I assure you—but he sought me out. He has given me a huge assignment. It's immense. Probably the most difficult test I've ever been presented with, and I am going to have to have your cooperation to pull it off."

Liz's phone rang in that moment. She crossed in front of Jamie and took it outside on deck.

"My mandate is to locate one or more oil pockets, three miles below, deep down under. That's a tall order, as well you know. For all your 'state-of-the-art' equipment—and this space-age ship here—you've come up empty to date. Mat Anderson is asking me to work a miracle and find it, and to do that I have to close out all distraction. That is the only way that I can focus the only tool available to me, my psychic sight, to find the exact coordinates USOIL needs to drill out here. It's an outrageous expectation, and of course you're all skeptical—who wouldn't be? But I'm going to do my damnedest to realize it."

Jamie looked right into Jimbo's eyes, her words intended for him alone. "But you do need to know that if I don't get the support and cooperation Mat promised, I'm out of here. I have no intention of trying to win a popularity contest, or convince you of anything at all, while I'm attempting to tap into the substrata layer of the ocean floor."

Jimbo looked straight back at Jamie, acknowledging her message. She wasn't going to put up with attitude, and the buck stopped with him. The woman had personality. He liked that.

"The main reason I asked to speak to you all before we sail tomorrow: I made it very clear when I signed on for this that we steer clear of the Orca sanctuaries. I want to be sure that you all got that briefing."

Sam interrupted. "We have carte blanche from the Canadians to navigate in their boundaries. We pass through the sanctuary on our way out into our target zone, right, Philippe?"

Philippe nodded, reluctantly. It was clear he didn't approve.

Jamie answered Sam sharply. "Wrong. I don't give a damn about government approval. I'm talking about what I need in order to do what I need to do. Period. You'll have to navigate around the sanctuary. Whales before oil; life over money. These were my terms before signing on: the whales have to be protected. No disturbance to those sanctuaries: no radar, no sonar, no interference." Again, she looked directly at Jimbo, speaking to him as the authority, completely dismissing Sam. "Captain, are we good?"

"We're good," Jimbo said. What he was thinking, but not saying, was, *"Right, I'm supposed to navigate this big baby through the wild Pacific with no radar? Dream on."*

"One last thing. Give me a chance. You'll see I'm not as weird as you think, and maybe you will learn something." She sat back down and gave a hug to Fin. "There is so much more than what you see and hear, and what you believe is real. There is so much more I can show you, if you will just relax and let me in."

There was an awkward silence. The team just sat there for a moment, obviously impacted by her words. In the end, whether or not they understood her, they had to get her on some level. Who could not be at least curious about the paranormal realms and dimensions that Jamie Hastings was reportedly able to enter and exit at will?

". . . and with that," Jamie said, closing, "I thank you for your time."

Liz, who stood by the doorway, gave her the thumbs-up sign when no one was looking. Jamie had made her mark once again: she had put Sam in his place, and gained a little respect from the others. Most of all, she had set the boundaries, which most definitely needed to be established from the get-go.

From the looks of Jimbo's toothy grin, Jamie knew she had broken through the bad first impression she had made with him, which was her fault for usurping his authority. But that was already behind them. Jimbo was impressed. Jamie was nothing like he had set her up to be in his mind. She was clear, she had a job to do, and she wasn't going to waste anybody's time telling ghost stories from the land of the "woo woo."

He stood up, addressing everyone in the room, but his attention was on Sam. "You heard it, people. Every one of us here needs to help Miss Jamie do what she has come to do. Like she said, even if we don't understand what it is she do . . ." he said, chuckling, "we're gonna help her do it anyway." He raised his beer bottle, as if to call for a toast. "Now, let's get this Lady ready to sail! Berto, run your stock checks, and Bobby, are Mike and the crew on board?"

Bobby nodded. "Yes, sir."

"Okay then, excuse us, Miss Jamie, I've got to run a final inspection. I'll see you at dinner." He walked over to the bar with his empty beer bottle and set it in the tray. Fin got up and quietly joined Jimbo as he was walking out the door, looking back at Jamie, undecided whether to leave with Jimbo or follow his heart and go with her.

He barked twice and Jamie smiled. She got the message.

Jimbo turned to Liz, who was still standing at the doorway. "How about you give Miss Jamie the captain's tour of the ship?"

"Absolutely!" she replied.

As she stood to leave, Jamie could feel Sam's eyes burning a hole in her back. What had begun as a healthy dislike for each other seemed to be escalating into a full-blown war. She followed Liz, who chattered her way through the halls and the staterooms, all the public spaces—even the bridge. Jamie managed to tune out the drone of Liz's mindless banter enough to get a sense of where she was, and what she had to work with.

Liz accompanied her back to her suite, where she had just enough time to grab a quick shower and freshen up before dinner, which she would have much preferred to eat in her cabin, room service style, but she knew she had to attempt to be social and take her place in the team.

She grabbed her purse and headed down to the dining room, where they had gathered. She was pleased to find they were respectfully waiting for her before sitting down to dinner. Jimbo motioned to her to take her seat at the head of the table, opposite him, and then the others took their seats as well. Jamie felt more comfortable—she was encouraged to see that the mood had lifted, and there was a sort of festive buzz in the air. And there was her new friend, Fin, who greeted her the minute she entered the room, before returning to Jimbo's side.

Alberto came through the swinging doors of the galley bearing an enormous platter of steamed shrimp, fried calamari, and fries—a real New Orleans–style spicy seafood dinner. The beer was flowing and they all dove in, filling their plates to the brim—especially Jimbo. Alberto disappeared back into the galley, returning with a mountain of cracked crab, piled high on the tray. Sam made sure the beers kept on coming. Jamie could eat nothing but the fries, which she served herself—but her plate was noticeably empty.

Jimbo feasted like a man who hadn't eaten for days. "Berto," he said, groaning with pleasure, "you have outdone yourself." He looked across the table, realizing Jamie was barely eating. "Hey now, Miss Jamie. We don't stand on formality around here—dig in!"

"I'm good, thanks."

"Good? Girl, don't tell me you don't eat seafood!"

"No, actually I don't."

"Oh man, you're a 'vegetarian'?" he said, like she was diseased.

Jamie knew her being a vegetarian in this group would only make her more of an oddity. "It's not a problem. I can always manage."

Jimbo asked Alberto, "Did we not get the memo?"

"No, sir."

"Well, hell! We sail in the morning, Chef!" He was annoyed, after Mat Anderson had made it very clear Jamie was to be given top VIP treatment aboard.

"Not a problem, Captain. I'll have Domenico stop at the market on his way tomorrow morning."

"You don't know what you're missin'!" Jimbo told Jamie.

"Sorry, I just don't eat anything with eyes."

Jimbo washed down a mouthful of fries with a big swig of beer. "Berto, you got anything 'without eyes' in the larder?"

"I'm already on it!" He disappeared into the galley and quickly returned with a beautiful mixed green salad in one hand, and an oil and vinegar cruet in the other. "Pasta is on the way," he said, reassuringly.

"No, thanks—this is more than enough," Jamie replied.

"Are you kidding? I can whip up a beautiful *pasta al pomodoro* in five minutes." Alberto walked away, back to his galley, not even giving Jamie time to refuse.

Jimbo peeled a few shrimp and leaned over to feed Fin, who was sitting there, patiently, knowing Jimbo never ate without sharing with him. He devoured the shrimp just as fast as Jimbo could peel them. "Ya hear that, boy? 'No eyes'!"

Everyone around the table was so busy eating, no one else spoke.

Jimbo served himself a second helping of shrimp. "Mmmm, mmm. Way to go, Chef!"

Amazing scents came wafting out from the galley: Italian cooking, the unmistakable aroma of garlic browning in olive oil. Within a very few minutes, Alberto returned with a fabulous plate of spaghetti with sautéed cherry tomatoes for Jamie, and for the others, more shrimp, smoked salmon, and fresh sourdough bread, right from the oven.

"So grateful," was all Jamie said. She really wanted to get the attention off herself, and to have the issue of her vegetarianism fade into the background, so that it didn't become another factor separating her from the group.

Alberto grabbed two goblets and a beautiful bottle of Chianti from the wine rack. He removed the cork from the bottle and then served her, sensing she would enjoy a fine wine. Having served everyone, he finally sat down, in the seat next to her, and then poured himself a glass as well. None of the others were wine drinkers, so he made no pretense to serve anybody but Jamie and himself. He raised his glass to Jamie, "To you, Miss Jamie."

She raised her glass as well and then Jimbo piped in. "Hear, hear!" he said, toasting Jamie with his bottle of beer, with the others joining in.

Alberto leaned close to Jamie and whispered, "Actually, I would much prefer a bowl of pasta myself, too, so don't you worry—I know how to cook for you, and these guys could stand a little more greens in their diets."

She liked him. Of everyone in the group, he seemed to be the easiest and most friendly of them all. And, of course, the most charming, which she noted for a second time.

Conversation ranged from predictions of the weather to technical things Jamie knew nothing about, and a sense of excitement prevailed. No one broached the subject of her work, and what they were expected to do, because there was no way of planning for what would happen. Orders from the top were simply to give her the space and tools she needed to do what she had to do—and it was left to everyone to figure that out. Their job was to manage the ship as usual, giving Jamie all the room and support she needed.

Having stuffed himself unmercifully, Jimbo was first to leave the table. He excused himself to go wash his hands and then, on returning, fell into his armchair. "Oh god, I think I ate too fast," he said, patting his swollen stomach. With the exception of Liz, who barely ate, everyone else was filled to the brim as well, and one by one they pushed away from the table, stuffed. Alberto cleared some of the plates and then returned with steaming towels. When they were done, everyone moved into the TV room, leaving Jimbo the privacy of his space, into which he invited Jamie for a little private conversation.

He pulled a cigar and a cutter from a case on the table next to his chair, and sliced off the tip, to prepare for a smoke. Almost defiantly, he held the cigar between his fingers, about to light it, and said, "Needless to say, you don't smoke."

Jamie smiled. Her premonition had been right—the fun was about to begin. "When the occasion calls for it, I have been known to smoke a cigar or two." She walked back over to the dining table, where her purse was hanging over the back of her chair. From it, she extracted a box of exclusive Cuban cigars. She carried it back over to Jimbo, placing it on the coffee table in front of him. "But I only smoke Cohibas."

Jimbo looked down at the table, amazed. He could barely believe his eyes: a full box of Cohibas—a rare, exquisite cigar by any standards, and expensive. Damned expensive.

"This would qualify as one of those occasions," she added, triumphantly.

He couldn't contain his delight. "A cigar-smoking, vegetarian, San Francisco psychic! Haha! That's rich, man. Wow. This is one unexpected surprise, Miss Jamie." He ran his fingers over the name on the box. "Cohibas. Now how in the hell could you know?" He immediately put his cigar back in its case, and then picked up the box before him, dramatically passing it under his nose from corner to corner, breathing it in—savoring it. "I am without words."

"Well, hey, Captain, they don't call me 'psychic' for nothing, you know?"

Jimbo held the box in his hands, a precious gift that he wasn't about to let go of, and he leaned back into the cushion of his armchair. He had a big Cheshire cat grin all over his face, like a kid at Christmas. "Call me Jimbo," he said. He peeled back the protective wax-paper wrapper ceremoniously. "Wowza. Cohibas Esplendidos," he said, and then carefully opened the hinge, broke the seals and meticulously extracted two cigars from the box. As generous as he always was, he never even considered offering one to anyone else. This was Jamie's and his bonding moment, and no one else was invited.

Taking time to enjoy the ritual, he performed the tip-cutting ceremony, preparing for the smoke of a lifetime. "Cohibas," he said. "This is really something, I tell you."

"Shouldn't we take these outside?" Jamie asked, knowing how invasive the smell of cigar smoke could be in closed spaces.

Jimbo's eyes were shining, reflecting the flame of the lighter, as he leaned forward to light Jamie's cigar. "Not with a box of Cohibas *inside*." He delighted in Jamie's style as she drew on her cigar, like a seasoned smoker, and then he lit his, breathing it in with gusto. "Oh yeah . . ." He got up and walked over to the bar, to a cabinet marked CAPTAIN'S STASH, from where he extracted a bottle of vintage scotch. He took two glasses and then set both bottle and glasses down on the table, and poured them both a drink.

Jamie raised her glass. "To special occasions!"

"Yes, ma'am. To many more."

She sipped her scotch and puffed on the cigar, while Jimbo watched her, fascinated.

"I do apologize, Miss Jamie. I admit it—I had you figured as some kind of off-the-wall, woo woo mama. Guess you could say I had a bias. I am sorry about that. I should have known better. I should have trusted Mat—he knows what he's doin'."

"Off the wall, maybe . . . but 'woo woo mama'? Now that's a new one!" she replied.

"You're one interesting woman, let me tell you." He downed the entire glass of scotch and immediately poured himself another. He'd been drinking all afternoon at the bar, had umpteen beers at dinner, and now he was belting back the scotch. Doc, who observed quietly from across the room, kept close watch on him.

Jamie sipped her drink slowly. She didn't really like the taste of hard liquor, but this was part of her rite of initiation with Jimbo. The scotch had to be drunk and the cigar had to be smoked. "So, tell me, how did you end up sailing ships?" she asked.

"Me? I've been on ships almost all my life—ever since I was a half-cocked stupid punk, old enough to enlist in the Marines. Shipped out to 'Nam before I had a clue what kind of a fool-ass thing I had done, but back then . . . it was either enlist or get drafted, so I thought I would 'be a man' and volunteer to serve my country. With the best." He laughed, sardonically. "I served under Mat Anderson—running patrol boats out there. He saved my life once or twice, too." He tapped the ashes of the cigar into the ashtray. "Followed Mat into the company and been here ever since, running their ships, lookin' for shit." Jimbo paused, looking down, and then he changed the subject, intentionally. He reached into his shirt and pulled out the leather cord with the shark's tooth, to show Jamie. "Got me a lot of trophies, too. Remember that big mutha white shark, Doc?"

Doc nodded. He didn't want to hear that same old story told again. Jamie looked over at Philippe, who was half-watching TV with the others. They exchanged glances.

Jimbo drank another full shot of scotch, smacking his lips, laughing. "Ol' Doc, he's out there swimming around one sunny day—right out there in the middle of the open ocean. You have to be crazy to do that. Now me, see, I never go into the water. Too much respect for what's out there. I mean . . . the ocean just is not human habitat. So, there I am, sitting out on deck, looking out at that crazy man out there and I see me this big ol' giant fin, moving fast . . . moving in close to Doc. And I start screaming at him, but he can't hear shit, 'cuz he's upwind of the ship." Jimbo gesticulated wildly, heatedly telling the story. "So I get up and I grab me the spear gun, and I shoot that white belly jaw's ass dead." He laughed again, smacking his knee with his hand, the cigar between his teeth. By now, Jimbo was so drunk he was slurring his words. "Ol' Doc, he almost died of a heart attack when he seen all that shark blood oozing all through the water—he thought it might have been his own leg or something at first, ain't that the case, Doc?"

Doc nodded again. He was not amused.

Jimbo laughed heartily, as he relived the story. "You should have seen him tear ass back up to the ship—I have never seen anybody swim like that in my life. And me, I'm looking off on the horizon and I see the ocean filling up with more of them big ol' whites, swimming around behind him." He stopped laughing, abruptly, and his mood shifted. "We pulled him out just in time, man ... just in time. Doc, he was pretty shook up, all right—never did see him go back out in the deep blue after that."

Fin, who had been curled at Jimbo's feet, was becoming restless and agitated.

"And I pulled in that cord with that big spear in his belly, and dragged that big white over to the railing ... I bet he must have weighed ten tons at least, and I cut myself out this trophy—right out of his jaws. Made sure he was good and dead first, you understand."

Doc interrupted. "He might have weighed a ton at the max."

"Hell, I'm the one who pulled him up to the ship. I'm saying he was a ten-ton mutha."

"Sure, Jimbo, whatever you say."

The dog now walked across the room to the door, out, and then back in again, barking. He went right up to Jamie and nudged her, and then went back to the door—looking back, to see if she was following.

"Looks like somebody's made a friend," Jimbo said.

Fin whined. Waited. Something strange was going on outside.

She put out her half-smoked cigar. "Excuse me a moment," she told Jimbo, and then she walked up to Fin, who waited anxiously at the door, where several jackets were hanging on a rack. She helped herself into one, and followed him out on deck—over to the railing, where he got up on his hind legs, with his front paws on the edge, and stood there, whimpering and crying, as he stared out into the darkness of the midnight sea.

At first she couldn't make out what it was that was agitating him, but then Jamie saw what he saw. There was a small pod of dolphins, leaping in and out of the water—not too far from the ship—and they were chattering and communicating with Fin. He barked, they chirped and whistled—it was a dialogue. He barked at Jamie, telling her he wanted to go into the water. She could hear him pleading with her.

Jimbo heard the barking from inside and called out, commanding Fin to come back in. He looked longingly at the water, wanting to go play with the dolphins.

Jamie watched in amazement. "Sorry, fella—the boss has spoken."

"Fin! Get your ass back in here!" Jimbo's booming command resounded through the doorway. Fin tucked his tail between his legs and he and Jamie returned to the lounge. He slinked straight over to Jimbo, obedient—but fearful, because he wasn't used to being reprimanded, especially by Jimbo, who usually cut him so much slack. Jimbo roughed him up, playfully. "You're okay, boy—I just want you to leave those damned dolphins alone, you hear me?"

Jamie was so intrigued. Apparently this wasn't out of the ordinary—Fin had direct contact with dolphins. She was eager to talk more about it, but it would have to wait until the light of day, after the captain had slept off his drunk.

"I worry about you, boy," Jimbo said, putting his head down close to Fin's and throwing his arms around the dog's neck.

Aware of how drunk Jimbo was becoming, Doc stood up and announced to everyone that it was time to turn in. "We've got an early-morning wake-up call and a full-day sail ahead, people. Let's call it a night." He started turning off lights, and Alberto picked up glasses, to run the dishwasher before closing up shop. Sam and Liz said their goodnights and walked out together. Philippe volunteered to take Fin out for a quick walk in the parking lot, so that he could do his thing before going to bed.

"You make sure and keep him on the leash," Jimbo said, "or he'll be jumpin' off the dock again."

Jamie ignored Doc and stayed, observing Jimbo. What an interesting man he was. Behind that tough exterior, she felt his vulnerability and loneliness, no matter how well he managed to keep it hidden. She could see him. Jimbo the sailorman had gotten lost somewhere out at sea, and never really ever made it home again. He was searching for something—a lighthouse to guide him back from some dark place in his soul. Filled with a sense of compassion and tenderness, she walked over to Jimbo's chair, leaned over, and hugged him. "Thank you for letting me in," she said, and then she kissed him on the head and left.

"Okay, Jimmy, that's it for tonight," said Doc. "C'mon, I'll walk you home."

Jimbo was still feeling that gentle moment—innocence—something that happened so rarely in his life anymore. "She's all right, this Miss Jamie, eh, Doc? A real class act." He reached for the bottle to pour another glass, but Doc took it from him.

"That's it for tonight, Jimmy. Doctor's orders."

"Where's the Fin man?"

"He knows where to find you—now come on, let's get you to bed."

Doc held out an arm, as Jimbo steadied himself.

"Just like old times, eh, Doc?"

"Yeah, Jimmy boy, just like old times," Doc grumbled, under his breath. He held Jimbo up, helping him walk down to his quarters, just barely managing to get him to the bed before he blacked out. As Doc was reaching up into the storage cabinet to get blankets to throw over Jimbo, Fin came quietly into the room and brushed up close to his master, licking his hand and whimpering.

Doc patted him on the head as he was leaving. "He's okay, boy. It's just another Saturday night."

And then Fin curled up in his bed, right next to his master: the captain who truly feared the sea, and his dog, who loved it for him.

9

The Ides of March

Jamie woke up feeling like the inside of an ashtray, stinking of smoke and still scorched from the burn of the scotch and cigar in her throat and mouth. She wasn't a smoker and she rarely drank hard liquor, and now she was paying for doing both: the price of wearing cool shoes for Jimbo.

The gentle sway of the ship in the water had rocked her through the night like an infant in the womb, and now, with the soft hum of the engines, she felt cocooned and so dreamy-like she just couldn't bring herself to get out of bed. She split the curtains over the head-board enough to allow a sliver of light to crack the shell of darkness in which she lay nested, waking from such deep sleep and slowly adjusting to daylight. Jamie lay there, meditating, wondering what gifts would be given to her on Day One of her passing, hopefully without incident, through the Ides of March.

And yes, she was superstitious.

The sound of male voices and some scurrying around outside on deck invaded, creating a sense of obligation to get up and get going. Begrudgingly, she leaned over to check the time: 10:30. She could not believe her eyes. How in the world had she slept that late? Surely one glass of scotch couldn't have knocked her out to the point that she would sleep more than ten hours! She threw on her robe and went into the living room, where she pulled back the curtains on a beautiful sunny day, with only ocean as her landscape. She slid open the doors and stepped out onto her private terrace—breathing the pure, ionized air and the vitality of the open seas deeply into her lungs, and reminding the cells of her body what oxygen was really like.

By the time she showered and dressed, and then walked out onto the main deck, the sun was bright and unexpectedly warm, considering the season. She stood at the railing, gazing out at the water, loving how the sun threw itself over and under the waves, bouncing light through the ocean like diamonds of the gods: Apollo's jeweled laughter. So very few people in the world really ever saw light that way, and she was filled with gratitude that she was blessed to be one who did.

Without a trace of wind on the water, *The Deepwater* drifted like a feather on gentle waves, in the soft morning light of early spring. Jamie saw Sam and Philippe, both dressed in trunks and T-shirts, busily pulling scuba gear out of the hold and checking the tanks. The main door swung open and Liz stepped out in an exotic bikini, with a diaphanous leopard-print scarf tied loosely over her hips—looking like she had just finished shooting the cover of *Sports Illustrated*. Both of the men stopped talking and gawked as Liz took center stage. Distracted, Sam tuned out Philippe and approached Liz. He had still barely noticed Jamie was even there.

"Can you help me suit up?" Liz asked, knowing how good she looked.

Sam could not resist ogling her body. "I can, but what a shame to cover all that up in rubber."

"Now, isn't that something a girl should be saying to her date?"

"Well, yeah, that might just be what she'd be saying."

"Are you going to come with me, then?"

"Oh yeah . . . I'm coming, for sure."

An unintentional intruder, Jamie tried to ignore the sexual banter.

She turned one of the deck chairs to face the water, and lay down with her back to them.

"Ah! I didn't see you there—good morning to you!" Liz said, calling over to Jamie.

Jamie waved from her chair, her back turned towards them.

"We're floating for a while. The captain's letting us take advantage of this amazing weather and the calm, so we're going in." As an afterthought, Liz added, politely, "Would you like to join us?"

Sam cringed. To his relief, Jamie thanked Liz, but said she had only just woken up and was still recovering from the night before. The two proceeded to the supply area, where Liz struggled into the wetsuit, with Sam watching lasciviously from behind as she bent over to get the difficult wetsuit pulled up on her legs and then over her hips. Sam could not help but stare, feasting on her sensuous curves and perfect body—just like she wanted him to.

"Are you going to help me out here?" She motioned to him to zip her up. With his hands on her back, slowly pulling the zipper up from her lower back, all the way up to her neck, the sexual tension between them sizzled.

Just when Jamie had decided to escape to the dining room to find herself a cup of coffee, Jimbo magically appeared, carrying a thermos and two mugs. He walked out to Jamie and greeted her. "Rumor has it we both missed breakfast this morning."

"I was hoping no one noticed," she said, looking up at him.

"Coffee?"

She reached out to take one of the mugs from his hands. "You must have read my mind."

He opened the thermos, and filled her cup. "I hear I got a little out of my head last night."

"So did I."

"I mean, I fell asleep with my clothes on . . . kind of more than just a little out of my head."

She took a sip of the coffee and grimaced. "Jimbo, this is the worst coffee I have ever drunk in my life!"

Jimbo winked at her. "Made it myself." He took a deep breath of sea air, which provoked a fit of phlegmatic, almost asthmatic retching—the smoker's cough. "I gotta tell you, though, I never met a woman who knew her way around a good cigar...don't you take that the wrong way, neither."

Farther back, near the gear locker, Sam got into his wetsuit. He and Liz disappeared down the stairwell to the lower deck and minutes later they appeared out on the Zodiac boat with Philippe, who was driving them a short distance from the ship, for safety.

"I guess those two didn't get the part about the big whites. They are sure as hell out there, lurking around."

"How is it that a master sailorman like you is so uncomfortable with the sea? It's kind of a paradox, don't you think?"

"Yeah? I suppose it is, Miss Jamie...I suppose it is. Think of it as 'respect.' I have seen enough to know you have to respect the deep and never, ever underestimate the sea. People don't realize it—not even the crew. We're on automatic pilot all the time; the ship is top of the line, pure navigational wizardry. But there is so much that could go wrong out here. The ocean is a wild, untamed rhapsody. And them big whites are always out there, roaming around, looking for something. Lest you forget—my best friend was almost shark bait."

Fin appeared out of nowhere. He walked in between their two chairs, greeting them playfully, and then he leaned up on Jamie's chaise, with his front paws over her legs.

"He sure is enchanted with you."

Again, Fin bolted over to the ship's railing and stood up against the railing, staring out at the water, and whining. He looked back at them, waiting.

"What do you want, boy? Your friends back?"

Fin was excited again. He came up to Jimbo's side, nudging him. "You mean to tell me he goes out swimming in open ocean with divers?"

"No ma'am. He goes out when the dolphins come."

Fin barked repeatedly.

"I'm not thrilled about him going out there either, let me tell you that . . . but what am I supposed to do? When they come calling for him, I can't contain him."

"You mean to tell me dolphins come looking for Fin? Get out!"

"You'll be seeing it with your own eyes in a minute."

Fin kept insisting, whining and nudging, until Jimbo stood up.

"Oh yeah. He's been jumping into the ocean ever since he was a pup. I don't think he even knows he's no fish!" Fin bit the cuff of his master's jacket, pulling him towards the stairwell. "All right, all right, boy—let's go. You just remember to stay close now, you hear?"

Jamie picked up her camera and asked to come along, and they both walked Fin down to the lower deck, where Jimbo opened the dive hatch. Fin leaped out into the water, where, to Jamie's amazement, two dolphins had just surfaced, about fifty feet from the ship. Fin swam out to them, adeptly, swimming and diving with them in the deep waters of the Pacific, just as comfortable in the ocean as he was running around on deck.

"Oh my god! Look at him—he's out there with dolphins! That is too much!" She slipped the camera band around her neck and started snapping pictures like crazy.

"Oh yeah. Ever since he wandered into my life he's been trying to swim away. Man, he loves them dolphins. They love him, too. That's how he got the name 'Fin.'"

Fin played with the dolphins, so comfortable in the water that he looked more like a seal than a dog. Jamie could feel Jimbo's anxiety building, though, and she knew he was afraid, with Fin out there in deep water.

"I figure he must have been a dolphin in another life."

"In another life? Did you just say that?" Jamie teased. "Now, would that qualify as a woo woo point of view?"

Jimbo never took his eyes off Fin. "Yeah, I guess so. I had this girl-friend, Ling, back in 'Nam for a little while. She was a Buddhist—she helped me understand a lot of things—taught me a lot."

Jamie held her camera on Fin and the dolphins, giving Jimbo space to talk about it if he wanted, or to run from the memory, without having to bare his soul to her. She just listened.

"In the middle of all that hell..." he said, his voice trailing away. Jimbo caught himself, showing too much, opening the valve—and he slammed it shut. "I realized... if more than four billion people on this planet believe in reincarnation, there has got to be something to it."

"Well, whaddya know?" said Jamie, affectionately. She under-stood that he wanted to take the conversation somewhere else, far from that time. Veterans of that despicable war never really wanted to talk about what they saw in Vietnam, or worse: what they did there. "I knew there was a kindred spirit down there, deep behind that crusty facade."

"Yeah..." he said, looking far away, his gaze fixed out on the horizon.

Without warning, the dolphins started leaping in and out of the water, appearing agitated. One of them kept slapping his tail down hard on the water, as if suddenly he was trying to scare off Fin, who was confused and unsure. Two other dolphins appeared from the below and at once the scene shifted from serene to threatening. Fin looked back at the ship, barking—and they disappeared, as quickly as they had come. Poor Fin was undecided whether to go out after his friends or swim back to the ship... and Jimbo could feel it.

"Okay, dude, get your ass back over here right now!"

Fin started swimming towards the ship. He had drifted farther out with the dolphins, and he was struggling to get in, breathing hard. Jimbo threw a buoy out into the water, which Fin grabbed hold of with his teeth. Jimbo pulled him in, closer to the edge of the dive well, and then reached into the water with his strong hands, lifting Fin, who by now was panting hard and shivering uncontrollably, out of the deep, by the collar.

"Damn, boy. This has got to stop," Jimbo said. Trembling uncontrollably, Fin shook himself off from his head down to his tail, dowsing them both in a shower of cold ocean water. Jimbo removed his jacket, and threw it over the dog, wrapping him in it tightly. "Easy, boy…" he said, holding Fin close to him in his arms, trying to get him to warm up.

"May I?" Jamie asked. She didn't want to interfere, but she did know what to do.

Reluctantly, Jimbo released his protective hold on Fin, and Jamie took over. Kneeling on the wet deck floor, she removed the jacket, then placed one hand on Fin's back and the other on his chest. Utilizing the power of the focused mind over matter, she brought immense heat through her palms, and then sent it into his body, through the tissues, and down into his bones. In less than a minute, he stopped shaking completely, and his breathing returned to normal.

Fin jumped up on her; he made sounds Jimbo had never heard him make before, as if he were speaking to her. The two of them were completely connected, in a sort of mutual trance, communicating across species lines. Jimbo still didn't know all that much about Jamie Hastings, but he knew his dog. He was witness to something extraordinary being exchanged between them and it was unmistakably real, and powerful.

From being curious and sunny, Jamie suddenly became very serious, as if a dark cloud had passed over her. The agitation that Fin was experiencing had something to do with the dolphins, and their state of anxiety. But there was more to it—something deeper.

As the thoughts ran across the screen of her mind, Fin barked, acknowledging that she was on track. He was that tuned in.

"He wants to show you something, but he can't—there's something hidden," Jamie said, curiously. "Something important." She squeezed Jimbo's hand. "You know what I'm talking about, don't you?"

Jimbo reacted evasively to Jamie's touch, or was it the words? He pulled his hand away and bent over to speak to Fin, shutting her out completely. "Yeah, you're hungry. That's what you're talkin' about . . . I hear you, boy—let's get some grub." Fin shook himself again. "I need to get up there and see what Alberto's got going on for lunch," Jimbo told Jamie, ending the conversation before it even really began. Whether something was hidden in the message of the dolphins, or deep in Jimbo's soul, he didn't want to know about it. Jamie knew she had accessed something he wasn't going to talk about, and she knew well enough to let it go. Perhaps she had crossed the boundaries, touching him that way.

Jimbo excused himself and led Fin back inside, leaving her, pensive, out on deck. Something called her to the bow of the ship—Mother Earth herself, no doubt. She watched the white cumulus clouds gather on the horizon. There, way out on the distant waves, she saw the first whale spouts, blowing high into the darkening sky.

While Jamie was lost somewhere in thought, drifting around between the waves and the clouds, trying to get a better view of the whales through her zoom lens, she heard the Zodiac approaching the ship and then what sounded like a winch, hoisting it back onto the platform on the lower deck. Minutes later, Sam and Liz reappeared from the stairway, carrying their fins and dive masks. Liz was noticeably upset. She handed her gear to Sam, and walked right up to Jamie.

"Did you see us out there? We were surrounded by at least twenty bottlenose dolphins."

"No! Where were you? I was watching Fin right near the ship—he had three or four of them with him. I never saw you."

"How could you have missed us? We were only about three hundred feet away—starboard." As she stood dripping water from her wetsuit, Liz started shivering. "The water is freezing cold."

Jamie pointed out to sea. "Look out there—I've seen three spouts so far...are they Orcas?"

Liz didn't even turn to look. "They were behaving so strangely. I've never been afraid around dolphins before."

Jamie didn't say anything, but she couldn't understand how anyone could ever be "afraid" of dolphins.

Sam walked up behind her with a big beach towel that he'd pulled from the hatch and he handed it to Liz. "I tried to tell her she was just freaked out over Jimbo's 'Tales of the Deep' last night," he said.

Liz snapped at him. "No, that's not it at all. I'm telling you they were aggressive—I felt threatened out there."

He went back to the locker and was quick to unzip the back of his wetsuit and step out of it, showing off his noteworthy physique. Dismissing Liz's concern, he called out to her, teasingly. "Maybe they were in the middle of a mating dance. You know what they say about dolphins."

Liz was no longer in flirtation mode and she was put off by his cavalier attitude about something that clearly had her so upset. "Sam! I dive all the time and I've never experienced anything like this. It was almost as if they were trying to trap me in their circle... it was just too weird."

"Where was Sam?" Jamie asked, just ever so accusingly. "Weren't you there?"

"I couldn't even see him. I was just surrounded by these huge creatures, swimming around me in circles."

Sam became defensive. "I was right there—you just got overwhelmed for a moment, that's all—a little disoriented. It can be intense when you find yourself in the middle of a pod, miles away from shore."

"You're not listening!" Liz replied, sharply.

"Whoa, you can lighten up a little bit," he said. "It was no big deal."

Jamie knew it *was* a big deal. "They were agitated out there with Fin too."

"Well, there you have it," Sam said, with finality. "Mystery solved. Fin must have spooked them."

Jamie thought about it a moment. "Jimbo says Fin's been swimming with dolphins since he was a pup. They came calling for him, that's what it seemed like, and when he went out they welcomed him—I watched when he swam out. And besides, they were talking to him like they knew him ... playing ... but then, suddenly, something set them off."

Sam walked over to the locker to hang up his wetsuit. "Right," he said, under his breath. "They were having a little coffee klatch, talking about the latest in sardine sandwiches."

When he came back over to them, Liz turned her back, gesturing to him to unzip her. "That is the first time I've ever been scared around dolphins ... that's all I know." She peeled off the wetsuit, and wrapped herself in the towel, standing there, shivering, from more than just the cold.

As Sam walked back again to the lockers, carrying her wetsuit, she whispered to Jamie, "I can't really explain it, but something very strange was going on out there—it was otherworldly."

"How do you mean?"

"I'm not sure."

Jamie could see how deeply shaken Liz was.

"I can't believe you didn't sense what was happening," said Liz.

"My focus was on Fin." Squinting from the sun reflecting against the water and the ship's sleek white walls, Jamie held her hand over her eyes to shield them. "Are you going to be okay?"

"Yes, sure . . . I'm fine," said Liz. But she wasn't.

The dining bell rang. It was time to go in for lunch and Jamie was hungry, having missed breakfast.

Sam came back with a big fleecy jacket for Liz, which was so huge on her she nearly disappeared into it. "We need to dry off and get dressed for lunch."

"You could use a bowl of hot soup, too," Jamie suggested. "I'll ask Alberto if he can whip something up for you."

Liz walked away with Sam, looking back over her shoulder at Jamie, quizzically. Jamie picked up her camera again and took one more look at the whales through the zoom. There were four spouts now, as far as she could make out.

"I am here for you, my beauties," she spoke, her words floating like thought bubbles over the ocean's spray. "Don't let the disguise of this ship fool you."

A second bell rang, calling everyone to lunch.

The table was loaded with a scrumptious smorgasbord of Italian food: Italian panini, a huge bowl of homemade potato salad, a platter of antipasto, and steamed broccoli. Once Jamie sat down, a uniformed waiter came from the galley with a beautiful plate of grilled fresh vegetables and a side dish of couscous—really beautiful vegetarian fare. She was amazed and relieved to see that the personality of the ship and the crew seemed to have shifted, and everything seemed more professional—and cohesive. Alberto, also uniformed, came from the galley with a pitcher of freshly made lemonade, which he placed at the center of the table.

"Miss Jamie," he said, pointing to the waiter, "I present you our steward, Domenico."

Jamie smiled at Domenico, intrigued by his classic dark Sicilian features and beguiling smile.

"You didn't meet him last night. You see, his wife is pregnant... any day now, eh, Domenico? So that is why he wasn't with us when you came aboard." Domenico disappeared back into the galley and Alberto took his place at the table, next to Jamie. One by one, the other members of the crew arrived, with the exception of Brady, on duty at the helm. Liz was still uneasy about what had happened out in the water; she was off in a cloud of her own, working through it all in her mind. Fin lay in front of his full dish of food across the room ... he clearly had not touched it. His head was down on the floor, and he seemed indifferent to everyone there— even to Jamie.

Jimbo came in last, as usual. The first thing he noticed was that Fin hadn't eaten. "What the devil's gotten into you, boy?"

Fin lifted his head listlessly, and then sank it back down between his paws, weighted to the floor.

"Hmmm. He's always ravenous after a swim. I guess after that shrimp feast, this dry dog food just ain't cuttin' it." He patted his dog on the head and then took his place at the head of the table, heartily helping himself to a heaping portion of potato salad and an Italian sausage sandwich the size of a small submarine.

Jamie was pleased to see that no alcohol was served.

All through lunch, Fin's abnormal behavior held everyone's attention. One minute he was lifeless and despondent, glued to the floor, and the next he was restless and edgy, a cycle that continued repeatedly throughout the meal. Towards the end, he sat next to Jimbo and started barking, incessantly, and then walked to the door, looking back to see if anyone was following—back and forth, repeating the behavior over and over again, waiting for Jimbo to get the hint and follow him outside.

Jamie excused herself and walked over to him, at the doorway.

"He wants to show you something out there, Captain," she said, in full support of Fin.

"Yeah, I know what he's whining about—there's more damned dolphins out there," he said, throwing his napkin onto the table. "All right, boy . . . hold your horses." Jimbo grabbed his cigar case and then he and Jamie followed Fin out the door, where Fin immediately returned to the railing, crouching down with his head wedged in the drain, between the railing wall and the deck floor. He stared out at the water, whining.

Jamie and Jimbo both looked out over the waves, but there was nothing there. "Sometimes, I worry he's gonna jump in when I'm not looking, and never come back." Jimbo took a cigar from the case and lit it. "I don't think I could live with myself if that ever happened . . . you know? Fin's my boy—he's my family."

That same loneliness that Jamie had seen in Jimbo the night before washed over him again, unconcealed and unapologetic, as if that part of him wanted to be found. *Whom had he lost along the way, besides himself?"* she wondered. It was *his* sadness, but still it rolled through Jamie in waves: the empathic chill of her heightened sensitivity. That was the double-edged sword of psychic vision and no, she couldn't turn it off, no matter how much she willed it sometimes—no matter how terrifying or painful it was to "see," or to hear the whispers of spirits lost in transit . . . and worst of all, to feel the suffering of others in her own skin.

Sam had to choose that moment to burst through the door, charging right over to them with the sensitivity of a raging bull, breaking the intimacy of that gentle flow of energy between them. "Captain, when you're ready to roll, just give me a thumbs-up."

Jimbo looked at Jamie, acknowledging something he wasn't even sure he could put into words, but she knew. Words were not needed. "Yeah, I suppose it's time to get to work."

"Miss Hastings, I've been instructed to prepare a briefing for you on the technological capabilities of the ship. Liz says she's already shown you where things are located on upper deck, so when you're free—you know where to find me."

How different Sam was in Jimbo's presence. Jamie figured he was just covering his back, in case she decided to make a complaint against him with the captain or higher up, to Mat Anderson. But that wasn't it at all. He was always respectful around the captain, and she just happened to be there.

When she got to the computer room, Jamie found Sam seated before an array of monitors and more high-tech computer equipment than she had ever seen in her life. Liz was beside him, her chair just a little too close to his—too intimate. They were engaged in a discussion about some sort of wave patterns—something way over Jamie's head—when she interrupted them. Sam got up to get her a chair, while Jamie stared in bewilderment at the complex array of strange gadgets and equipment. "The captain said to put all the tools at your disposal, so here they are," he said. "Everything but the actual navigation of the vessel itself is directed from here."

"It's not as complicated as it looks," Liz said, reassuringly.

"All of this to run this ship? Amazing..."

"All of this in search of oil," he said, correcting her. "Where would you like me to start?"

"I'd like to know more about the sonar equipment—that's what concerns me the most." Jamie took her seat slightly behind the two of them. "You'll need to bear in mind that my technological savvy is limited to sending the occasional email."

"That's like asking me to explain how to fly a 747 to a guy who never learned how to ride a bike."

"Well, I guess your boss has faith in you, Sam—so show me how to fly."

He swiveled his chair around so that he was looking at Jamie as he spoke. He seemed more professional now that he was in uniform, in his business environment, and assuming authority over his area of expertise: not that he was by any means more likable. "If you'll tell me what you are specifically interested in knowing, I'll do my best not to get into the minutia of how it's managed technologically."

"Fair enough," said Jamie. "Talk to me about the sonar equipment."

"Can you be a little more specific?"

"I want to know how sonar is being used in the ocean, and how effective it is in searching for substrata oil deposits."

"Right. I'll try to keep it as simple as possible. 'Sonar' is an acronym for 'sound navigation ranging.' We send a pulse into the water—we call it 'pinging'—and it bounces back off objects in the water, natural or otherwise, and from the ocean floor." He typed something on the keyboard and a series of data, unintelligible to Jamie, appeared on the screen. "The problem is it's deep, and we get a lot of false readings from stuff in between."

"Stuff? You mean like whales, navigating their waters?" Jamie interrupted, sarcastically.

Sam ignored her. "And then there's the problem that there's rough terrain down there, so we get these echoes from all over, at many different angles. They bounce off the valleys and hills and cave openings, which causes a lot of distortion and misreads." He played around with the keyboard commands and a complicated chart appeared on a different monitor. "So, basically, we measure how deep an object is, or how deep the seafloor is, by how long it takes these ultrasonic waves to hit and come back up to the surface, where the equipment monitors the exact depth, based on a ratio of that return."

"Gotcha."

"*The Deepwater* is equipped with what we call a COTS-based, open-systems architecture that the Navy employs on all U.S. combat submarines." He typed COTS on the keyboard and now a complete manual of information appeared on the monitor in front of Jamie.

"We can create and utilize very intricate algorithms, which give us a much broader scope and allow us to create our own digital maps of the ocean floor."

"Whoa! Now you've lost me," said Jamie. She simply couldn't get her mind around science—especially the science of the military.

"There are basically two kinds of sonar: passive, which just listens, and active, which is basically what the Navy uses in anti-submarine tracking and other military applications. That's what we've been using to get down there."

"You use military-capacity sonar testing?" Jamie shrieked.

"Well, yeah. This is an oil company research vessel. We've got state-of-the-art equipment on this baby."

"But it's been reported that Navy sonar tests are making the whales insane and driving them to suicide!"

Liz spoke out, almost defensively, on Sam's behalf. "Actually, Jamie, that is a matter of conjecture. I mean, it certainly hasn't been proven."

"What kind of proof do we need? We know that a lot of mass strandings happen immediately following some of those military sonar blasts. You're telling me this ship uses the same-force equipment?"

"Hold on. We work with ELFs—extremely low frequency waves. They operate at around three hundred hertz . . . not like the big guns the Navy is using. Hell, they use MFAS! That operates between three and four thousand hertz."

"Sorry," said Jamie, "but can we speak English here?"

"Mid-frequency active sonar. Now that shit is bad for the whales."

"So you're telling me that private corporations are free to use this killer military equipment to chart the ocean floor? That's outrageous!"

"Well, we're not just looking at the seafloor—that's already been mapped out. We're looking for oil deposits, don't forget."

"I surely won't."

"We also utilize special seismic air gun equipment, better known as the 'towed air gun array.'"

"Oh, my god. What is that?"

"Didn't Mat Anderson brief you at all on what we're doing out here?"

"The only brief I got from Mat, to be honest, was how the *Deepwater* operation was failing," Jamie retorted. "Now what about this 'air gun' whatever-it-is system?"

"Imagine a large piston with a plunger that discharges compressed, high-pressure air bubbles into the ocean—a powerful sound base. That's why it's called the 'air gun.' It's a little hard to explain to a layman. Sorry... I mean 'laywoman.'"

Jamie shook her head in aggravation. This kid simply could not avoid making his digs, no matter what.

"This creates what we call a 'pressure wave field,' which gets pushed downward, actually beneath the seabed, and moves through the deeper earth below it—and then eventually reflects back up to the surface."

"That's got to be great for the whales and dolphins."

"High-level hydrophones record sound signals as they are reflected through rocky sublayers of the seabed. And we get an idea of density, cavities, and potential oil deposits from reading the signals."

"Good god," said Jamie. She had such a sense of dread over just this hint of what she was up against, in her fight for the whales and dolphins. Imagine what the big picture was really like! "All of this disruption of such sacred space."

Liz could feel Jamie's angst intensifying. "I don't think Jamie needs all the intricate details."

Sam exploded. "Sacred space—the oceans of this planet? You are so out of touch with reality! No offense, but what did you think goes on day and night, everywhere around this big globe? There is no sacred space left out there in the ocean. You've got global fishing on a massive scale, the cruise industry and private recreational boats, jet skis, and what have you . . ."

Jamie cut him off mid-sentence. "You can stop there—I get your point."

"I'm not done yet. Then there are your military vessels and operations, major international naval testing and reconnaissance, oil drilling, oil-research sonar-testing vessels. It's a virtual disco inferno down there. It just goes with the territory."

"Whose territory are we talking about? As I recall, the oceans are the 'territory' of the beings that inhabit it . . . not humans and our over-the-top military-style bombardment of the waters—and not oil-hungry corporations sucking the life out of the planet, and filling the oceans with their ineptitude."

Sam put his head to the desk, pretending to bang it against the surface. "Oh, please! Tell me I don't have to apologize on behalf of the company for all the evils perpetrated on the oceans."

"It wouldn't hurt for you to stop and think about what you are doing to contribute to their destruction."

"So then, with all due respect, Ms. Hastings, what are *you* doing here?"

Jamie replied, tersely, "I'm here to try to prevent USOIL from creating an irreparable fissure in the Pacific Ocean's floor, like they've done in the Gulf of Mexico—using equipment like your stupid gun array system. And face it, with all your 'state-of-the-art' technology, USOIL's strategy certainly hasn't been successful so far, now has it? Do tell, Chief Technician—has it?"

"Hey, strategies come from the top. I just run the equipment and read and record data. That's what I'm trained in and that's what I do. If you've got a problem, talk to the boss."

"What about Philippe? Isn't he supposed to be looking out for marine life, while you go charging around pinging up the ocean floor—and god knows what else?"

132

Sam turned his chair, giving Jamie his back. "If you want to know what Philippe's doing, talk to Philippe. I'm sharing what I do with you, as I have been told to do. I'm an engineer, not a whale conservationist."

"You bet I will." Jamie got up abruptly and headed for the exit. "Thanks for the technology lesson. I'm done here."

"Are we finished? We haven't even touched on the radar," he said, insolently. He made no bones about how much pleasure he derived from getting under Jamie's skin.

"No thanks. I've had all the technology I can stand." Jamie left, leaving Sam and Liz looking at each other, bewildered.

"That didn't go very well, now did it?" Sam said.

"Well, you did set it up to fail, didn't you?"

Sam started flicking switches and slamming things around on the desk. "Like they're not using substrata sonar in the desert over there in Pakistan? What's the big deal?"

"The whales," Liz replied.

"What about the whales? I can't believe we're even having this conversation. We're looking for oil out here. I can't help it if there are whales swimming around in the meantime. I mean, is this woman clueless, or what?"

"Far from it. I just think she was blown away by the potential damage we could cause—in all fairness, we both know what kind of power we hold in our hands, now don't we?"

"Well, what did she think she was coming out on, the *Love Boat*?"

"Hey you. Cut her some slack. You made it sound like we're running a killing machine here. Why do you dislike her so much, anyway?"

"I never said I disliked her," Sam barked.

"Yeah, right."

"I'd just like to know the real reason she's on board. I'm not buying this idea that she's going to have this 'vision' and bingo—we get the pot of gold. Give me a break." He looked over the entire network of computer equipment. "Like a human mind can do more than all of this? Nobody's going to tell me that she can reach down below the ocean floor in her mind and smell oil—or 'see' it—whatever the hell she supposedly does. Sorry, I'm not going for it."

"Don't forget her track record, luv. What if she can?"

"Can what?"

"What if she really can just pinpoint where those reserves are—just from seeing them psychically?"

"If she can see what's going on beneath the seafloor? You believe this bull?"

Liz simply said, "Yes, I do."

"Well, then she probably knows what's going on up on deck, right now … don't you think?"

"And what exactly is going on up here?" Liz replied, seductively.

"Well.… It seems to me like one hot lady wants to play with fire." He leaned over, and pulled Liz to him. They kissed gently at first and then it got passionate—they were all over each other. Footsteps passing outside the door startled him and he pulled away abruptly, thinking Jamie might have decided to come back. He cracked the window shade and saw it was Brady walking past the door, which was closed, and there was no way he could have seen through the blinds. "We better cool it a minute here," he said.

Liz sat upright in her chair, distancing herself. "Agreed."

They had to lay off while they were on duty, or for sure they would get caught in the act, and neither of them wanted that—especially Liz, who was on trial, doing her internship for six months.

Sam tried to switch gears. "I guess I better not even tell her about *Poseidon*. One thousand pulses per second—that is guaranteed to permanently blow her mind."

"I think you managed to blow her mind enough for one day."

"Something else is going on here. This whole thing is too weird —I just want to go on record that I'm not buying any of it."

"Oh for god sakes, man! Like what?"

"I don't know. But nobody's going to convince me that we're going to wake up one morning, while we're floating around in the middle of the ocean, with Jamie Hastings dishing out the coordinates for the drills. That is just fantasy island." He flicked several switches, then leaned over to the intercom and buzzed the bridge. "Captain, we're ready to roll here—minus one psychic."

Jimbo's voice fed back through the intercom. "You mean to tell me you already scared away Miss Jamie?"

"Apparently she doesn't do technology, sir."

"Yeah, well . . . don't forget the orders come from the top, so mind your manners."

"I'm doing my best, Captain."

"All right, good. Now let's get moving here. We've only got four hours of light left."

The radar antennae and other equipment at the top of the ship began turning, slowly at first, and then quickening.

"We're right on and tracking, sir."

Jimbo looked up at the two navigational monitors over the command board, just as a strange anomaly appeared on the screen. It whizzed across both monitors with amazing speed and then, in an instant, they went completely blank. For a moment, he thought the whole ship had lost power. He tapped on his microphone to see if it was working. "Sam, I've lost both screens. What just happened?"

His call interrupted Sam and Liz, who were otherwise mesmerized by the escalating sexual fire they couldn't seem to put out. The more they tried to restrain themselves, the more things heated up. They were right in the middle of another passionate kiss when it happened, and neither of them saw the flash, nor did they notice the screens had gone black.

Sam turned on his microphone. "Huh? That's weird. Hold on." He fiddled nervously with the computer equipment until the monitors came back on.

"I'm back up now, both screens. Did you catch that?"

"Sorry, Captain . . . catch what?"

Jimbo was silent for a moment, and then in a comedic, theatrical voice he said, "Thought I heard one of them big whites sayin' . . . 'you better watch your asses'!"

"Damn, Captain, did anybody ever tell you you've got a Jaws fixation?" Sam retorted, but inwardly he was wondering if somehow Jimbo was on to them. Romancing the intern was absolutely out of the question if he wanted to keep his job, no matter what kind of a foxy babe the company had sent to tempt him. He would have to answer to his father if he screwed up the USOIL gig—and no good-looking woman was worth that.

"Like I told you, Sammy boy: it's a matter of respect." Through the intercom, they could hear Jimbo singing in falsetto, imitating Aretha Franklin: "R-E-S-P-E-C-T, find out what it means to me . . . just a little respect, won't you come on, hey baby . . ." Sam and Liz chuckled, but Sam still wondered if he was getting a cloaked message, and he backed off Liz immediately.

"So strange, Captain. I have no clue what just happened. There are so many security systems backing us up—no way the system could have gone down and come back up in seconds."

"Does everything check out?"

"Yes, sir, we're back on. All monitors fully operative."

"Okay. Run a systems check in the morning."

"Will do." Jimbo was the one person to whom Sam deferred. He was, in some ways, in awe of him. He looked up to Jimbo as a role model, a man who walked to a different drummer, someone he could talk to: the kind of man he secretly longed to be. In his eyes, Jimbo was the free spirit he would never become, no matter

136

how he tried. He'd had too much indoctrination from his father, the congressman.

"So, where's Miss Jamie?" Jimbo asked, shifting gears.

In that moment, resenting how the mere mention of Jamie interfered with his camaraderie with the captain, Sam realized that he was actually jealous of her. That was the real problem. He resented how she had come in as a figure of authority, and how she had so effortlessly connected with the captain. *"And then the little suck-up with the cigars. Nice touch,"* Sam thought, talking it through in his mind. The feeling was akin to sibling rivalry. It was the first time he got in touch with his adversity to Jamie Hastings. He didn't want her interfering in his relationship with Jimbo, and he sure as hell wasn't going to be outdone by her.

Liz leaned into the intercom to answer. "She stormed out, after her first and probably last briefing with Sam."

"Don't you go scaring her on me, kid. We need her to 'smell the oil,' remember?"

"Yeah, right. Three miles down." Sam leaned back in his chair, shielding his feelings of insecurity from Liz, while they exchanged sexual glances, both eager for night to fall so they could carry on in the privacy behind closed doors.

Jimbo turned off the intercom and entered one speed dial number on the ship-to-shore radio. His hand cupping the mouthpiece, he said in a low voice, "We're in the zone. And they're here." He hung up without saying another word . . . and without waiting for a reply.

Out on main deck, Fin ran back and forth excitedly, all around the ship. His annoying behavior was becoming a distraction for the crew. Bobby finally grabbed him by the collar and put him on a leash, to try to get him to calm down, before walking him up to the bridge. "I don't know what's up with Fin," he told Jimbo, apologetically. He felt it wasn't his place to reprimand the captain's dog. "He's all over the place. Crazy like. I took him down below to do his thing—so that's not it." He unhooked the leash. Fin walked in and went right over to his bed, barely looking up at Jimbo, as if he knew he was in trouble.

"Now you listen here, boy. You got to cool it for a while. You just stay with the Big Kahuna and stop making everybody crazy."

Fin looked up, sighed, and put his head down to sleep.

"I'm going to go get a few hours of shut-eye before my shift, if that's okay with you, Captain?" Bobby said, turning to go.

"Sure thing. Domenico didn't answer his pager. Tell him we need some coffee up here on your way down."

Bobby nodded, and disappeared down the stairs.

By early evening, the wind had picked up substantially, and the water, which had been smooth as glass in the morning, was getting rough, with four-foot waves slapping the ship from stem to stern. Jamie had gone to her cabin to clear her mind of Sam's technology briefing, and to get an idea of the oceanscape beneath them, through meditation, taking herself down below the waves to observe the ocean floor. As conditions worsened, she started to feel seasick, which kept her in body awareness, so much so that she could not even get close to a meditative state. Her faculty was shut down completely, and all that she could think about was the roll of the ship. When she could bear it no longer, she left her stateroom and went looking for Doc. Surely, she figured, he would have a remedy in his medical supplies. She returned to the living room, where the staff was socializing over drinks, enjoying leisure time. Nobody else looked the least bit affected by the rolling pitch of the ship.

The first one to see her come into the room was Liz, who was playing a game of backgammon with Sam. "Whoa! You're looking pretty green, there, Jamie. Are you all right?"

Jamie steadied herself, leaning up against the wall. "Let's say I'm still trying to get my sea legs."

"I've got Dramamine—shall I get it for you?" Liz asked.

Jimbo was relaxing in front of the television. Doc got up to go to get something from his supply cabinet, but the captain waved at him to sit back down. "You don't need meds, man. The best cure for seasickness is an ice-cold beer."

Feeling sicker by the minute, Jamie staggered across the room, struggling with the ship's motion, and sat down near Jimbo. She put her head in her hands, completely incapacitated.

Jimbo got right up out of his chair to get her a beer from the refrigerator. "It's the hops. Best thing for seasickness—trust an old salt." He was gentle, but he knew he had to help her get her mind off it. "I promise not to smoke a Cubano tonight."

Jamie took the beer gratefully. She was so squeamish that even the thought of smelling cigar smoke made her stomach turn, and she knew there would be no way food was going to touch those lips, beer or no beer. Not this night. She excused herself and got up to leave, but Jimbo insisted she stay in the living room, so they could help her through it.

"The thing about seasickness is—the more you think about it, the worse it gets," Jimbo said. "So stay here with us—we'll put you right in no time." Reluctantly, she yielded to Jimbo's advice. "You get comfortable here, a little TV... Fin right here. Alberto!"

The chef popped out from the galley, where he was preparing dinner.

"Bring some saltines for our guest! Miss Jamie be havin' the green meanies."

Alberto came back out from the galley with a dish of saltines and he stood over her, making sure she at least nibbled on one, which she did, and convincing her that she needed to eat at least one or two, if she could get them down. "I made a beautiful *melanzane alla parmigiana* tonight for everyone—it's vegetarian, too! You just tell me when you are ready to eat—any time of the night, and I will warm it up for you," he said.

Eggplant? What possibly could be heavier on her stomach than that? The mere thought of it made her feel like leaning over the railing.

The dinner bell sounded and everyone took a seat at the table, with the exception of Bobby, who was on duty at the helm, and Jimbo, who went to housekeeping to grab a blanket for Jamie. While the others started eating, he wrapped her up in it and stayed with her, making sure she was comfortable. He didn't want her to run back to the cabin—that was the last place she needed to be. It was at the back of the ship: she would feel the motion even more there and she would be closer to the fumes, even if only a faint trace actually made it up to main deck.

Fin, who at last had calmed down from the frenetic behavior of the day, stayed with her, instead of following Jimbo to the table. They healed each other, just being quiet together. No amount of persuasion from his master would lure Fin away from Jamie; he just lay there, close, holding her in the protective field of his energy, and becoming more calm and relaxed in hers.

Domenico served up Alberto's delicious fare. Sam was right: in a perfect world, the cooks *are* Italian. Spirits were high and the conversation flowed, with Jimbo always at the center of attention, recounting another one of his famous stories. He had them all in stitches, telling a long tale about getting caught with his pants down, making love to somebody's wife in a port halfway around the world. They loved him and humored him, knowing that a lot of his stories were mere fantasies and that others were built around secrets that would never be told.

Jamie felt like such an outsider sitting there, bundled up in her blanket. She couldn't help but notice how much more relaxed they all seemed without her presence at the table—as if her being amongst them stripped the fun out of their whole dynamic. She knew she was perceived as being different from them and, then again, these were mostly people who had spent so much time together they had formed solid relationships. She was the new entry—still disconnected. There were obstacles to overcome and she knew that it wouldn't happen overnight.

By the time dinner was over, she was amazed at how much better she felt. The beer and crackers trick worked: not enough to regain her appetite, especially not for eggplant parmesan, but enough to be over the nausea, and she was thrilled for that.

Jimbo joined her, once dinner was done. "The beer, right?"

"The beer did it," she replied, grateful for his help.

"Don't forget, Miss Jamie, I've got your back."

One by one, people left the table. Domenico cleared it immediately and then he and Alberto disappeared into the galley, where they still had to prepare to serve the crew in their mess hall.

Brady stood by his dining chair. "Hey, anybody up for some casino action?"

Sam, Liz, Doc, and Philippe all signaled that they were in, while Jimbo excused himself. He retired to the captain's chair, seated across from Jamie.

"What about Alberto and Domenico?" Brady asked.

"They're tied up for a while," Doc said. "They can come in later."

Everybody sat back down. Brady got out the deck, chips, and a notepad and started divvying up the chips, keeping track of everything on paper. Stakes could get high sometimes, on those long evenings out in the middle of the ocean.

With the game under way, Jamie and Jimbo tuned out the others and got into a deep discussion.

"I hear you spent some time with Sam. All clear?" he asked.

"All too clear."

"Meaning?"

"Meaning Mat forgot to mention that you had weapons-grade sonar equipment on this ship."

"Weapons? Sonar isn't a weapon, Miss Jamie."

"Tell that to the whales and dolphins who are getting their brains blown out of their heads."

"Aww, now, that's a little bit drastic…"

"You're damned right it's drastic, Captain." Jamie was intense, and her anguish was palpable. "These are sentient beings."

"You know what? I'm thinking it must be a real bitch, feeling and seeing all the things you do. I don't think I'd want the vision you got."

"You don't have to be psychic to feel pain. Or to care."

Philippe overheard them talking from the table. "Deal me out a minute." He walked over to where Jimbo and Jamie were sitting. "Is this a private conversation?"

"Hell, no!" Jimbo motioned to him to sit down and join them. "Got no private conversations on this ship that I know of." Jimbo went over to the bar to pour himself a drink.

"So, what exactly is your role here, Philippe?" Jamie said, in a low voice.

"I work for the Canadian Marine Wildlife Preservation Department," he replied. "Our concern is to study how marine organisms interact with each other and the physical environment—especially as it is affected by human behavior."

"Do you monitor the effect of sonar as well?"

"We study the overall impact, I guess you could say."

Jimbo returned with his scotch, and another beer for Jamie.

"And wouldn't you agree that with a huge Orca sanctuary so close and migration lines cutting through our trajectory, that sonar would be disruptive?"

"Say what?" Jimbo said, listening in.

"We haven't got enough data to conclude that sonar testing is damaging to the whales," said Philippe. He looked up at Jimbo, knowing he had to be careful how he talked to Jamie: careful not to get political.

"How much data do you need? This ship can blast out over three hundred hertz—what does that do to them? To their music?"

"Their music?"

"You will agree there are all kinds of musical emissions coming from the Cetaceans?"

"Well, sure. I suppose."

"And will you admit that a lot of whale and dolphin beachings regularly occur after Navy sonar tests?"

"That could be one of the reasons. We really don't know for certain." It was clear Philippe felt pressured.

"With all due respect for our military, there's no question that they don't seem too concerned about the effect of their secret weapons on the environment."

Sam glanced over at them, as he drew a card from the dealer. "Sounds like the conversation is getting a little heavy over there," he said to Liz, under his breath.

Jimbo bristled. "Now hold on a minute, Miss Jamie. Nobody is going to be talking against the Navy on my ship. I don't want to hear it. The military is trying to protect the world—not destroy it."

"Really? They're doing a pretty bad job so far, I'd say," she said, standing up to him. "Seems like all the military knows how to do is destroy, Captain. What we need protection from *is* the military— are you sure you haven't got that backwards?"

"They're out there protecting the borders, trying to hold things together," he said, looking into his glass.

"What borders? I thought the term 'international waters' spoke for itself."

"Damn it, Jamie. There is a lot that has to go on to protect against terrorism, let's leave it at that."

"Oh yeah, right, I forgot. The terrorists. What is it—one if by land, and two if by sea? And who is protecting us against the protectors, Jim? Who is protecting the whales and the dolphins, whose only borders are the curves and jagged edges of the Earth's landmasses? Don't you understand that, for them, there is no escape from sonar weapons?"

Clearly unwilling to get embroiled in a conversation that would find no way to resolution, Philippe got up. "On that note, I'm back in the game. Excuse me." He walked back over to the table.

Liz threw in her cards. "You'll have to excuse me, guys . . . I'm getting a headache. I'm out." She served herself a cup of tea from the buffet. Sam studied her from behind. She smiled seductively at him as she walked out.

Sam looked at Jamie with the usual air of disapproval. He threw his cards into the pile and asked to be cashed out. "I'm out, too." He said his goodnights and walked out after Liz.

"You see there?" Jimbo said. "You went and spoiled the party. It serves no purpose talking like that . . . no purpose whatsoever."

Doc and Brady tallied up the chips and put things back in the cabinet, just as Alberto and Domenico came out to join the game.

"What happened?" Alberto asked.

Doc, a man of few words, just said, "Game over."

Jamie leaned closer to Jimbo and spoke straight from the heart, staring him in the eyes. "I do see things, Jim. Some are in the shadows, some are in the light—and it isn't always the first impression, but I do see behind the curtain. I see the Hidden."

Jimbo leaned even closer. "That's cool. You go ahead and see what you need to see . . . but remember, we aren't monsters out here. If you want to get along with everybody, you're gonna have to lighten up and stop preaching. You make it sound like you're working against us, instead of for us. We're all just doing our jobs—just like you. It's not easy living out on the water for weeks on end. People out here, see, they don't want to go there."

She stood up, preparing to walk out. "Who will care about the whales and the dolphins, Jimbo? Who *is* willing to go there?" Lost in her own thoughts, Jamie said goodnight and then left Jimbo sitting there. She walked out, down the hall to her suite, never even noticing that Fin was following not so far behind.

Back in her suite, she couldn't wait to go to bed and forget the tensions of a difficult day. As she was brushing her teeth, preparing to go to bed, she peered out the bathroom window, amazed to see whales out on the horizon, breaching in the moonlight. She rushed into the bedroom, to her camera, and snapped a picture just in time, before they disappeared from sight, and then she turned off the light, and fell asleep.

Unlike that first night in harbor, it was a fitful, nightmarish sleep, one that had her tossing and turning wildly all through the night. In a vivid dream, Jamie relived the horror of the tragedy back in New Zealand, with the dying whales. She was standing on the wet sand, shivering, in a soaking-wet nightgown. Hundreds of whales and dolphins lay dying on the beach, where the tide had receded, and more kept coming in, throwing themselves onto the sand, dying all around her. She walked up to one of the whales, whose calf was lying there beside her, and implored her to return to the water. The whale looked at her and started crying, and so did the calf—they just looked at her in complete desperation. Jamie pleaded. She implored them to turn back to the ocean and find their way back to living.

She tried to push the whale back out into the water, but of course there was no way she could move the immense body.

She felt the cold of the whale's death overtake her own body, and a voice uttered the words *"Beware the Ides of March."* And then, an enormous explosion sounded, louder than the booming blast of a bomb. Jamie saw blood oozing from the whale's blowhole. She tried to stop the flow, throwing her arms over the whale, but she was already dead. And so was her baby. The dead whale stared at her from the cold, gray beach, the light in her eyes dimmed forever, with Jamie standing next to her, covered in her blood.

With that horrible image in her waking mind, the memory flooding back from the beach in New Zealand, Jamie woke up, crying. She began to sob uncontrollably, feeling the pain so deep within her she could barely breathe. There was no one to call, no one she could talk to. Surely no one on the ship would understand, and no one seemed sensitive enough to even care.

She got up, afraid of sleep, and took a hot shower, as if she still had the blood on her body—so real was that image. Wrapped in the bathrobe, she searched the suite's small kitchen, where she found an electric teapot in one of the cabinets. She took a box of herb teas from her bag and made herself a cup, and then just sat quietly on the sofa, hoping dawn was not long in coming. So many thoughts flooded her mind—all sad and despairing. She drank her tea and then crawled back into bed, so tired, trying to calm her spirit.

Jamie reached for her camera to look at the picture she had taken earlier of whales out on the horizon. To her amazement, what was looking back at her in the frame was not distant whales in the moonlight, but rather an eerie close-up of a whale's eye, looking right at her. She stared at the camera, incredulous. How was it possible? What was she seeing? Was she in a lucid dream?

She sat bolt upright in bed, wide awake—this was no dream. She turned the camera off and back on again, and there it was still—imprinted on the camera's screen: the eye of the whale.

And a voice that echoed through the hallways of her mind kept repeating and repeating: *Beware the Ides of March.*

10

The Whale Rebellion

Jamie felt caged and restless in the night, waiting for morning to lift her from the burden of a dreamscape filled with death. Despite the luxurious surroundings, she felt uncomfortable, a captive guest, of sorts, on a ship headed nowhere: cut off from the world. She stepped out to the terrace, briefly, peering into the night. She looked out upon nothing but darkness, with not a sound, not a light—only the lapping of the waves, hitting up against the ship. From their position in the great Pacific, with no sight of land in any direction, she felt unbearably confined and restricted. She realized then that a month at sea, aboard *The Deepwater,* was going to be impossible, and that her deal with Mat was ill conceived from the onset. She would have to make amends, but her instincts told her that she would be getting off the ship well before April, as she had originally agreed. Everything about it was wrong from the start: her first encounter with Sam, the tension, her dream, the ominous eye in the camera . . . and that visceral sense of doom, hovering over her, like storm clouds gathering over dark fog. She tried to shake it, but she could not.

Hungry from the night before, she opened all the cabinets in her kitchenette, looking for something healthy to munch on, but all she found was the usual hotel fare: potato chips, nuts, and chocolate bars, and plenty of booze in the bar. The tin from Max's was empty—not a crumb. With an hour or more to go before sunrise, she decided to find her way into the galley and make herself some breakfast, or, at the very least, heat up some leftovers from dinner the night before. Coffee and a couple of slices of toast would more than hold her over until the galley opened. Anything to get out of that room ... her bed ... the dream. It lingered, haunting, taking her back to that day and the requiem of death that sounded, over and over again, in her mind.

She dressed and threw some blush on her cheeks, and then grabbed her jacket and cap, warm gloves, and the camera, hoping some early-morning photography would capture the incredible spectrum of light that paints the horizon, over the great waves, the way the sun does when it rises on the water.

When she opened the door to leave, she found Fin, curled up against the doorway of her suite, sleeping. He was shivering, in the cold of the unheated hallway. Had she only known, she would have welcomed him in with her, a companion through the long night. She couldn't believe this amazing animal was there for her, guarding her space through the night and waiting for her to wake up. She reached down to embrace Fin, so filled with gratitude and joy that he knew to be there in that moment. He lifted her spirits in an instant, and brought the joy back.

"Hooboy, Finny, you are a sight for sore eyes," she said in a whisper.

Fin was playful—a couple of overzealous barks and the whole ship would have been awakened in the middle of the night. Jamie got into her jacket and hat and together they found their way down the poorly illuminated corridor, where only the emergency night-light lit the way. When they got to the lounge, she remembered where Doc had turned off the lights, so she was able to light up the public spaces—but she had no clue where to look for the thermostat. They would have to freeze until somebody woke up. She and Fin stole into the galley, thieves in the night, and there she fumbled around trying to find the coffeepot. She'd never seen a ship's galley before and everything was so ... big. She finally found the coffee and filters, and put the pot on to brew—then she opened the refrigerator and found everything she needed: bread, butter, an assortment of jams, and cream for her coffee.

Fin sat quietly, waiting for his share of the bounty. She fed him the first two slices, and put another two in the toaster. As she waited for the toast to pop up, she gazed through the galley window, where, in the distance, the first hint of morning glowed indigo out on the horizon.

Pouring herself a cup of hot coffee, she thought she saw whales, far ahead of the ship. At first, she could just barely make them out. It was still dark and they were a significant distance away, but she could feel them—there was no mistaking Orcas ahead. And they were many. Jamie could never have imagined she would ever prefer not to be in the presence of whales. Something wasn't right about it, even though the unnatural presence there was their intrusive ship, not the whales. Still, their appearance that early in the morning, leaping black silhouettes against the violet ray of Earth awakening, made her feel apprehensive.

Transfixed, she stared out the galley window. More whales were gathering, rapidly now. She could hear the force of their tails, slamming down hard against the water's surface—as the dolphins had done, the day before, with Fin. These animals were clearly stressed, and the momentum was building, somehow, across species lines: the incident with Liz, the strange dolphin behavior with Fin, and now Orcas.

Fin heard them, too. He whined and gestured to Jamie to go back out on deck, just as insistently and with the same urgency as the day before.

"No way, boy," Jamie said. She topped up her cup of coffee, buttered the toast, and carried a tray back out into the living room, to the sofa. There she would wait for day to break and the cold night's silence to be pierced by sounds of the others, moving about in the morning hours. Fin curled up at her feet, waiting patiently and watching for signs. When she finished eating, he jumped up onto the couch, right next to her, something he would never have dared to do in his master's presence, but he knew, with Jamie, house rules didn't apply.

"I won't tell if you don't," she said. She hugged him tightly, and then lay down with her head on his back. The warmth of him close to her was reassuring, and she was starting to relax under the blanket, almost falling back to sleep, when, somewhere between the worlds of perception in her mind, she heard a whale call—just as clearly as if she were out there, in the water with them. She leaped to her feet, listening—a live audience to their distress calls—and she heard it again. She went back to the galley window, to find there were more whales, closer in—exhibiting those same behavioral patterns.

Something was seriously wrong. She could taste it.

With Fin following close to her side, Jamie searched near the galley door and finally found the key rack. Following her intuition, she took the key to the Tech Office and headed for the doorway, like Sherlock Holmes in pursuit of a clue, with Watson in tow. What she would find there, she didn't yet know. What she was sure of, however, was that whatever was creating the agitation in the whales and dolphins had to be connected to that room.

Once inside, Jamie stood before the array of equipment with no idea whatsoever. What was she looking for? How could she find it? "Oh great computer god, show me where we are," she said. She fiddled with a few switches, clueless, and then startled herself when one of the monitors actually came on. Frustrated, knowing she was out of her element completely, she walked back down to the main deck, into the hallway, past Sam's cabin. She could hear voices coming from the room and decided to be bold, and knock.

He already hated her, so she figured there was nothing to lose.

Sam cracked the door just a sliver, wearing nothing but a pair of boxer shorts. Through the opening, she saw Liz, naked, in bed behind him—no surprise there.

"What the hell?" he demanded of Jamie.

"Forgive me, I realize this is off the charts—I'm sorry. Something is very wrong, I can feel it. I need you to tell me where we are in relationship to the whale sanctuary."

"Are you out of your mind? It's five in the morning!"

"Five? Oh, thank god it's that late."

"Five a.m., Jamie...five!"

"I know. I'm mortified."

"Why didn't you just go up to the navigation room and talk to Bobby? We're on automatic pilot anyway, for god sakes."

"I didn't know that. I took a big liberty and went to the Tech Office and tried to turn on the equipment myself, but I didn't know what I was doing."

"What do you think you're doing? That is highly sensitive equipment!"

In the background, Liz threw on Sam's shirt and came to the door. "What on earth is going on?"

"It's the whales. There's a bunch of them, not far ahead of us. They're amassing. I think we've entered the sanctuary," said Jamie.

Sam threw his hands up in the air. "I give up."

"Please, Sam. I might have done something stupid—I turned a few switches in there."

"Jesus, Jamie! Let me get my pants on." He closed the door in Jamie's face, while she and Fin stood in the hall, waiting in the cold. Inside, Sam slipped into a sweatshirt and his wrinkled pants from the night before. Liz searched for her clothes, which were strewn all over the room, to dress to go with him. "No, you stay here... keep the bed warm. Hopefully, this will only take a minute." He sat on the edge of the bed, putting on his socks and shoes. "I so did not sign up to sail with this whack job."

"Don't you find it curious, though?" said Liz. "It was the dolphins yesterday—they were so strange."

"I refuse to engage in a conversation about Cetaceans at five in the morning." Sam opened the door, tucking his shirt into his pants, and then he stepped into the hall, where Jamie and Fin were waiting. They raced up to the Tech Office, where, fortunately, all Jamie had done was to turn on one of the monitors. The main systems board was untouched. "I can't believe you would just walk in here and put the ship at risk, meddling where you have no idea what you're doing."

"I'm sorry—I didn't know what to do—no one was awake."

"There's always someone on the bridge—just a few doors down."

"I didn't know that," Jamie replied, apologetically.

Sam fired up the system and then sat down at his desk chair, typing on the keyboard, checking the system. "Sorry," he said, with his back to her, "but isn't the point of you being here that you're supposed to be able to see these things? What part of your psychic genius am I missing?"

Jamie was embarrassed. She wasn't one to react like she had, involving other people, especially in this instance—and especially disturbing Sam, the least likely person to be cooperative, in the middle of the night.

"Here you go," said Sam. He pointed his cursor to a marker on the screen. "This is our GPS position. We are not in the sanctuary. Can we go back to sleep now?" He turned off the computers. "Please don't ever do that again. You need answers? Go to the helm first—there's a protocol to follow on a ship."

"I still haven't gotten the protocol memo. I wouldn't even know where to find a life jacket, if I needed one!"

In all fairness, he had to admit that was true. His was the responsibility of explaining how the ship operated when Jamie first came aboard, but he had dumped her with Liz and walked away. "I tell you what," he said, "I won't mention this to anyone . . . you forget seeing Liz in my bed."

"Liz, who?"

To her amazement, Sam smiled at her—for the first time.

"Back to sleep?"

"I'm up now—I'll grab Liz and we'll see you at breakfast."

Sam closed the door behind them, stashing the key in his shirt pocket, and then he proceeded back down the hall to his cabin. Jamie was too wired to even consider sleep, and Fin was pushing to go out on deck.

When they came back down the stairs, she could smell the sweet aroma of fresh baking bread wafting from the galley. "Mmm. What's that heavenly smell, boy? Something good is in the oven." Jamie bundled herself up in her jacket, hat, and gloves, preparing for the cold of the morning out on deck. She was eager to see if the whales were still out there, and Fin had to get out—it seemed as if he needed to go down to the lower deck to his allocated toilet space, in a hurry. The minute she opened the door for him, he bounded out the door and disappeared down the stairs.

She stepped out into the chill of morning at sea, intent upon studying the whale activity, to pick up whatever information they might be trying to send to her. Mindful that she had spotted the Orcas ahead of the ship, she wanted to set herself up at the bow, but there was no protection there from the cold ocean winds. She settled for her place near the living room entrance, and after wiping down the deck chair with towels, she set herself up for whale watching. Only now, the Orcas were nowhere to be seen.

Fin came bouncing back up the stairs from the lower deck, and ran right over to her. He was restless, going back and forth to the railing and looking out, as he had done before, searching the sea. Jamie looked everywhere, but they were gone. She began to have doubts. Had the shadowy Orcas actually been a vision, or were they real, physical beings out on the ocean? Sometimes her psychic sight was so powerful, so real, she couldn't tell the difference. And then, in the penumbra of those early-morning hours, it was all the more possible that she was seeing between the veils, pulling from the shadows of night. Only Fin was there to corroborate her perception of the physical presence of the whales—but even then, he surely could see and hear the spirit world as well as she—if not better.

Pulling her thoughts back to the workings of the ship, sounds of pots clanging in the galley and the first footsteps of the crew moving about brought her focus back to the reality of where she was, and what she was there to do. It hit hard and with immense clarity, once again, that she would never be able to fulfill the task set out for her. There would be no oil for Mat Anderson—the whales were in the way of all of that. Less than forty-eight hours since her arrival, she could already see that her being there was an intricate part of a divine plan that was manifesting as a completely different scenario from what Mat had designed for them both. It had nothing to do with oil—that was just the vehicle that had set it all in motion.

Someone from the other realms, the spirit side, spoke the words *"Go deep. Listen to the messenger. Find what's hidden."* She allowed those feelings and information to flow through her, trusting that, as the hours passed, she would gain clarity—answers to the mystical puzzle held in those words—and that all would be shown to her.

The screeching of a flood of seagulls snapped her back to the matters at hand: the mechanics of the ship and its impact on the waters. Fin leaped up and ran forward, to the ship's bow, barking like mad. The Orcas were back—only now she was witness to a huge pod, and she could see newborns leaping out of the water, surrounded by their guardians. Was it a nursery, straight ahead?

She tried to estimate how many were out there, but counting was impossible. They were everywhere, hundreds, it seemed. It was a rare spectacle of nature that, in any other circumstance, would have filled her with joy and celebration. And yet, as breathtaking as it was to see such beauty, Jamie's reaction was not one of joy, but of alarm.

The ship's motors had just fired up and they were headed straight towards the pod. From the bow, Jamie could see the equipment at the top of the ship: the radar and other unidentifiable devices had begun spinning, and in minutes were rotating at full speed. Almost immediately, the whales became agitated, exhibiting the same behaviors and signs she had seen in the dolphins the day before.

Jamie flew up the stairs to the bridge, but, contrary to what Sam had told her, no one was at the helm. She then raced to the Tech Office, and there was Sam, staring sleepily into the screen, sipping from a mug of coffee. She was breathless. "Thank god you're here."

Sam was flippant. "Is this a recurring dream?"

"Turn it all off!" Jamie ordered.

"Turn what off?"

"Everything. Cut the motors, turn off the radar. Now!"

Sam sighed. "Well, what will it be, Jamie? Off, on . . . on, off—what?"

"There is a huge pod of Orcas ahead of us—there are at least a hundred, and they have babies. I've never seen anything like it."

"Yeah, funny thing about the ocean. Whales live here," said Sam, dryly.

"Don't you understand? There's a pod with their young out there—how dare you turn on all this equipment against my express wishes—turn it all off!"

"Turn what off? Do you even know what you're talking about?"

"We need to steer away from this pod, that's what I know."

"I have nothing to do with navigation—didn't we already have that conversation? Go to the bridge—the captain should be up there now."

"I went there first. Nobody was there."

"Listen, Jamie, you can't go ballistic every time you see a few whales in the water. This is the open ocean."

"This isn't a 'few' whales. There is a community of them out there—maybe hundreds. I want proof we're not in the sanctuary."

Sam turned on the intercom. "You there, Captain?"

"And a good morning to you," he replied.

Upon hearing his voice, Jamie raced out of the room and went right to the bridge to find Jimbo. The intercom was open, and Sam could hear the whole conversation come down.

"I thought it was beyond clear that we were to avoid this sanctuary, Jimbo. Don't tell me we're not in it. I don't believe it."

"And a good morning to you, too," he said.

"Sorry. Good morning, Jim. We're in the sanctuary—yes, or no?"

"Just passing through. Cutting through these waters saves us a ton of time and fuel, and we're no threat to any whales."

"How much clearer did I need to be about this? Did you or did you not get briefed by Mat Anderson?"

"You're going to have to chill out about this—it's no big deal. We're just passing through."

"Can't you see the whales ahead?"

"Yeah, I see them. Not unusual to see whales in the ocean, Miss Jamie—and they know how to swim out of the way, imagine?"

"How can you sit there and tell me 'it's no big deal'? You live on the water. Have you become so detached that you can't feel what's going on out around you? There are mothers and babies out there!" Jamie was almost hysterical. "And what has Sam turned on? All the equipment—what's going on?"

Jimbo had had just about enough of Jamie and her histrionics.

"Look, Jamie. I can't have you interfering with the navigation of this vessel. I have my orders. They come from headquarters."

"All right," she said, snapping at him. "They're going to have to change, or you can drop me back at the harbor. Get me Mat on the radio, right away."

"Call Mat at this time of the morning? On a weekend?"

"Do it anyway," Jamie insisted. "I'll take full responsibility."

Laid back in his chair, eavesdropping on Jamie and the captain, Sam saw a large object shooting across the radar screen. He sat up attentively, tracking it, and quickly froze the image and ran a printout. From nowhere, another appeared on the same trajectory as the first; but faster than he could hit the key to print again, they both vanished without a trace—a virtual impossibility.

He grabbed his radar print, and burst into the bridge, interrupting them. "Captain," he asked, "have you got a minute?" It was clear from Sam's sense of urgency and the sideways glances that he wanted to speak to Jimbo in private.

Looking past Jamie, Jimbo said, "Talk to me. What you got?"

He walked up to Jimbo and spread the printout on the desk.

Jimbo looked at it, showing no expression at all. "Hmm," he said, nonchalantly, "What the hell is that—a sub?" He looked up at his own screens, but there was nothing visible.

"You got me, sir. It's nothing I've ever seen before—just picked it up on radar."

"What's its position?"

Again, Sam looked over at Jamie uncomfortably. "The thing is, it just disappeared off the screen, as fast as it came on."

Jamie stepped in between them to see the printout.

"Exactly where was this, in relation to our coordinates?" Jimbo asked.

"It was about two miles ahead, then another showed up right behind it—before they both disappeared off the radar screen."

"God, Jimbo, that's right in the middle of the whales," she said.

"Yeah, we'd be having a much bigger problem than upsetting a few whales if there were a couple of submarines ahead of us, now don't you think? Relax. Probably a malfunction in the equipment—it happens... a false reading, most likely."

"Malfunction? How curious," Sam thought. He studied Jimbo, trying to figure out what his game was. Radar doesn't malfunction by showing distinct objects in the field. He figured the captain was making light of the information because Jamie was present... and yet he could just as easily have had Sam hold off until they were alone. What bizarre behavior—it wasn't like the captain. He looked at Jimbo quizzically, unsure how to respond. Jimbo told him to keep tracking it and to keep him informed if it showed up again. Sam left the room, befuddled. Things were backwards—it should have been Jamie leaving the room with no answers, not him. Jimbo just nodded at him and then he folded the paper in half and placed it in the desk drawer, giving it relatively no importance.

"Wait—do you mind if I take a look at that?" she asked.

Reticent, he reached back into the drawer and handed the paper to Jamie, who placed it on the desk next to Jim, running her fingers over the image.

"Are you going to tell me you can get a hit off that?"

"Possibly." She closed her eyes and held her left palm over the blip on the graph.

Jimbo kept his gaze fixed on her, anxious for her to open her eyes. After several minutes, he interrupted her: "What do you read?"

Jamie opened her eyes, slowly. She looked a bit dazed. "Do you believe there's an extraterrestrial presence on this planet, Jim?"

He was nothing short of flabbergasted, but he held back, hiding it from her. "Should I?" he replied. It was all he could muster as a response.

Jamie knew she had to be careful about what she shared. She

wasn't going to give away anything more than what she thought he would be able and willing to hear. "Shouldn't we all, Captain Jim?"

"Well now, my dear Jamie, if you can run your hands over a map and tell us where the oil is, I'll believe in just about anything—even little green men!"

Static from the intercom interrupted their discussion.

"Captain, can you hear me?" It was Philippe.

"Yeah, I hear you, Phil. What's up?"

"Can you come down on main deck, sir? We have a situation down here."

"What kind of situation?" Jimbo asked. He turned to Jamie and said, "This is one crazy way to start the morning."

"I think you'd better see for yourself, Captain."

"Talk to me, Phil. What's the problem?"

Philippe hesitated. "We've got about fifty whales up close around the ship, and more are swimming in, from every direction."

Jimbo replied, "I'm well aware of the Orcas. I've got Jamie up here already screaming about it."

"No sir. These are Humpbacks. The ship is surrounded by a huge pod of humpback whales."

"Humpbacks in Orca territory? C'mon, man, you're the biologist! You know that's not going to happen."

"Captain, I've walked the whole deck, stem to stern. I'm telling you we are surrounded by humpback whales. You need to come down and take a look at this, with your own eyes."

"They're just changing shifts up here. I'm waiting on Brady and then I'll be down."

"What in god's name is happening?" Jamie headed out the door. "Are you or are you not running sonar?"

Jimbo looked guilty, but said nothing.

"Tell Sam to cut the damned sonar, Jimbo—now!" She ran out the door, down the stairs, and out to the deck. There was Fin, crouched down at the drain, where he could look out at the ocean. She could not believe what she was seeing. Swimming up alongside the ship, several huge humpback whales appeared to be almost closing in on them. As she stood there, in utter astonishment, Philippe approached her. He looked completely bewildered.

"Never in my life have I been witness to any whale behavior like this."

One whale in particular, a big female, was slapping her fluke at the surface, spraying so much water over the ship it reached the height of the main deck.

"This is dangerous!" Jamie said, looking down at her. She could feel the great mammal's anguish, which projected Jamie, once again, back to the beach. She felt the spirit of the mother whale in New Zealand, in the mighty being below, reminding her of the voice from the other side: *Go deep. Listen to the messenger. Find what's hidden.*

Philippe pulled her away from the railing, where they were both getting drenched in the spray, and walked her closer to the doorway. He unzipped the walkie-talkie from the inside pocket of his waterproof parka. "Captain, are you there?"

Fin stayed up against the railing, fixated.

"Yeah, Brady is on his way up, and then I'll be down."

"You need to come down here now."

"I said I'm coming! Hold your horses."

Jamie grabbed the walkie-talkie out of Philippe's hands and shouted into it. "It's the sonar! The whales are screaming . . . they can't bear it! Tell Sam to cut the sonar immediately!"

Jamie and Philippe watched in consternation as the scene beyond the railing of the ship became more threatening by the minute. Huge humpback whales swam menacingly close to the ship, and more were coming in, joined by their natural enemies—the Orcas: side by side, united, in some sort of rebellion against the ship. As impossible as that seemed, against everything that is known about Cetacean behavior, there they were, holding the ship hostage.

First Liz and then, moments later, Sam appeared on deck, stunned by the scene that surrounded them. Sam went over to the railing, to see for himself. He couldn't fathom that he was looking out on at least fifty humpback whales, all swimming alongside the ship. "What the hell?"

"Are you ready to listen to me, yet?" Jamie snarled, brushing past him on her way back up to the bridge. As she approached from the upper-deck hallway, she caught Jimbo in conversation, talking on the ship's radio.

"...I had to, sir. I have a situation out here."

Mat's unmistakable voice came through loud and clear. "How could you lose it, Jimmy boy? Turn the damn sonar back on."

"Boss, we've got about fifty pissed-off Cetaceans encircling the ship, and there's another fifty coming in. I have never seen anything like this in my life."

"Do what?"

"The ship is surrounded by five thousand tons of distressed whales. We still don't have a clue what's going down."

"I don't give a goddamn about a bunch of whales—do you read me? What part of this don't you understand?"

Jamie listened, stealthily, from the hallway.

"I don't think you're really getting the picture here, Mat. I'm talking we are surrounded by, and I repeat: about five thousand tons of agitated whales, up close and uncomfortable. The ship is big, but it ain't that big! It's already an emergency."

"Am I really hearing this? Don't forget what you're there for, Captain."

"Gotta go, incoming from the Coast Guard—I'll keep you posted."

"Wait a min..."

"Over and out."

Jamie took her cue to enter. "Please, Jimbo, you need to cut the engines."

"Jamie, I don't have time for this right now."

He dialed the Coast Guard. "This is *The Deepwater,* do you read? Over."

The radio reverberated with the sound of static, but no one replied. "This is the captain of *The Deepwater,* do you read me? Over."

"Yes, we read you. Over."

"I'm passing through the Orca sanctuary at 128 degrees and I'm in a little trouble out here. Over."

"Hold on, I'll get navigation," the first voice said. "Hey there, Captain Jimbo, it's Tom here—what can I do for you?"

"Tommy, you better sit down for this one. I'm surrounded by a pod of about fifty big Humpbacks out here, right up close on all sides. Can't even count'm. And I've got a huge Orca congregation ahead. Don't know how to move. We're in some serious trouble out here. Over."

"Did I hear you correctly, Captain? Over."

"Yeah, you heard me all right. I'm completely surrounded by estimate fifty or so whales, maybe more, and there's a bunch more swimming towards us. They're in some strange, aggressive behavior mode. Seems directed at the ship. Over."

Tom started laughing. "Jimbo, did you have too much to drink last night, or is this another one of your practical jokes? Over."

"This is no joke, Tommy. These boys are in a wild frenzy like I've never seen before, and they're closing in on the ship. What's the best course of action? Over."

Back in the Coast Guard office, Tom and two other officers were seated in front of their computer monitors. As the conversation ensued, the two other men rolled their desk chairs back to listen to what was transpiring. "Jimbo, there simply is no protocol for a ship being attacked by a gang of whales. Over." Tom looked at his colleagues, and winked. He was still convinced Jimbo was joking with him.

"Well, dang me, Tommy—you think I don't know that? There's no punch line here, if that's what you're waiting for. This is an emergency. Over."

It was the first time he'd ever heard fear in Jimbo's voice. It made him realize, at last, that, however unprecedented the situation was, it was real and the situation seemed to be accelerating rapidly. "Get yourself out of there, Jimbo," he said. "What's holding you up? Over."

"If I try to navigate out, I could have a mass kill on my hands, at the very least. If I cut the engines and try to wait it out … hell … there's enough whale muscle out there to capsize the ship. This is a first for me, my friend—I don't know how to move. Over."

"Stand by," Tom said, taking time to consult with his fellow officers.

Jimbo and Jamie looked at each other, both aware of the danger. He waited nervously for instructions, while Tom and his colleagues conferred. Jimbo was a skilled captain. Though it made no sense at all, if he was talking "emergency," then *The Deepwater* was in trouble. That was all they had to know.

"What's your position? Over."

"I'm in the north end of the sanctuary. Over."

"We think the best thing for you to do is to cut your engines and lay low. You've got enough steel in the water to hold your position. Wait for them to move on. Keep us informed when you are free to clear out. Over and out."

Jimbo cut the motors. He hung the radio back on its hook and to Jamie, he said, "I should have been listening to you all along …" He threw on his jacket just as Brady was walking in.

"What's our course of action, sir?" Brady asked, looking duly alarmed.

"I'm not sure yet. Take the helm until I get back up here." He stashed a walkie-talkie into his jacket pocket, and then he and Jamie ran out from the bridge, down into the lounge. They exploded out the door to the deck to find the entire crew standing around, watching the whales, spellbound. The water around the ship was so engulfed with their huge forms that it was almost black from the density of their bodies, three and four deep, and more were closing in: Humpbacks and big male Orcas, side by side, against man—or so it appeared. The question was: why?

Fin was completely out of control, running circles around the ship, barking nonstop. Jamie finally managed to grab him by the collar.

"Fin! Shush now! You need to quiet down." In her hands, Fin became immediately submissive. Despite the chaos all around him, he simply lay down at her feet, waiting for her to take command— and she did just that, while everyone else just stood there, immobilized—even Jimbo.

"Philippe, have we got a hydrophone?"

Philippe nodded and looked at Sam.

"No, I don't mean the high-tech stuff. Have you got a good old-fashioned hydrophone?"

"Yes, we have one—it's on the lower deck."

"I don't like this idea, whatever you've got in mind," Jimbo said. "Try to throw a phone out, right now, in all that confusion? They be eatin' it, at the very least."

"Let's get it," Jamie said, ignoring him, and she and Philippe ran down the stairs, with Fin following on her heels. Philippe disappeared into a storage room and emerged, minutes later, with the hydrophone, on a thirty-six-meter coil of cable. Jamie was now close enough to the water level that she could almost touch a few of the whales who were close in, hovering next to the hull of the ship.

"All right, everybody, you heard the lady—let's get down there!" said Jimbo, following her lead.

By the time they got down the stairs, Philippe had thrown the hydrophonc over the side and lowered it into the water, just missing the huge female Humpback, who was swimming so dangerously close to the ship that the device almost hit her.

Just as quickly as Jamie placed the headphones over her ears, she had to rip them off. The intensity of the whales' anguished cries and the thrashing about of their enormous bodies, reverberating through the water, was so much more than she could bear, and besides, she didn't need a hydrophone to hear their calls. She handed the headphones to Philippe.

"Listen to this."

He placed the set over his ears and was almost physically blown back by the intensity of the sounds. "It can't be," he said, incredulous. The enormity of the sound, this whale collective sounding its distress and agony through the waters, was overwhelming.

"Can you get this hooked up to speakers?"

Philippe nodded, stunned.

"I want everybody to hear this, especially Sam."

While Philippe scrambled with the equipment, Jamie sat listening intently to the screams of almost one hundred whales, converging, under extreme duress, unfathomable in their immensity and despair. She was attempting communion with them all. Fin howled like a wolf under the pull of a full moon, only adding to the frenzy and confusion. He stood at the railing, crying incessantly, responding to their calls with sounds Jimbo had never heard come from him before. He howled madly, and nothing anyone could do would silence him.

The speakers finally came on, belting out the cries of desperation so that all could hear. No one could have been prepared for the devastating calls from such impossible numbers of whales, in distress, surrounding the ship. Not one of them had ever even considered the enormity of a whale's song, much less the expanse it could cover in the sea. And here now, with this massive presence around them, the intensity of the whales' traumatized, collective voice was terrifying.

As they stood almost paralyzed by the scene that surrounded them, the huge humpback whale scraped against the hull, pushing up against the side, rocking the ship dangerously. And all the while, Jamie kept hearing someone speaking to her from amongst them.

"... It's what's hidden ..."

The mighty female was so close, Jamie could almost touch her. She peered over the ship's railing, and there, once again, she found herself almost face-to-face with the great whale—in yet another tragedy, unfolding. She stared at Jamie, fixated upon her, and through that one eye facing up out of the water, she communicated the despair and urgency of the entire community, no less desperate than on that day of dying on the beach.

Jamie turned back to Jimbo, who stood there, immobilized. All he could see was the impossible—whales attacking a ship. "She's speaking to me," Jamie cried. *"Help us ... we need your voice."*

For the first time in his life, Jimbo felt totally impotent. He stood watching the scene unfold all around him, unsure and confused.

"Listen to this! Oh my god, can no one else hear? *'Help us, before we all are gone.'"*

Drowning in the sounds blasting from the speakers, the crew looked helplessly on while Jamie walked through her torment alone—but for Fin. What she could hear was unimaginable to them: spoken messages from the animal kingdom? They all were still locked in the world of their senses, where they could hear the physical cries and haunting calls of the whales and dolphins through the stereo, but they could never believe that she heard messages, nor could they feel the despair in Jamie's soul.

Not one of them, not even Philippe, had the vision to even question what possibly could have caused this unfathomable behavior. All they knew was that it didn't fit into their box of reality. Across the minds of the captain and Sam, who had, indeed, activated the sonar in the breeding nurseries of Orcas in season, only a subtle trace of guilt fluttered—not for the damage and pain they might have inflicted on this community of living beings, but, rather, because they had proceeded through the sanctuary against Jamie's express warnings and demands. There was no way, in their minds, that cutting through a channel in the ocean where a few Orcas might prefer to birth their young could have provoked anything like what they were witnessing firsthand. This was something so enormous, it had to be more than that.

When had it ever occurred that whales attacked a ship? Never, in any record of man sailing the oceans, had there ever been an account of Cetaceans behaving in such a way with humans. And yet here it was, unfolding before their eyes. The great ocean mammals, targets for the hunters, seemed to have become the aggressive predators of man.

Jamie leaned precipitously over the railing, speaking to the whale. "Please trust us. Move back ... let us get out of your way, so that none of you is hurt."

The whale rolled to her side, lifting her huge fin up at Jamie, revealing that, somehow, the cord from the hydrophone had become entangled around her blowhole. The more she moved, the more she became entrapped and distressed. Jamie grappled with the cord, trying to free her, but, before anyone managed to catch her, she lost her footing—slipping on the wet flooring. In one calamitous instant, she hit her head violently up against the steel railing and went crashing to the floor with a vengeance. Blood started gushing out of her head, running down over her face, and dripping onto the floor. Fin was the first to race to her side, barking hysterically. Jimbo was second.

"Jesus! Where's Doc? Get him over here—stat!" He ripped off his jacket and covered her, kneeling down close. "You just lie still, Jamie. Just lie still, don't try to move." He removed his sweater, rolled it up, and carefully placed it under her head.

"Where the hell is Doc! Move, people! Dom, get me some blankets fast."

Doc smashed open the glass to get to the first aid supplies. He moved into action immediately, treating the wound as best he could and then wrapping bandages around Jamie's head, to try to stop the bleeding long enough to get her up to sickbay. "She needs stitches, immediately," he told Jimbo.

Jamie lay there, white as a sheet, but for the deep crimson stain of her own blood trickling down over her eyes.

Fin was inconsolable. He ran back and forth, trying to get close to her, barking uncontrollably. Nothing Jimbo could do could contain him.

"Berto—take that damned dog up into the mess and don't let him out—he's no help right now!"

Beyond the immediate tragedy surrounding Jamie, right off the side of the ship, the great whale had begun thrashing wildly— one hundred tons of fear slamming up against the ship. With Doc tending to Jamie, Jimbo took command of his ship. He looked up at Philippe, who was in such confusion, he seemed to be in a state of shock himself. "Phil, pull those damned speakers and get that freakin' cord off that whale—just cut it off if you can. Now! Bobby— call the Guard. We may need medical emergency assistance—go! Liz..."

Doc interrupted him, looking grave. "She's bleeding heavily and I'm not sure about her spine. I don't think we should move her."

"Can we handle it here?"

"I don't know what kind of damage we're talking about—she needs a hospital, Jimmy. Code Red."

Bobby was already up on main deck. Jimbo screamed into the walkie-talkie: "Make that 'Code Red,' Bobby—we need a medivac helicopter."

"Yes, sir!" Bobby called back as he raced up to the helm.

Domenico returned with the blankets, which Jimbo tucked around Jamie's trembling body while Doc treated the wound. Between the shock and the loss of blood, she was becoming delirious. She stared up at Jimbo, muttering incoherently. "Don't let them ... the towers ... help ... the music ... help us ..." She tried to lift her head, but couldn't move.

Jimbo held her hand, tightly. "Don't try to move, Jamie—you have to stay real still. It's going to be all right. Let us take care of you." The bandages were already soaked in blood. "You're going to have to sew her up, Doc—right here and now."

Doc carefully unwrapped the bloody gauze from her head. Her hair was matted with blood and more poured out from the gash in her scalp. On a ship that was rocking precipitously, with emergency conditions on board, he tried to hold a steady hand long enough to shave around a head wound that was gushing blood, on a person who was still conscious enough to feel everything. He called over to Liz, who was nearly frozen in panic, to assist. "There's a needle and surgical thread in there," he said, pointing to the medical case.

Liz couldn't move, the blinding fear paralyzing her completely.

"Come on, girl! I need your help—snap out of it!"

She came hesitatingly, repulsed by the blood, and kneeled down next to him, waiting for instructions.

Jamie squeezed Jimbo's hand with every last drop of strength she possessed. His face was blurry to her now, and she knew she was losing consciousness. Still, she was present enough to speak, and she had been given a message that had to get to Jimbo. Her voice was so faint, he had to put his ear close to her mouth. "They're going to destroy them all, Jim," she whispered. "It's a lie ... they're using you.

It's not how you think," she muttered, slipping out of consciousness. "They're going to destroy the colony. You have to know. Please help them. It's a lie ... it's all a lie."

And then, she blacked out.

With the imprisoned whale now thrashing desperately up against the ship, Philippe couldn't even consider attempting to free her, without risking his own life. Then again, he didn't possess the same kind of selfless courage as Jamie to even try. He ripped the plug of the stereo from the wall, silencing the unbearable sounds, and then cut the rope from where it was secured on deck, enabling the whale to eventually fling it off and free herself. The great creature flapped her fluke down hard on the water, once again, and then pushed through the army of whales and swam away from the ship.

The hydrophone sank slowly down into the depths of the sea, having done what it had to do for Jamie, and for the whales.

Jimbo looked desperately at Doc, who was checking Jamie for a pulse.

"It's okay. We've still got her, but we need that copter, bad."

Jimbo called up to the bridge for an update.

"Twenty-five minutes, Captain," Bobby replied. And then he said, "Mat Anderson called, asking for an update on the situation."

"What did you tell him?" Jimbo looked all around him, disaster and chaos unfolding. All he needed now was Mat breathing down his neck.

"I told him that, as far as I could see, you had everything under control, sir, but that you were busy down on lower deck. I didn't provide any details."

"And he was okay with that?"

"Yes, sir, he said it was good to hear that, and that he would be talking to you later on for a full report."

"That's my boy, Bobbo. Looks like *you're* the mind reader around here."

"Yes, sir."

"That's our official line from here on out, until we get things sorted. Make sure everybody's clear on that—any questions come to me and me alone."

"Got you, Captain."

In the wake of Jamie's dramatic accident, Doc was naturally the calmest of everyone present. He was trained for every kind of medical emergency, having seen it all in his day. During the war, he'd pulled boys out of the swamps, with their legs half gone. He looked up, reassuringly, at Jimbo. "You go do what you need to do—I've got this."

The captain stood up, with Jamie's blood on his hands. He knew she was hanging on to life by a thread.

"It's a blessing on one hand that she's out; she won't have to feel this," Doc said, trying to reassure him.

"I'm havin' a hard time finding the blessing in any of this," Jimbo said. He turned to Sam, who had stepped away from the railing and braced himself up against the wall of the ship—never offering to help—clinging to his own fear. Not once did he move from that spot, as if his terror had frozen him there. Only then, when he saw the anguish in Jimbo's eyes and realized that he was in trouble, did Sam finally get out of his own way enough to reach out.

"Captain," he said, "are you all right?"

"Yeah, it's not me we need to worry about." Jimbo stared out at the water, mystified. "We should have listened to her. She warned us over and over again." Several whales were slapping their big flukes down hard on the surface waves, spraying the ship with sheets of seawater. "The minute we get Jamie on that helicopter," he said, "we move out of here, no matter what happens. We've got to get the ship out of here, out of the way."

"Yes, sir."

"And we leave quietly—nothing operating from your end, you

got that? This is where we all start paying attention to Jamie—the woman knows what she's talking about."

Sam nodded, holding his head down. As insensitive as he could be, he still couldn't help but feel partly responsible.

"Let's move. Domenico, go grab the gurney."

"Bring the head brace—it's in the supply cabinet—and get me more blankets!" Doc shouted.

While Jimbo watched him treat Jamie, tragedies they'd shared raced through his mind: lives that had been taken on his guard, and others that he'd saved. And now Jamie was lying in her blood, unconscious. He had to extract himself, and focus on getting the ship out of danger, but it was so hard to release from her. Doc could see his torment—he'd seen it many times before. He assured Jimbo that he had Jamie under control, as best as he could amid the precarious conditions on deck. With that, the captain ran up the stairs to the bridge, trying to outrun the doubts that kept clouding his vision, but dark shadows from Jamie's warning obscured the light of his reasoning mind.

"It's a lie . . . it's all a lie." Her words echoed through his mind and would not be silent. The more he tried to push them away, the louder they rang—the truer they became.

Both of his officers were there, holding the helm. "Anything I can do for you, Captain?" Bobby asked, concerned. He'd been with Jimbo the longest, after Doc, and he could second-guess Jimbo's moods and his thoughts.

"Just hold on while I get myself together here, Bobby." Jimbo's mind was racing wildly. He couldn't focus enough to think things through, bouncing back and forth from what he once knew was impossible, to what Jamie knew was not. Everything was upside down; he was walking a tightrope between realities. No matter how insane it seemed, the whales were there for her—they had been warning her all along, and it had taken this to get him to listen.

His mind played out the moment she ran her hand over the radar printout. If only he'd come clean with her then, and trusted her with what he knew.

"Do you believe there's an extraterrestrial presence on this planet, Jim?"

"Should I?"

"Shouldn't we all, Captain Jim?"

From the bridge, Jimbo had a 360-degree view of the ship. They were completely surrounded, still, by the whales' frenzied bodies. His responsibility was to the ship and the people on it, and he needed to shake off the doubt, and his fear for Jamie, and get them out of danger.

He walked through the steps he needed to take, in order to still his mind. "Start with Mat." What was he going to tell him about what had happened? How much did he need to hold back? And could he trust Mat? He decided to send an SMS, to buy time, until he was clearer and he could talk to him rationally. He typed out a brief message, revealing as little as possible: *Accident on board. Jamie head injury—medivac to hospital. Waiting news. Heading back in. Will get back when I know more, J.*

Back on deck, Doc prepared to operate on Jamie—to stitch up the wound and stop the bleeding. As best he could, he took all the necessary precautions. He slapped on a pair of gloves, sterilized the wound, and then injected Jamie with an antibiotic and a tetanus shot before performing the rudimentary surgery. It took twenty stitches just to seal the wound and get the bleeding to stop, but the greater concern was the possibility of bleeding inside the brain and possible permanent brain damage. He wrapped her head again, relieved to see the bleeding had just about stopped— waiting, counting the minutes for the medics to fly in and get her to a hospital.

He worried that they would not be in time.

With all attention on Jamie, it took a while for anyone to notice that, uncannily, the violent rocking of the ship had stopped. The whales became very still, hovering right next to the ship, almost immobile, as if they knew that Jamie's life was in the balance. Doc carefully secured the head brace before Sam and Domenico lifted Jamie onto the gurney. Doc strapped her in securely, and then, with Philippe's help, Sam and Domenico carried her up to the main deck. Doc threw the medical gear back into the kit and brought it up with him, looking back at the bloodstain left behind, and an angry sea filled with giant whales, beyond.

To Liz, who was still grappling with what had happened, Doc said, "Tell Mike to get one of the crew to come and scrub that out."

"I'm going with her," Liz replied, ignoring his command.

"You'll have to ask the captain for permission." Even though the ship was run informally, there was still a line of command, and she was in no position to make that decision.

"I don't need permission. Don't let them fly without me." She ran up the stairs after him.

"Okay then, but make it fast—when that copter sets down, nobody's going to be waiting on you."

She disappeared down the hall to her cabin. Sam and Domenico rolled Jamie into the entryway, just inside the main doorway, waiting—nervously watching the clock. Jimbo came back downstairs, secretly hoping some miracle had occurred, and that he would find Jamie back on her feet again, but knowing that wasn't going to happen. He didn't need to ask Doc how she was holding up. After so many years, he knew how to read him. The urgency of Doc's movements . . . the anguish in his eyes: Jamie was critical.

To see Jamie Hastings, such a big presence, so full of life, lying there unconscious, close to slipping away . . . was surreal. No one spoke, for fear of giving voice to the thoughts they all were thinking.

They stood around her, stunned and silent, each confronting his own conscience—especially Sam.

He had never even given her a chance.

Fin scratched persistently at the glass door, looking woefully out at his master from the mess hall, but Jimbo ignored him. Fin was more than he could deal with. As out of control as Fin was, he would be another bit of drama that nobody needed and then, Jimbo knew Fin would be traumatized at the sight of Jamie, so lifeless . . . so close to death.

Jimbo wanted to go with her, to protect her, but he had no choice. The ship was in jeopardy. He was the captain—he had to stay and bring her out of it.

Liz came racing back from her cabin, struggling to get into her jacket. She had an overstuffed overnight bag over her shoulder. "I'm going with her . . . she's going to need someone."

Jimbo nodded in agreement. He went to the bar, opened the cabinet with his private stash, and poured himself a double shot of scotch, which he drank down in one hit. He set the glass down hard on the table and looked over at Doc, who he knew disapproved, to let him know not to even think about saying a word about it. Not even one word.

"Set me up one of those, will you, Jimbo? Once Jamie's on her way, I'm going to need one, too."

Jimbo took another glass from the bar and left the bottle and glasses on the table, knowing that would be a ritual they would share, in Jamie's honor, once she was in the air.

At last, the unmistakable drone of the helicopter whirred in the distance, and they all moved out, wheeling Jamie to the heliport pad at the stern, readying her for transfer. Overhead, the pilot and the doctor seated next to him stared down at the scene below them, incredulous. Who could believe what was actually happening down below? From their position, it looked as if the ship had become engulfed in a cluster of floating logs, but they had had the briefing—they knew these were whales: it looked like a hundred or more. It was like a scene out of a movie—pure science fiction—only it was all too real.

"What in god's name is going down?" said the pilot. He spoke into the radio, "*Deepwater*, we are coming in for a landing. Over."

Bobby sighed a breath of relief. "We are ready and waiting. Over." He prayed they could set her down easy, without spooking the whales any more than they already were.

The helicopter put down carefully on the ship's helipad, and the men moved into fast action. The medic in the back opened the hatch; Jimbo and Sam lifted the gurney into the cabin. The medic hooked her up immediately to an intravenous drip and all manner of life-support equipment. Doc tried to brief them, but, with no time for anything but the most perfunctory details, the doctor waved him away—even one minute lost could mean her life.

Jimbo reached in and took Jamie's cold hand. "Come on, Jamie, hang in there. I'm ready to hear them whales speak," he said.

Liz turned to look back at Sam, oddly detached from him now, and took a seat in the back, next to Jamie's gurney. They closed the hatch and took off immediately, while Jimbo and his crew looked on, left to deal with the insanity that surrounded them, and a desperate sense of foreboding that Jamie would not be coming back.

Buckling her seatbelt, Liz looked out at the apocalyptic scene, an immense sense of dread overtaking her. As the wind from the helicopter blades splayed the water beneath them, she could see whales spy-hopping out of the waves. What she didn't realize—what she couldn't know—was that they were searching for the Emissary, knowing she was gone, and with her, a message from the deep that had not gone unheard . . . only unanswered.

11

A Near-Death Experience

Within minutes of landing on the roof of Vancouver General, the hospital emergency crew had Jamie racing down the elevator and into the emergency room, into the expert hands of the ER medical team. Liz tried to stay with her, but a nurse rushed her out into the waiting area, where she was helpless to do anything but that: wait . . . and maybe pray.

An admissions clerk approached her almost immediately, with a pile of forms and bureaucratic red tape, but Liz explained she was not family and couldn't provide any information. Jamie was all but a stranger to her, and she couldn't answer even the standard questions: Did she have insurance? Who was the next of kin? What medications was she taking?

She realized how shallow she'd been with Jamie. What did she really know about her? She'd just met her only three days earlier—even if it seemed a lifetime since she had seen the woman first drive up at the harbor. Did she have a family? Who needed to know that she was lying in the emergency room of a hospital unconscious, possibly dying? About all she could tell the admissions nurse was Jamie's full name, that they were from the USOIL *Deepwater* research vessel, and that all billing and insurance matters would have to be handled through the head office, directly. For a girl who never stopped talking, she was curiously at a loss for words.

She called Sam on his mobile, which he fortunately picked up, and told him to have someone call the hospital immediately, since the staff was already pushing for confirmation of Jamie's insurance coverage, and—most of all—they needed someone to sign permission slips in case surgery was required. Sam reassured her that Doc was already taking care of it, and that they were talking with the appropriate people in headquarters, who were on the case as well. As for signing permissions, that would be her mandate, and her responsibility.

In that same moment, the nurse nodded from behind the desk. "We've got them on the line now, thank you," she said, calling over to Liz.

Sam pressed to hear any news on Jamie's condition. Everybody on the ship was still in shock and disbelief at what had happened, and they were waiting, worrying. All Liz could tell him was that Jamie was still unconscious and that they were working on her in the ER. Other than that, she had no information. It was still too soon, and all she or anyone else could do was wait.

"Call me later," she said, and then hung up, abruptly.

While Jamie lay unconscious, being examined, tested, punctured, radiated, scanned, and transfused, her spirit floated out of her body: first, hovering over the room, watching the doctors working on her, from above the bed, and then floating higher... leaving the physicality of her existence all behind. She could still hear their voices, but as she lifted higher and her body awareness yielded to the pure light of spirit, she let go completely. The scene of her imminent death and the team's desperate rush to save her faded from full color to pastel, and then it blanched completely, like a distant memory that was all but forgotten. As she drifted, all there was left to feel or to hear of the body and the room was the remote sound of the beeping monitor, reminding her that she was not completely dead—not yet. It perforated the veil between the dense, physical world, in which her physical form was encapsulated, and the expansive spirit realms, through which she floated, boundless, surrounded in the bliss of her own immortality, and the infinite light of Source.

It was wondrous: leaving her body behind; letting go of the pain it held; letting go of the fear. She was swimming in crystalline waters, and everywhere around her, the spirits of dolphins and whales wove a musical nest in which they held her to the light, like an infant in its mother's arms, singing to her eternal being. Everything was music: the opus of an endless symphony, the music of the spheres.

The mother whale she'd linked with in New Zealand came to her. Jamie knew she would. She knew that their souls would reunite, and here they were, so soon after: soul-to-soul—ancient sisters. The magnificent whale poured back into Jamie's essence the fountain of love she'd swum away in: that day when her time of going had come, and Jamie had seen her through. Jamie heard a voice, echoing through the ethers.

"I am the messenger," said the great whale. "Know me . . . I have so many things to show you." With that, she swam beneath Jamie and lifted her to the surface, teaching her to breathe in the new world, as she did with her newborn, who lay by Jamie's side on the back of the great mother. And then higher . . . and higher still, they rose together, breaching in the light of stars—surfing the cosmic waves.

Through countless universes, where the stars, pinholes in the screen of sacred darkness, leaked the light of god through the illusion of nothingness, they rose into the infinite light, and journeyed in the ecstasy of Oneness. Only when they had known it in all its brilliance and glory, did she deliver Jamie to the dolphins. They were there, waiting to greet her on reentry into the deep, bouncing their sounds off her being, healing her with their music. She swam by their side, guided through a dark tunnel in the deepest waters, their eyes shining the way through. Always moving towards the bright light, Jamie delighted in the beauty of luminous sea spirits: she could see them all. Everywhere around her, their vaporous, glowing light bodies flowed in the current and the gentle sway of the sea. Celestial beings, angels were they—illuminating the fantastic voyage into the brilliance.

Before her, she beheld a city of lights—a civilization of light beings, no less than heaven on earth. There were huge underwater ships, unlike anything she could have ever imagined: translucent worlds unto themselves, and so light, so fluid—like gigantic jellyfish, illuminated from within.

Music abounded. The ocean was filled with celestial sounds— and the melodies of the whales.

"Doctor... we're losing her."

"Paddles."

"We're flatline."

"Stand back."

The doctor placed the defibrillator around Jamie's heart and hit her with a first bolt. No response.

A monstrous blast ripped through Jamie's ocean in that moment, and the music of the great whales turned to screams. Terror. The colony vanished instantaneously, faster than the sound itself.

"Nothing, Doctor."

"Stand back." He rubbed the paddles together, waited ten seconds, and then hit her again.

A second blast ripped through the water. This one hit her in the back and she started sinking to the bottom, while everywhere around her, dolphins and whales lay dying, in agony. Where was she? Where was the light? What were these enormous microwave towers doing in her dream?

She fell to the ocean floor, landing with a thump—just next to the hydrophone, which was poking out of the sand next to her. Lying there, back in the pain of her body, a voice spoke out.

"This is really happening. It's not a dream. It's real. You are the chosen one . . . only you can help us now."

She reached out, but saw no one. "Take me with you . . ."

"Help us silence the great drums . . . please help us."

"I want to go with you."

"It's not your time. You are needed. Wake up, now . . ."

"Wake up, Jamie."

"We've got a pulse, Doctor."

"Jamie? Can you hear me? Open your eyes."

The attending physician, Dr. Arun Varja, was standing at the foot of the bed, reviewing her chart and discussing her condition with the nurse, when he noticed activity on the brain-wave monitor. "Jamie, can you hear me? Wake up; wake up, Jamie."

In her unconscious state, trapped between worlds, she saw herself, lying pale and lifeless; she saw the doctor and nurse who watched over her. She didn't want to be back, but there she was. The great Humpback had delivered her back to life, for the time being. She was still there, by Jamie's side. The whale's giant tear fell over her hands like a gentle waterfall, before washing out into the sea. Jamie tried to open her eyes, but could not. The whale slowly faded away and she floated there, somewhere between life and death, unable to move forward or back.

The hours passed, with no progress at all. Jamie was officially in coma, with no response to any attempted stimuli from the doctor. Liz pushed for news, and finally was given word that Jamie was comatose, and still in ER. She went to the hospital cafeteria to have something to eat, waiting for a chance to speak with the doctor, and then returned to the waiting room, hoping for news. Into the evening, Liz waited, unsure how to move . . . what to do. In the unnerving setting of the hospital waiting room, she ran over the events that had led to the accident, reminded of the incident she'd had with the dolphins, and tried to put it together in her mind.

The admitting nurse finally came to speak to her. "I'm sorry—there's no change so far, I'm afraid," she said. "It might be better for you if you return in the morning. It's getting late."

"No, no thanks, I've got to be here," Liz replied.

"There's a motel just up the street. Why not try to get some rest?"

Liz thanked her again, but she wasn't going anywhere.

In the ER, meanwhile, the electroencephalograph showed a flurry of brain activity. The doctor was called in immediately.

"Come on, Jamie. Open your eyes," he said, loudly.

Jamie could hear him, but she couldn't open her eyes. She simply could not.

"Jamie. Come on, girl, open those eyes."

Jamie found her way out of the haze of that gray zone she had been in for hours, and she awoke in that moment. She looked curiously at the doctor, disoriented, not realizing where she was or how she had gotten there.

"Welcome back," he said, patting her on the hand.

"Where am I?" Even with her eyes open, she could barely see. Her vision was cloudy and blurred.

"You're in the emergency room in Vancouver General Hospital. You gave us quite a good scare."

"What happened?"

"There was an accident on the ship. You had a severe head trauma—lost a lot of blood. Do you remember?"

Jamie was still trying to bridge back to the body. She had lost almost a full day. She was dazed, and still extremely confused. "I am swimming . . . the tunnel . . . the city of lights deep down there. Let me go."

"Come back to us, now, Jamie. Right here."

"The whales," Jamie mumbled.

"You were on the ship and you hit your head. Do you remember?"

Jamie winced from the pain of her wound. "We have to stop the killing drums." Tears flowed from her eyes. "I am their Emissary."

Varja turned to the nurse. "I'm going to need that CT scan."

"Yes, Doctor," the nurse replied. "I'll check downstairs and see how backed up they are."

He spoke in a loud voice, trying to keep Jamie stimulated. "You have a very serious head wound. I need you to calm down now and take it slow. Can you lift your index finger for me?"

Jamie responded.

"That's good." He raised three fingers. "How many fingers am I holding up?"

Jamie strained to see. "Two."

"Okay," he replied, noting on the chart that her vision was impaired.

Jamie became agitated. "You don't understand! There's not much time left. We have to stop them."

"It's okay . . . it's over now. You're safe."

"No, it's not over . . . only they can stop it."

Varja whispered to the nurse, "Looks like we're going to need to sedate."

"I saw the towers . . . electrical waves—was it? Nothing lives . . . no one."

"Everything is fine, just relax now. We need you to just rest now. You're in good hands. Quiet your mind."

"Don't you understand? We have to help them. Please." She struggled to get out of bed, and in one sharp movement, ripped the needle out of her hand. Blood started flowing. The nurse grabbed her hand and held it up, to stop the blood flow, applying pressure on the vein. Once they got her back in bed, the doctor and nurse worked together, testing for another vein to jab, since that one had now collapsed. They had to get her back on the saline drip immediately.

"We need you to cooperate with us. You are not out of the woods here. Do you understand me?" Dr. Varja said, forcefully.

Jamie nodded, too weak to fight. "Let me go," she muttered. "Take me back with you." She was beginning to hyperventilate.

He turned to the nurse. "Infuse half a milligram of midazolam."

She exited the room and returned with a hypodermic needle, which she injected directly into the drip.

"I've just administered a sedative to help calm you down. I want you to just breathe slowly and let yourself relax."

Jamie reacted quickly to the medication. Her eyes got heavy and finally closed.

While the nurse was taping Jamie's hand to secure the needle, Varja asked, "Do we have family here?"

"No, Doctor. Just a colleague—she's down the hall." She looked on the admitting report. "Her name is Elizabeth Bartholomew."

Varja exited to go look for Liz in the waiting room, but found her, instead, standing right next to the doorway, within ear's reach. "Are you here for Ms. Hastings?"

"Yes. Is she okay?"

He was wary about giving out information. Hospital policy— only family was privileged to patient diagnosis. "Ms. Bartholomew?"

"Yes, I came in with her."

"Has her family been contacted?"

"I don't know, Doctor—it's been a crazy scene here. We flew in by helicopter. I just accompanied her. I don't know what else has been put in motion. Please give me some information—we're all worried sick."

"She's just come out of coma."

"What a relief!" Liz said, interrupting.

"...but she is still incoherent and very disoriented. She doesn't understand what has happened. Her speech is slurred—she's delirious, she has hallucinations. These symptoms, I'm afraid, could indicate brain damage."

"Hallucinations?"

"Well, she is somewhere between here and a 'city of lights' at the bottom of the ocean. This could be a transition, or it could mean bleeding in the brain. The experience of lights triggering—that could indicate pressure on the brain tissue. We don't know at this stage."

Liz tried to conceal her reaction.

"We had to defibrillate after she went into cardiac arrest. We still don't know what caused it."

"Her heart stopped?"

"Yes, we lost her for a few minutes. She's definitely been through extreme trauma. But for now, she is stable."

"Oh, man. Poor Jamie."

"Unfortunately, we did have to sedate her. I would have preferred not to do that—we need to run a series of neurological tests, but she was in a high state of agitation and intense pain, so, for now, I decided that was the safest course of treatment."

Liz sighed. "What a freak-out."

"The head of neurology, Dr. Katarov, will be in early tomorrow morning. We will need his expertise."

"Right."

He looked at Liz, curiously. "What exactly happened out there?"

"Oh my god! I'm not even sure. The ship was surrounded by whales—we don't know what caused it. I guess you could say the same thing applies: we just don't know at this stage."

Varja was more than skeptical. "When you say the ship was 'surrounded by whales,' what do you mean, exactly?"

"We were caught up in some kind of freak situation—there were...god...maybe a hundred whales surrounding the ship. No one knows what could have triggered them to do that. That's why she fell. Jamie was trying to free one of them, after it got entangled in the cord from the hydrophone. She was standing there one minute, and in the next she was down—soaked in blood."

The doctor looked at Liz as if she were the one hallucinating.

"I know it sounds insane, but that is what happened."

"Was she conscious when she hit her head?"

"I'm sorry...I don't know. It all happened so quickly."

"Do you know if she suffers from epilepsy?"

"I really don't. I only just met her a few days ago."

"Can we check her purse for medication? We need to know what she's taking."

Liz felt so foolish—she hadn't even thought to grab Jamie's purse on her way to the helipad. "Sorry, in the panic, I guess no one thought of that."

The doctor finally resigned himself to the fact that Liz was going to be of no help whatsoever. "Well, the next twenty-four hours are going to be crucial. We need to advise next of kin. It's best if they come to the hospital."

"I know she's from San Francisco. They'll have to fly in."

"That would be a good idea."

"But she is going to be all right, isn't she?"

"We'll know better once we've been able to run more tests. First, we need to get her to a calm, conscious state. Hopefully, in the morning we can do a complete neurological workup." He started walking towards the nurses' station. "Can you come with me, please?"

"Our ship doctor has already spoken with your nurse. I was there in the lobby when he called."

"Good, then. Next step is to get them to phone the family."

"That sounds pretty ominous, Doctor."

"It's normal procedure to call in the family," he replied.

"It sounds like you think she's not going to make it."

"I didn't say that, but it is a serious trauma. She came in comatose, she flatlined in emergency—we had to bring her back from that. The good news, though, is that she's out of coma. She is able to speak and she has motor response—those are all good signs." He handed Jamie's chart to the nurse. "That's all I can tell you for now."

"May I stay with her?"

"I don't see why not: a few hours anyway. Once we've moved her to ICU, you will be able to visit her. For now, though, we're holding her in ER until we've got a bed up there. I'll be checking on her personally in the morning."

Liz thanked the doctor and watched as he walked away down the hallway, before dialing her mobile. She spoke furtively. "Sorry to disturb you."

The male voice on the other end replied, "What's up?"

"Jamie Hastings took a bad fall and nearly cracked her head open. I'm here in the hospital ER. She just came out of coma." She didn't want to get into the insane story of the whales—that could come later.

There was a silent pause. "Who else is with you?"

"Nobody, I flew in with her alone."

"Good."

"Doctor said she was talking out of her head. Delirious. She was trying to tell him about the colony."

"I'll be there in ten."

"They're moving her up to intensive care. I don't know the room yet."

"Stay with her. I'll find you."

As soon as she hung up, Liz overheard the nurse on the phone.

"We need a bed for an ER," she said into the phone. "Patient name Hastings. 368B? Got it—I'll get her signed out of ER and then send her up right away, thanks." She leaned through the partition and said to Liz, "We're in luck. They've got a bed for your friend."

12

Black Ops

The whales clung to the ship until the helicopter disappeared, carrying Jamie away. Then, just as mysteriously as they had come in to hold the ship hostage, they swam away, releasing *The Deepwater* back to the open sea. It was almost impossible to believe any of it had ever happened—as if they'd all slipped through a crack in the universe and then sailed back in from the other side.

The crew was eager to get home, awaiting instructions from the captain. They were all somewhere between shock and denial, aware that they had lived through something supernatural, even if they didn't know what or how. They wanted to touch land, and ground out, which was understandable, considering what they'd all been through.

Jimbo was troubled. He stood near the railing on main deck, drink in hand, reliving the accident over and over again in his mind, and hearing Jaime's words resounding through his brain. *"They're using you . . . it's a lie."* He couldn't let go of them. Despondent, Fin sat with his head on Jimbo's leg. He searched for Jamie everywhere, knowing she was gone, but he couldn't understand how she'd gotten off the ship. He ran around, checking the docking ramp, well aware land was nowhere in sight. He returned to the lower deck, where he could smell Jamie's blood on the floor, and he despaired, whining and crying for her for hours, until he simply wore himself out.

Everyone was exhausted: Doc had drunk only one glass of scotch and had fallen asleep on the couch; Alberto and Domenico were in the galley, throwing together the first meal of the day; Brady and Bobby were at the helm, awaiting orders; and Sam had gone up to his office, with strict orders from Jimbo to leave all sonar and radar systems down.

Jimbo gave the order to head back in to the harbor. He needed time out in the fresh air, trying to clear his head. There was so much he still had to work out. What was he going to report to his boss in Houston? What if Jamie didn't make it? He emptied his drink into the ocean and then kneeled down, stroking Fin's neck. "If only you could talk to me, boy."

Fin nodded his head up and down. He was thinking, "If only you could hear my thoughts, like she could."

Alberto appeared from the lounge. "Is there anything I can get you, Captain?" he asked. "We've got the galley open."

"You know the drill, Alberto—let's get some java brewing."

"Five minutes."

"I'm headed up—maybe you can feed this guy here?"

"Okay, come with me, boy," Alberto said, and the two of them left. Jimbo stayed until he felt the engines start up, then he proceeded up to the bridge. As he passed by Sam's office, he heard him talking on the radio.

"Yes, sir," he said, "I can confirm that."

Jimbo listened furtively from the hallway.

"I'm simply saying they were extraordinarily large anomalies, and I…"

Before he could complete his sentence, Jimbo walked in on him and hung up the line. "Jesus, Sam, now why did you have to go and do that?"

"Do what?" Sam couldn't believe Jimbo had had the effrontery to simply cut off his call with the home office.

"I thought I told everybody to answer no questions—were you not paying attention?"

"Captain, I was only answering a direct question from Logistics. They call me every day—I report data. You can't think I would disregard express orders from you."

"I'd like to think not, Sam. That would be a serious lack of respect," Jimbo replied.

"Sir?" Sam said, quizzically. One thing he'd never lacked when it came to Jimbo was respect.

"Call them back and tell them you found the glitch. Nothing else to report."

"That was no 'glitch,' Captain. I saw these things move across the screen. You've got the proof sitting in your desk somewhere."

"So, you're still not reading me? I'm talking about a glitch in the equipment. Make the call," Jimbo said, with authority.

"Captain, is there a reason you want to ignore this information?"

"Damn, kid. This is no time for this. There's things goin' on that you really don't want to get yourself involved in, boy."

"I'm just trying to understand."

"I'm talking about shit you can't possibly understand—do you read me?"

"No, sir, I don't. Would you mind telling me what's going on?"

"I'm not really sure."

Sam dialed and got the home office back on the line. "Sorry, it's me, Sam. We're having some problems with our equipment out here. I can't find this thing: not a trace. But I do have a glitch in my main screen. I'm embarrassed to tell you this, but I think that may be all it is."

The voice on the other end replied, "No problem. We'll check back in with you tomorrow."

Sam hung up with the home office, and looked to Jimbo for an explanation.

"Well done, Sammy. And now do me one more thing—pretend like you never saw whatever it is you think you saw." Jimbo went to the door. "Just wait for my orders." He walked out, and headed back to the bridge to relieve Brady and to have a little private think time, telling himself the time had come to set things right.

Sam worked the computer feverishly, still searching to find the images from the radar-tracking screen, for his own gratification. But they were gone—not a trace anywhere within the system. He couldn't fathom why Jimbo would want to hide something so potentially important.

He burst in on Jimbo, who was just setting himself up at the helm. "Sorry, I just can't let this go without asking."

Jimbo leaned back in his chair, tired and weighted down by a sense of responsibility for what had happened to Jamie. Moreover, his mind was working overtime, running her warning through his mind, like a recording on automatic reply. "What's that?" he said, distractedly.

"Come on, Jimbo. You've got the image. There were two huge objects, moving so close to us. I'm not making this stuff up. The computers show no memory of it—like they've been wiped clean. What does this have to do with the whales? It has to be related."

"What the hell do you think you picked up out there, kid?"

"I don't know," said Sam. "All I can see is that you're hiding something, and I'm here in the middle of it—trying to make sense of what's happening. If I need to hold back information from head-quarters, you need to tell me. Shit, Jimbo, talk to me."

"There are things I can't tell you . . . not yet. Just give me time to get my mind right." Jimbo overrode the automatic satellite guid-ance system and set his course for the harbor. "I'm bringing this ship in ahead of time. I'll fill you in once we get there. Round up the crew for me, and let's roll."

Frustrated, Sam headed for the doorway. He hesitated, wanting to ask for more, but Jimbo cut him off before he could utter a single word.

"I will fill you in, Master Sam, once we get back to shore."

Liz sat patiently by the bed, where Jamie was hooked up to every kind of monitor, oxygen tubes, and the intravenous drip. Beyond the natural state of confusion from all she'd been through, they now had Jamie in a pharmaceutical fog, sedated, and on pain medication. She struggled to wake up. Her will was so immense, she was able to push through it all, knowing one thing: she had to deliver the message. At last, she opened her eyes, surprised to find Liz there next to her.

"What am I doing here?" she asked, groggily.

"Heya. How are you feeling, lady?"

Jamie grumbled, incoherently. "How did you get here?"

"I flew in with you on the helicopter."

"Helicopter?" Jamie was completely nonplussed. She had no recall whatsoever.

"You were bleeding out pretty badly—and you lost consciousness for several hours. Jimbo called for a medivac to come in for you and I jumped on, to be with you. You're here now, safe in the hospital. Everything is going to be okay now."

Jamie looked past Liz, through the dividing curtain between her and the next bed. It was backlit from the light in the hallway. She saw a shadowy silhouette of a man, sitting in the visitor's chair, but there was no patient in the bed next to him. She was too out of it to know if she was looking at someone's spirit—perhaps a recent passover—or if someone was actually physically there. Whatever it was, there was a darkness to it: an inky, vile energy—just a few feet away, lingering close to her. Jamie spoke in a soft voice, cautiously. "I need you to listen to me. It's important."

"I'm right here for you."

She struggled to get the words out, slurring her speech. "The whales. They came to show me the weapon. There are these towers . . . do you know?"

"Towers?"

"The oceans are filled with them."

"Say what?" Liz said, raising her voice.

"They call them the 'great weapon.'"

Jamie touched her fingers to her head, running them lightly over the bandage on her scalp. She was in immense pain. "There is a whole network of them, blasting the oceans . . . and sonar . . . excruciating sound waves."

The nurse came with Jamie's medications, interrupting them. "Ah, you're awake. That's good to see!" She pushed the foot pedal to raise the head of the bed, so that Jamie could sit up, and then handed her a little paper cup with several pills and a water bottle with a straw. "Drink these down for me, now, and we should be done for the night."

Jamie took the pills as ordered, her hand shaking as she put one at a time in her mouth to swallow. The nurse held the water bottle for her while she sipped through the straw. "I've got the most unbearable headache," she said, squinting, as she looked up at the nurse.

"I'll get the doctor to come right away," the nurse replied, and then hurried out to find him. Sudden, acute headache pain was the first sign the ICU nurse knew to watch out for.

Jamie did her best to lean closer to Liz. She was attached to so many tubes and monitors, she could not move that easily. "This is real. The drums . . . the towers. They are killing the music."

Liz stood up, and leaned Jamie forward so that she could fluff up her pillows. Jamie grabbed her arm.

"Please don't let me die again, until I'm done."

"What? Jamie . . . you're safe and sound now. There's nothing to be afraid of."

"Don't let them kill me."

Liz gently pulled her arm away. "You're talking crazy."

"You know who I'm talking about." Jamie looked pleadingly into Liz's eyes. "I'm the Emissary. There's a whole civilization—a city of lights. A million or more beings. They're trying to help."

"Where? Where did you see this?"

Jamie's words were becoming more jumbled as the medications kicked in. "In the deep."

"Where?"

"Below the sanctuary. Why do you think they gather there?"

Jamie's eyes were at half-mast. She couldn't bear to look at the overhead lights.

"Who? Who gathers there?"

"The whales. They're the guardians. They're the . . . the . . . musicians."

The nurse returned with Dr. Varja. He asked Liz to step outside and then moved in close to Jamie.

"I'll be right outside, in the hall. Right here, I promise," Liz said.

"The nurse tells me you've got headache pain?" he said to Jamie with concern.

"Yes, it's excruciating."

He took an ophthalmoscope from his lab coat pocket and examined Jamie's pupils, shining bright light into each eye, looking for signs of swelling in the optic nerves. To the nurse, Varja said, "Tell them to clear the slate downstairs for this patient—I want a CT and MRI done immediately." When Jamie told him she also had tingling in her arm, he told the nurse, "Stat!" and she ran out of the room to make things happen with lightning speed.

The head nurse came into the room minutes later in a huff. "Doctor, we have several emergencies ahead of this patient." She was a fussy woman with puffy eyes and a lot of attitude.

"I said 'stat!'" he barked. Then he spoke to Jamie. "I'm concerned about the possibility of cerebral hemorrhage. We need to run more tests, so that I can rule that out."

Jamie nodded, in agreement. She knew the doctor was doing his best for her. He had a purity about him that she trusted.

"We need to call your next of kin. Who can we contact?"

Jamie was so spaced-out she couldn't even remember her mother's phone number. "My mom ... Amanda, San Francisco."

"Good, we will try to reach her now."

"Don't frighten her," Jamie said.

"Of course not," he replied. The nurse came in to report they were making room for Jamie in X-ray. "They'll be up for you shortly," he said officiously. And he walked out.

Liz returned as soon as the doctor had gone. "I'm so sorry, Jamie. I wish I could take the pain away for you."

"I need to talk to Jimbo."

"They're coming up for you now—I can get him a message if you like."

"No, I need to talk to him," Jamie said, insistent.

Within minutes, the orderlies came to take Jamie down to X-ray. As they pulled the bed out, monitors and drip intact, Jamie implored Liz one last time to speak to Jimbo.

Liz stroked her hair. "It's going to be better tomorrow, I promise."

After they wheeled Jamie from the room, Liz pulled back the curtain to find her superior, Dr. Emery Wells, seated next to the empty bed, out of view. An emotionless shell of a man, he was the picture of evil—everything you would never want in a human being, much less a physician. He had dark black eyes—no light passed there, and a coldness that seemed to emanate right from his skin into the vacant space around him. No one that empty could possibly be running warm blood in his veins. He stood up, acknowledging Liz, and they walked out together, without even speaking.

Dr. Varja stood at the counter of the nurses' station, giving instructions to the nursing team. One of a dying breed of truly dedicated physicians, he wasn't planning to leave until he had results from Jamie's CT scan. "Dr. Wells? I'm surprised to see you in ICU this time of night."

Wells looked at him with the cold, hard stare that comes of omnipotent authority. "I got a call from the CEO of USOIL, asking me to take over here. Ms. Hastings is one of their VIPs."

"Really? That's odd. I still have not been able to speak to anyone other than Ms. Bartholomew here."

Liz looked awkward, but said nothing.

"And how can I help you?" Varja asked, suspiciously.

"Ms. Hastings has actually been in treatment with me for over a year now."

Varja looked surprised, if not incredulous. "Really? What for?"

"She suffers from occasional episodes of delirium, extreme anxiety, and almost phobic paranoia."

"How bizarre. Whatever was she doing on a ship in the middle of the ocean, then?"

"I don't really feel that's relevant, Doctor," Wells said, authoritatively.

Beyond his personal dislike for the man, Varja felt there was something very wrong about the director of psychiatric medicine intervening in Jamie's case, even if he *was* one of the administrators of the hospital, and chairman of the board—and even if he *had* been treating her privately. She had been flown in by helicopter, died and come back, and quite possibly had a blood clot in the brain. She was still critical. Whatever psychiatric issues she'd had before ending up in the trauma room in ER, they were insignificant compared to these life-threatening developments.

"I'll be taking over this case."

"You, Doctor?"

"She is my patient, and I know her medical history."

"I beg your pardon, but whatever her history, this patient has just been through emergency care and was unconscious for nearly twelve hours. We have reason to suspect brain damage here."

"I understand that. I'm moving her to the Psychiatric Facility, where my staff and I can keep a close personal watch over her."

Varja was flabbergasted. "Move this woman? You can't be serious. We've only just brought her out of coma."

"I don't recall ever having had to explain myself to an attending physician. Do I need to remind you that I am the chairman of the board of this hospital?"

Varja stood his ground. "Doctor, I mean no disrespect here, but I have been involved in this case since she was wheeled in, comatose. I have reason to suspect cerebral hematoma. She needs to be in ICU until we can be sure she's stabilized, and we've been able to do all the necessary evaluations to make that determination."

"I want to treat her personally, and that is best accomplished by placing her in the facility. Let's get her released and signed over to my care. Is that going to be all right with you, Doctor?"

Varja looked at Liz, who had been silent the whole time. He was absolutely dumbfounded that any doctor would even consider moving a patient in Jamie's condition out of the ICU, much less relocating her into a psychiatric facility, miles outside the hospital. What was the connection between these strange characters: Dr. Wells, a psychiatric doctor; Jamie Hastings, a woman in deep trauma; and this young woman, who didn't fit with either one?

Dr. Varja was adamant that Jamie Hastings remain in the intensive care unit, with the backup of a twenty-four-hour operative emergency room just one floor away. "But there could be subdural bleeding," he insisted. "We're going to need to see the results of the CT and MRI before making those decisions."

Emery Wells was not there to listen to Varja's medical opinions. "The decision is made, Doctor. You can send over the test results with the patient. We are a medical facility, a part of this hospital, in case you've forgotten."

Dr. Varja realized there was nothing he could do to prevent Wells from moving Jamie if he wanted to. There was no one superior to Wells, to whom Varja could voice a protest, and he was well aware that insisting would mean his job. Still, he was a doctor, and his ethics and professional opinion were both being challenged by this strange intervention. "I suppose I don't have much say in the matter. But I will go on record as saying that this decision goes against all my medical judgment, and that you have overridden my authority."

"Authority, good doctor? I am the authority here," Wells said aggressively. "I suppose you can always take it up with the board, if you have a grievance."

Wells put his hand on Liz's shoulder, walking her down to the visitors' lounge to speak to her privately, leaving Varja standing there, incredulous. Once they turned the corner, out of Varja's sight, Wells pulled a syringe from his pocket and slipped it into her purse. "I want you to use this if she starts talking too much."

Liz looked despairingly at him. She didn't sign up for murder.

"It's only a sedative—you have nothing to worry about. They'll take her downstairs to X-ray now. Then, they'll wheel her back up here, for her release, and within the hour she's on her way over," he said. "I'll meet the ambulance outside. You stay right there with her—once we get her checked in over there, I'll drop you at the Westin. We've already got a room for you. And you stay there until I call you."

"What am I supposed to tell them? Sam will be calling."

"You tell them she's fine, sedated, no visitors. And then throw your phone in the ocean. You won't be speaking to anyone else for a few days—except me. Clear?"

"Clear."

"You can fill me in on the whale situation tomorrow."

"You know?"

"Just what I gathered from listening in on the captain's conversation with the Coast Guard. I am interested in the details—I'm sure you have plenty more to tell. Tomorrow, when things are in place. I'll be back in an hour."

They walked back around the corner. Liz returned to Jamie's room, and Wells approached the nurses' station, where Dr. Varja was signing papers. "Sign the release, Doctor. I want this patient in the ambulance and on her way, within the hour."

Dr. Varja leaned up against the counter, stupefied. Moving Jamie out of the hospital could mean her life. But there was no one he could appeal to: Wells was that man—the highest official in the hospital. Varja shook his head, trying to make sense of what was happening.

Wells walked back down the hall to the elevator, and slithered off the third floor just as sneakily as he had come in.

13

Truth, Revealed

While Liz waited for Jamie to return from X-ray, she grabbed the opportunity to call Sam. Strange, how cold she felt, as if she'd never even touched him. The mask was off now; that ship had sailed.

He picked up immediately. "Wow, I was just about to call you! What's the news?"

"She's stable. She regained consciousness relatively soon and they've been running tests all day, and now they've sedated her. She'll sleep through the night. I think the worst is over."

"Phew! That is excellent news. Everybody here will be glad to hear that. How are you holding up?"

"Well, I'm knackered, as you can imagine. I'm going in to town now and take a room somewhere."

"I'll call you later?"

Liz wouldn't be talking to Sam later. Probably never again. "I need to sleep now," she said. "Bye, Sam." Before he had a chance to reply, she was gone.

She removed the battery and the chip from her cell phone, and stepped out into the hallway, where she had seen a large waste bin marked "bio-hazardous waste." While no one was looking, she tossed them both in and closed the lid back down securely. She was done with *The Deepwater*—no further contact. She turned on her new government-issue phone, as instructed, and waited for Jamie to return. They wheeled Jamie back up to the third floor, but since she was being released, they didn't hook her back up to the monitors—against everyone's better judgment, on orders from Dr. Emery Wells. She would be leaving in a matter of minutes.

The nurse came in with her. "We've got the release papers. We're just waiting for the test results and then we'll transfer her out to the ambulance."

Jamie was still drowsy, but much more alert than before she was taken downstairs. Liz walked to her bedside, and caressed her hand. "Hey there," she said, "how are you hanging in there?"

Jamie was aware enough by now to realize that something wasn't right, but she still had no idea she was being kidnapped, or that the hospital had its hands tied to prevent it. She didn't feel safe with Liz, but there was no one else there for her. Where was Jimbo? She trusted him and she knew he was ready to listen, but of course, he was with the ship. Jamie knew she was trapped, too weak to move—too confused to even try to think for herself. For the very first time in her life, she was completely dependent on others—strangers, who didn't love her.

"Did you call Jimbo? I have to speak to Jimbo."

"Yes, Jamie, we called him and we've called your family too. Everyone is rooting for you. And I've assured them everything is under control."

"No, it's not."

"Well, let's just say you're out of danger now, which is the most important thing. You've been in and out of consciousness for a while now. My god, Jamie, what a trauma you've been through. You're a survivor, though!"

Jamie looked at her, vacantly. There was so much she still couldn't put together. "I can't remember..."

"The doctor said you were delirious. Do you remember? You

told him you were underwater, swimming around with the whales or something."

"I was on the other side."

"He said you were hallucinating."

"They took me to a city."

"That's right, you told him there was this big colony or something down in the ocean floor, imagine? You were really far out there for a while, I'm afraid. Must have been the effect of all these medications and then, you have been unconscious for quite a while."

"I died."

"Oh my god, yes, that's right. Dr. Varja told me your heart stopped—they had to use a defibrillator. How did you know that?"

"I saw everything."

"Sorry? You saw what?"

"I saw the city… the whales showed me everything. I was there."

"Well… the doctor said you were hallucinating."

"I was *there*. And now I know the story."

There was another patient in 368A, next to her bed. Liz asked Jamie to speak more quietly, so that she didn't disturb the woman.

"There are these towers everywhere. And these beams," she muttered, "… the device… long rays… sonar. It's all designed to shatter Earth's frequency. It's happening now."

"Jamie, what are you talking about? What device?"

"The towers, the drums, they're all connected to stop the pulse—it's the ultimate weapon. That's why they're killing the whales, don't you understand? The whales carry the music, the pulse…" Jamie held her free palm to her head, grimacing from the pain.

Liz whispered, "How do you know about this?"

"The whales… they told me… they showed me. You have to believe me. This is the final war for the Earth. The real one."

Liz pushed on. "Where is this underwater city? Can you locate it?"

"There's more than one. And there are millions of light beings in the oceans: it's a parallel civilization."

"Why have they never been identified—why hasn't anyone located them?" Liz asked, prodding her to reveal what she knew.

"They cloak themselves. They can disappear from 3D. But I can see them. I can see them all, and I have the eyes of the whales to take me there."

"Is it near the sanctuary?"

"Of course. They came first—the whales gravitated to them." Jamie struggled to sit up in the bed. "You don't believe me, do you?"

"I do, Jamie. I believe you see this."

"Yes, of course, perfect answer. You don't believe they're there, but they are. There is a parallel civilization, right on this planet, and nobody knows about it except those who are trying to kill them." Through her clouded vision, through the dulling of her extrasensory perceptions, Jamie saw, once again, the black mask she'd seen over Liz's face in the beginning. That was the moment of reckoning. She knew, then, that she was in the hands of a dark force.

Liz asked Jamie, again, to lower her voice.

"You're not on my side, are you?" Jamie said, pleadingly, through tears of exhaustion and a growing sense of hopelessness. She scrambled for the emergency call button, to call in the nurse without alerting Liz, but couldn't reach it. "You fool. You don't get it, do you? None of us will survive it—not even you. Why can't you see? Don't you see what you're doing?" Jamie screamed for the nurse, trying to save herself. No one answered—the nurses were away from their station, doing rounds.

Liz tried to calm her down, but Jamie was inconsolable, screaming for help, leaving Liz no choice but to take the syringe from her purse and inject it into the drip. Jamie tried to pull the needle out from the back of her hand, but she was already immediately immobilized from whatever was in the pharmaceutical cocktail Liz had slipped her. "By the time you realize what you've done, it will be too late … too late … too …" And she was out cold again.

Liz sat there, frozen. She wasn't sure what was going to happen next, and she had no message from Wells. More than an hour had passed—what was he up to? Nervously, she awaited his directive.

Accompanied by a nurse, Dr. Varja walked into the room carrying an envelope containing the test results and Jamie's chart. He was stern. "I don't know who you are, but I will tell you this. Everything is documented, with witnesses. If this woman doesn't make it, you and the doctor will have to answer for your actions. I am reporting that she is being taken out of intensive care against medical advice and without my consent. I will report it to the police as well."

The nurse checked the saline drip, which would be wheeled out with Jamie, and tucked two extra blankets around her.

"In my country, we believe in karma. If you understood how karma works, you would not be doing this." Without waiting for Liz to say a word, Varja stormed out, leaving space for the orderlies to come and transfer Jamie out the ER exit. They waited inside the door for the ambulance to arrive. Liz looked outside, searching for Wells, who had still not arrived. What she didn't notice, off at the end of the parking lot, was an unmarked taxi parked within sight of the entrance.

In it were Jimbo and Sam.

They watched a limo drive up next to the ambulance, and Emery Wells step out. Jimbo didn't recognize him, but he knew, from one look at him, that he was from the Agency. The government worked that way—one rarely knew who was pulling the strings more than one level higher. A minute later, Liz appeared from the doorway, with Jamie, out cold in the hospital gurney. The orderlies lifted her into the ambulance and locked the doors behind her, ready to take her away.

"Wow! There's Liz," Sam said, reaching for the door. He still didn't realize what was happening.

Jimbo grabbed his sleeve. "Wait. Stay back."

Emery walked right up to Liz. They exchanged a few words, got into the backseat of the limo, and then drove off before the ambulance, which followed close behind.

"Shit," said Jimbo. "They've got Jamie." He opened the partition to speak to the driver. "Stay on the ambulance—out of sight."

"Are you going to tell me now, or later?" asked Sam.

Jimbo lowered the brim of his hat as he looked out the window, trying to get a glimpse of the man in the limo as it drove past them. "Tell me all you know about your girlfriend."

"Liz? I'd hardly call her a girlfriend."

"What do you know about her, Sam?"

Sam was evasive. "Not much, to be honest. I met her when you did. What gives?"

"Are you sure you never saw her before that—back in Houston, perhaps?"

"No way. I would have remembered. She flew in from London, far as I know, straight here." As they followed stealthily, a safe distance from the ambulance, Jimbo continued to drill him.

"Anything else you know about her, that I don't?"

"Look, what do you want me to say, Jimbo? She's a cute chick, nice ass . . . fun to be around. What else was I supposed to know?"

"Did she ever talk about how she got chosen for this gig?"

"The London office . . . that's all I know. They recruited her from applicants at Cambridge. The girl is a genius—I mean, she knows more about sonar technology than I do. Beauty and brains, man. Come on, Jimbo, what's this all about anyway?"

"Where's your phone?"

Sam reached in his pocket and pulled out his mobile. Jimbo took it from his hands, pulled off the casing, and took the battery out. He slipped it back into Sam's coat pocket.

Jimbo looked Sam straight in the eyes. "She's an agent."

Sam laughed, nervously. "An agent? For what?"

"You've been screwin' around with the wrong babe, Sammy boy." Jimbo watched as the limo and then the ambulance pulled into a driveway, where a sign read "Vancouver General Hospital—Psychiatric Facility." He opened the partition again, and told the driver not to follow them in, but just to keep driving. "Drop us at the Crow's Nest, back at the harbor. Make it as fast as you can, without attracting any attention."

The driver hit the gas. Sam was trying to make sense of what was going on, but it was so crazy, he couldn't figure anything out. As they walked towards the bar, Jimbo finally broke cover, knowing he had no choice but to confide in Sam. He needed him.

"Listen up. We've got a few minutes, no more. I need you, Sam. You have to get your head around this, real quick." He looked around, making sure no one was within ear's distance. "The *Deepwater* operation isn't what it seems. We're not really worried about oil. It's a cover for a secret NSA directive to make contact with an underwater alien base. That's what we're really doing out there— we're trying to locate it and open communication."

There was a chill in the air. Jimbo raised his collar against the wind. Sam just stared at him, thoughts ... images swirling around in his head.

"We have the best people—trained remote viewers, equipment comin' out our asses, but we could never get a freeze on it. That's why they called in Jamie."

They stopped in the middle of the walkway. "Jesus, Jimbo, what kind of crazy are you giving me here?"

"Nobody expected you would pick up these ships on the radar.

That was their craft you were seeing. You weren't supposed to ever know any of this—you were part of the cover. You understand? It's all a cover. But I never understood about Liz—who was she? Mat never told me much about her, so I never asked. She never really fit, though. I couldn't have suspected that a young babe like her would be ranked over me. These people know what they're doing. I just never understood it until now."

"Damn, Jimbo—understood what?"

"Liz, man. She answers to another authority. Higher up."

Jimbo pulled open the door into the Crow's Nest, which was half-full of drunken sailors, belting back the booze. Sam and Jimbo walked in and grabbed a corner table, which still had not been cleared of empty beer bottles and a half-full basket of stale popcorn.

Sam spoke in a whisper. "Who are you, Jimbo? How do you know all of this?"

"I'm Government, boy. Covert operations. I served under Mat Anderson in 'Nam and I've been reporting to him ever since. Do you get this? We've been trying to establish contact with an underwater alien colony that we know is out there—beneath the sanctuary. We had similar locations out off the California coast, but we could never pinpoint them. That's what we're doing out there—do you want to try and grasp that for me?"

Jimbo walked over to the bartender and threw a ten-dollar bill on the bar, leaving Sam with his jaw still slammed down on the table. "Hey, dog, set me up a couple of brewskies and throw me some metal for the phone." He grabbed the beers, scooped up the coins and put them in his pocket, and went back over to Sam. "You gettin' this, kid?"

Sam took an enormous gulp of beer. "I know a little bit about remote-viewing programs. But you're going to have to give me more than a minute to get my head around the rest."

"Okay, now follow this through. Jamie Hastings had almost

immediate contact with the whales—these are highly conscious beings, man. The woman is totally plugged in. We know a hell of a lot more about them than you can even imagine, but that's a story for another time. When the shit started coming down, and those big whales came in around the boat, she was on to something. They were there for her, you understand?" Jimbo drank thirstily from his bottle. "She was lying there, about to lose consciousness, but she whispered to me, 'They're going to destroy them all.' That's what she said, all right. I wasn't sure what she meant. Liz was there—she was straining to hear, but Jamie whispered into my ear. It was me she was talking to. Who was going to destroy the whales? Those beings down there? That didn't make sense, but of course I couldn't ask her. I had to wait and see what would come next…I had to play the part. I had to report back to Mat."

Sam just shook his head. "Let me get this. You're an agent, Liz is too—but you didn't know it, and Jamie's talking to whales about aliens. Did I leave anything out?"

"You did. You left out the respect, Sam. You think I'm playing games here? Jamie, she's the key. She told me she was their Emissary. The Agency wouldn't want her to ever be able to tell that story—you get me? She made me realize there's something else goin' on…some shadow shit higher up, and the plan wasn't about making contact, like I believed. Before she went out, she told me I'd been lied to—she said, 'it's all a lie'—they've been using me. The plan is to destroy that colony—destroy those lives. I've been fooled all along, believing we were working to bring in a new era for humanity—part of the Disclosure Project. But that's not it. They want destruction. This shadow shit goes higher up, even higher than presidents."

"Are you telling me Mat Anderson's part of this? He plays golf with my father!"

"Yeah…Mat. I served under him in 'Nam. Let's leave it there for now."

Sam ran his hand nervously through his hair and took another gulp of beer. "So what are we doing, Jimbo? Why are you divulging all this to me now?"

"I need you, Sam. I'm thinking Jamie's in big trouble and we're all she's got. It's still not too late to save her. You have no idea what they have in store for her in that hellhole of a psychiatric prison."

"I can call my father. He can get her out."

Jimbo slapped his hand down on the table and laughed out loud. "Yeah, sure—right on. In the world where I live, Sambo, your daddy is a joke—he's just part of the smokescreen that keeps people from seeing what's really goin' on, behind the scenes. You say three words to him on the phone, Jamie's dead meat. Everything's monitored—they got everybody covered. You work on *The Deepwater*? Every single call you make is under surveillance—even when your phone is turned off, somebody's listening to you breathe, man. That's why I took the battery out. Make sure it stays out. They're already looking for us, and we're not even lost yet. Wake up, boy, we're talking heavy players here."

"What happens now?"

"We have to move fast. I have to be able to trust you, and you haven't got much of a choice but to trust me, too. If Jamie's talking about what she seen out there—god knows how doped up she is—then they're gonna take her out, once they get what they want from her. Are you with me?"

"You know it, Captain."

"Welcome to Jimbo world, son. You just said 'hello' to a whole lot of trouble."

Back in Houston, Mat was having a great old time in bed with Louise when his "emergency-only" mobile, which he never turned off, rang. He leaped out of bed, threw on his boxers, and took the call in the next room. It was his superior, Emery Wells.

"How much do you know about what's going on out here?" Wells asked, sharply.

Mat tried to get his mind around to why Wells would be calling. "Apparently not enough, if y'all are calling me."

"So you have no idea what's happened with your psychic?"

Mat felt the adrenaline pushing through his body. "What's happened?"

"I would think your captain should have been the one to report to you, not me. Have we had a breach in security?"

Mat paced the room. "Never. He follows orders and asks no questions. Never has. I'd put my hand in a fire on that one."

"Like he'd do for you, I imagine, but then . . . he'd get burned, now, wouldn't he?"

"Can you please tell me what's happened?" Mat said, worried.

"Where is your captain now?"

"They're still out there, laying low, at the sanctuary."

"You're sure about that?"

Mat was nervous. No, he wasn't "sure." He'd been distracted, playing with his secretary. For once in a rare moment, he had disconnected.

"Where else would he be, sir?"

"We've got *The Deepwater* showing in port, Anderson."

"What?"

"Find your captain."

"Yes, sir."

Mat couldn't believe Jimbo would bring the ship in without informing him. Not Jimbo. He quickly slipped the battery back into the other mobile phone and there it was—Jimbo's message. *Accident on board. Jamie head injury—medivac to hospital. Waiting news. Heading back in. Will get back when I know more, J.* He could have kicked himself for literally getting caught with his pants down. "My mistake. I didn't get his message."

"Not a great time to fall asleep on the job, is it?"

"No, sir," Mat replied. "No, it is not."

"L called me—she flew in with your guest. Your office hasn't been able to locate you for hours. Seems almost everybody but you knows what's happened. I want you to make sure your captain stays away from the hospital."

"What's the situation there?"

"Messy. You know how much I dislike messy situations."

"How is Jamie?"

"She's resting. She's been talking up a storm, though. I think we managed to convince the attending physician that she's prone to bouts of delirium. We had to get her to a quiet place before she said too much else."

Mat knew what that could mean for Jamie. "Don't let anything happen to her. We need her."

"I see her more as a liability than a necessity."

"We need her, sir."

"You seem to have forgotten who makes the decisions around here."

"No, sir, I have not. I just know what she can do, that's all."

"Wait for instructions. Oh, . . . and get that broad out of bed." He hung up on Mat abruptly.

While Mat stood there staring at the phone, trying to decide his next move, Louise called out to him.

"You comin' back to bed, or what, baby?"

He went back to the bedroom and threw his pants on in a hurry. "You need to go—I have shit coming down all over."

"You're kicking me out of bed? Well, I never . . ."

"Sorry, sugar, business calls." He threw back the covers. "Get dressed," he said, ". . . fast."

"And you call yourself a 'gentleman'?" Furious, she got up, naked, and stormed into the bathroom. Mat called down to his driver, instructing him to be waiting for Louise at the entrance. She came back out, slipped into her clothes, and marched out of the bedroom to leave. Just as she was about to slam the door behind her, she turned back to Mat. "You are one son of a bitch, Mat Anderson," she said, and stormed out.

14

The Race Against Time

Mat called the ship radio. No one answered—by now it was almost midnight on the West Coast. The ship was in port, so there was no necessity for anyone to be at the bridge. He speed dialed Jimbo, but his cell was off, which infuriated Mat.

He called Jimbo's senior officer, Bobby, who was fast asleep in his quarters after a day of extreme tension, trauma, and fatigue. The weather was turning, too. Getting the ship back into port had been a tough ride. He was wiped out, exhausted.

Bobby scrambled for his cell phone, trying to focus after being jolted out of a deep sleep.

"Bobby?"

"Yes, sir."

"Where's Jimbo? Get him on."

"Sorry, sir, far as I know he's not on board," he said. Bobby sat up at the edge of the bed, knowing he wasn't going to have the luxury of falling back to sleep.

"Where the hell is he?"

Bobby looked at the time on his phone—11:45. He really didn't know where Jimbo would be at that hour. He'd been sleeping. He tried to be as evasive as possible. "He and Sam were heading out to the hospital last I heard, but I crashed early."

"Goddamn it, track him down."

"I'll check his quarters—do you want to hold?"

"Yeah, of course I'll hold. Find his ass."

Bobby slipped into his jeans and walked just a few steps down the hall, where Jimbo's cabin was. He knocked, but there was no answer, as he suspected. He returned to his cabin. "Sorry, sir, he's not there."

"Damn."

"Did you try calling him?"

"Of course I called him—he's got his freaking telephone turned off. I want you to find his ass."

"Sir? How am I going to do that without a phone?"

"That's not my problem, Bobby. He should have left instructions. Call the hospital—check the bars. Tell him to call me no matter what time of night it is."

"I'm on it."

"Report back to me when you've tracked him down."

"Yes, sir."

"And tell him to turn his freakin' phone on and leave it on."

By now, Bobby was wide awake. He knew better than to look for Jimbo at the hospital at that hour, and so he called the most likely place—the Crow's Nest. Jimbo was a regular there, and Bobby knew all the bartenders. Sure enough, the bartender confirmed that Jimbo was there, knocking back a few beers.

"Hold on, I'll get him for you," he said. "Jimmy, I got Bobby on the line here."

Jimbo leaped out of his seat and grabbed the phone. "Hey Bobby, what's up?"

"Just got a furious call from the boss. He told me to find you and have you call him back, pronto. And I quote: 'Tell him to turn on his freaking cell phone.'"

Jimbo was cagey. He didn't want Bobby to know any more than

he had to, to protect him, and he wasn't about to say too much on the phone. "What did you tell him?"

"I told him you were headed out to the hospital, but I fell asleep early, so I didn't know where you are—which is the truth. How's Jamie?"

"We couldn't see her. But they say she's stable—we'll know more tomorrow. Sam and I just came by for a few brews, chillin' out."

"Please call Mat right away and get him off my back."

"No sweat, I'll call now. What about the crew—where is everybody?"

"As far as I know, they're all nice and warm at home. Brady and I are out here, holding guard. There's a big storm comin' in."

Jimbo hesitated, thinking on his feet, making his game plan as he went along. "All right, here's what's doing. I want you to call them little darlins back to the ship, and keep that private. Repeat: private, between us. Got it?"

"You kiddin', Captain? They'll shoot me! What gives?"

"I don't have time to explain a whole lot. Just say we have an emergency—tell them the storm's coming in and I've called them back to duty."

"How about in the morning?"

"How about … like, yesterday? I need them on that ship, Bobby. And get that Lady ready to sail."

"You want to go back out, in storm conditions? Sorry, sir, forgive me, but how long have you guys been drinking over there?"

"I won't take offense to that, Bobbo. But yes, we may have to take her out. This is the real thing—just tell them we're still in emergency mode." He looked back at Sam. "Call Doc first."

"Got it."

"And if Mat calls again, you tell him you conveyed the message. I'm calling him now, as soon as we hang up."

"Okay, Captain."

Jimbo slipped a tip to the bartender, and then walked past Sam to the pay phone. Faking a drunk, he called Mat's number. "Hey boss! Word's out you're looking for me. What's up?"

Mat was dressed now, pacing the room. "What's up with me? How the hell could you leave me hanging, with everything that's happened? I thought you were on my team!"

"Whoa, what are you talking about? Did you get my message?"

"I got it. Too late."

"Too late for what?" Jimbo burped, theatrically, into the phone.

"Too late to know about it before my boss did. How did that make me look?"

"Hey, I've had a pretty full plate here, but hell—I sent that to you in real time, Mat. Anyway, it's all okay now. Everything's under control."

"Update me first on Jamie H."

"Fortunately, she's all right. Bad accident, man. She was just hanging off the side of the ship, with all those whales. It was one freak situation. We had about a hundred whales all around us at one point, closed in on the ship."

"Right, we can talk about that later. What about Jamie?"

"We got there too late—no visitors allowed. She's in the ICU. Strict rules and all that. Liz told Sam that Jamie had been sedated and to come back in the morning, after the doctor makes his rounds. Phew! What a scare. Blood all over the place."

"You should have reported back to me."

"I'm sorry, boss. I figured you'd read between the lines—I had a whole lot of stuff to deal with. You never called, either. And then well, hell, we're tired. It's been a damn rough time out there."

"You don't need to be drinking in the middle of all this, Jimmy."

"I beg to differ. I never needed a drink more in my life!"

"Stop drinking. That's an order."

"You got it, boss. I was just about to go grab a hotel room, get away from everything for the night, and jump into a nice hot shower. I'll check on Jamie in the morning." He looked out the window—rain was coming down in buckets. "Hoowee—it is pouring out here."

"Don't worry about Jamie—we're in direct contact with the hospital. You make sure the ship is safe."

So there it was. Mat was definitely in on 'the lie.' Whatever doubt Jimbo still clung to was ripped from the bitt. Then Mat said, "Where's Sam? I imagine his daddy is going to be asking for a status report once he hears about the storm brewing out there."

"He's out looking for Liz. She told him she was going to a hotel for the night, so he went in to town to look for her—in the middle of this crazy storm." Jimbo put his finger to his lips, signaling Sam not to make himself heard. "They seem to have a hot thing goin' on, those two—I know it's against company policy and all but, hell, you can't really blame the kid. I mean, they sure knew how to pick a pretty young thing out there in London, eh, man?"

Mat chuckled, relieved that he had nothing to worry about with Jimbo. "Listen, crazy man, lay off the sauce and get your ass back on board. I'll need you tomorrow morning."

"Yes, sir. Does that mean I can't get laid tonight?"

"Sorry, Jimbo, it'll have to wait. And turn that damned phone on!"

"Will do, once I find it . . ." He hung up with Mat, but not before grumbling, loud enough for Mat to hear, "Now where in the hell did I put that thing?"

Mat laughed, feeling the tension roll off him. He decided to go for a quick run and grab a bite to eat in preparation for a sleepless night.

Jimbo hung up the phone, stunned for a minute. The man he'd served for almost forty years, the man he trusted with his life, was working black ops for the Agency. Jamie was right. It had all been a lie; he was being used. He wondered how far back it went that

Mat signed up for the dark agenda. For how long had he been lying about the mission?

Jimbo walked past a couple of rough-looking, burly fishermen, whom he heard talking about the storm, worried. Jimbo had been so absorbed in thought, he had barely paid attention to the news. They looked up at the TV, over the bar. Breaking news flashed across the screen: CNN was reporting a huge earthquake, right off the coast of San Francisco—9.3 on the Richter scale!

Jimbo raced over to the table, where Sam was glued to the screen, which read *Tsunami warnings are in place for the entire West Coast of North America.* "We have got to get out of here," Jimbo said.

He downed his beer, then he and Sam bolted for the door. The rain was teeming down around them, like nothing either one of them had ever seen, and they were soaked through in a flash. They heard the crackling sound of lightning, but they couldn't see any—it sounded more like a hot, sizzling wire. Jimbo looked up to make sure there wasn't a high-tension wire dangling somewhere, but there was only rain—buckets and buckets of rain. And the sea was rough, and rising. "Holy shit, man," he said, shivering, "let's go back inside and call a cab."

No sooner had he said the words, than a cab pulled up and they jumped in. Jimbo gave the driver an address and he drove off, through a veritable flash flood, taking pains not to lose control of the car. He pulled up in front of an old apartment building, not that far from the pier. Jimbo handed the driver a twenty-dollar bill and told him to leave the meter running.

"Hey man, I'm going off duty. I can't drive on these streets—this is insane."

Jimbo pulled out another twenty for the driver. "Ten minutes—don't leave."

Jimbo and Sam got out of the car and ran up to the doorway, the rain coming down in sheets. The lights were out. Jimbo pounded on the door and his part-time girlfriend answered. She had a cigarette in one hand and a candle in the other. A heavyset, sexy-looking woman, she was just what Sam would have imagined would be Jimbo's type.

"Well, welcome home, stranger. Nice of you to pop in for a visit before I go floating away in the monsoon."

"Hey, baby. This here's Sam. Sam, Lorna." They stepped into the dry porch.

"You are soaking wet, boys! Hang your coats out here and we'll see what we can do to warm you up. I've got a fire burning, but the electricity's out."

They hung up their coats, but still were soaking wet, and cold.

"We've got about ten minutes—and we're out of here," Jimbo said, gruffly.

"Yeah, well, come on in and run right back out, why don't ya'?"

They walked up close to the fireplace.

"You heard about the earthquake?" Jimbo asked, rubbing his hands together before the fire.

"Earthquake? I didn't feel any earthquake, but I'm cut off here. The whole street is blacked out."

"Huge earthquake in San Francisco—tsunami warnings out for the whole coast."

"Good lord! That is not good news."

Jimbo walked into the next room, like he clearly knew the place. "I need some clean, dry clothes and then I have to go. You know the drill."

"I do indeed. Can I get you some hot coffee, Sam?" She had a kettle sitting next to the fire.

Jimbo poked his head out. "Make that for two, mama, and then get your boots on—you're going to have to move out."

Sam was shivering, sitting in his soaked clothes. The hot coffee felt good. Jimbo came out, bare-chested. "Here you go, man, these ought to fit you all right." He handed Sam a T-shirt, a heavy sweat suit, and a dry pair of socks.

"Where can I change?" Sam asked, awkwardly.

"Don't you worry about a thing, honey. You've got nothin' I haven't seen before." She poured a cup of coffee for Jimbo, and walked into the next room, leaving Sam the privacy to get undressed. When she came back in, she said, "What's happening this time? It's always something with that man, I swear to god."

Jimbo called out from the other room. "Did you not hear me, woman? There's a tsunami watch out. Now get your boots on, girl. You're movin' out."

"And just where am I supposed to go?" she shouted back at him.

"You're going to higher ground." He walked out dressed in slacks and a shirt and tie—not exactly storm gear. Both Lorna and Sam were surprised. He opened a closet in the living room and threw a full-length raincoat across the back of the couch. Then he fumbled around, reaching up to a shelf at the top of the closet, from where he pulled down a shoebox containing two guns and ammunition. He loaded them both and stuck one under his belt; the other he tossed to Sam, who looked horrified.

"I don't want to have anything to do with any gun," Sam said.

"Let's hope we don't need to use them."

"I don't know anything about firing any gun, Jimbo."

Lorna was alarmed. "Now wait one minute. What have you gone and gotten yourself into, James?"

"You know better than to ask questions you don't want to hear the answers to. Now get yourself dressed up warm and grab what you can, 'cuz you are leaving for higher ground—and we can't be sure the place will still be here when this is over."

Lorna became frazzled. This was no drill. "You can't just blow in here and blow out with those things, and not tell me what's happening. I can't take this shit, Jimmy."

He took the keys from the rack, signaling Sam to get up and get ready to go. "I need the car. Now I want you to listen good. There's a tsunami coming, it's more than likely. I've got a driver out there, waiting for you. Here's a hundred bucks," he said, pressing the bill into her hand. "Tell him to drive as far away from shore as possible, as high up as you can climb—into the mountains. You hear me? You need to move fast, girl. He is not gonna wait for you to think it over."

"Can't you take me with you?"

"It's too dangerous. You hear? I know what I'm talking about. Now get yourself together and get out. I have to go. We don't have time to talk it through." He touched her cheek, tenderness they rarely shared. Something about it scared her, a sense they were parting for the last time—a final goodbye.

He got into his trench coat. Sam took a dry parka from the coat rack, and off they went, leaving Lorna standing in the middle of the dark room, panicked. She thought about what she could take with her—what mattered most—then grabbed a few framed pictures off the wall and stuffed them into her purse. She poured the coffee on the fire, dowsing the flames, even though there was no way that apartment was going to burn. From the bedroom, she took a few dry clothes from the chest of drawers and stuffed them into a grocery bag, and then she scrambled for her rain boots and coat.

With no time to figure out what possibly was going to happen next, or where she was going to go when she got to the top of the hill, she ran out from her dark, empty apartment to the taxi, to escape to the mountains inland.

15

Rescue

Jimbo took the wheel. The tumultuous rain crashed down all around them so hard that keeping the car on the road was nearly impossible. He couldn't even see out the windshield much more than a few feet in front of him. "Why the hell does everything have to happen all at once?" he said, trying to wipe the humidity off the inside of the window. Sam switched on the heater, which, in Lorna's beat-up old car, was about as helpful as using an eyedropper's worth of hot water to defrost a freezer.

He stayed on the main roads, driving as fast as he could, but the floodwaters down by the waterfront were already as high as the car's fender. Finally, as they climbed out of the area and approached the Psychiatric Facility, the streets were easier to navigate, and he was able to push it. "Let's hope we're not too late," he said, as they drove up to the empty parking lot. He cut the lights as soon as they turned into the driveway, and crawled in, enveloped in the dark rain of the storm.

Jimbo turned to Sam. He could see the fear in his eyes, but he knew the kid would come through for him. "You're gonna follow me in, exactly three minutes after I enter that door. Have the gun ready and cover my back. That's all you have to do." He reached into the trench coat pocket and pulled out a knitted ski mask. "And wear this—we don't want your old man or anybody else to know you were anywhere near this thing."

Sam took the mask. "What about you?"

"Don't you worry about Jimbo—I'm not new to this cloak-and-dagger business." He pulled the handle of the door to get out. "Three minutes exactly, from the time I open the door. Gun out. Follow my lead."

He got out of the car and ran up the walkway to the facility. Sam slipped the mask on, counting down the seconds until he had to get to the door.

A night nurse and an orderly were watching the news of the earthquake on television. San Francisco was reportedly devastated; reports were just starting to come in from local news stations in the Bay Area. All the waterfront areas were leveled; the financial district and several high-rise buildings were literally wiped off the map. It appeared the anticipated "big one" had at last hit the city. They watched, consumed by the bad news, distracted.

Jimbo's entry into the lobby in the middle of the night, without any notice at all, startled them. "Evening, ma'am," he said, walking up to the counter. "We've got a pickup for a patient, Ms. Jamie Hastings." The water rolled off his coat, forming a puddle at his feet.

"A pickup at this hour—in this storm? This facility is closed for the night."

"Yeah, I hear that—it's some crazy weather out there—waves washin' over the piers down at the harbor . . . some streets flooding down there too."

The nurse looked at Jimbo suspiciously. "And you're out in this weather, trying to transfer a patient at midnight?"

"Yes ma'am. I don't ask questions, I just do my job. I have orders to transfer her to Vancouver ICU immediately—something about her test results."

"Yeah? You have an order in writing?"

The nurse picked up the phone. A wall of a man, the orderly stood up, menacingly. Jimbo had no choice but to pull the gun on them, making his moves and writing the script of Jamie's rescue as he walked through his own movie.

"That's not such a good idea. Hang up the phone, ma'am, and you sit right down, big man. No reason anybody has to get hurt here, but I do know how to use this, and I will if I have to... so please. Don't do anything I'm gonna have to feel bad about later."

Sam walked in on cue.

Without taking his eyes off the two of them, Jimbo instructed Sam to check the supply room off to the side of the office, and find something to tie them up with. Sam disappeared into the storage room and came out with two straitjackets, which he held up for approval. While Jimbo held the gun steady on them, Sam first tied up the orderly, then the nurse. With the gun pointed right at their heads, they knew better than to resist.

"I appreciate you being civilized about this all. No reason anybody has to get hurt here tonight. Where is she?"

"Down the hall, to the right, room 157."

"You have staff on duty?"

"We're the only ones left for tonight," the nurse said.

"Okay, good. We're going to lock you up in this room in here—you can see how it feels to be in a cage, like these poor people are, for a little while. You make any noise, I will kill you. Push any buttons, do anything to get in my way, and I will kill you. All I want is the woman, so if you have any brains at all, you'll just sit quiet and let me take care of my business. You got it?"

They both nodded.

"You don't want to be dead for something as simple as that, I'm pretty sure."

Sam pushed them into the storage room and locked them in. The surveillance camera system monitors were behind the desk. Jimbo disconnected the system, hoping the nurse had been telling the truth, otherwise they were going to have company. He flipped through the medical charts until he found Jamie's—that was going to be a big help to Doc. He handed it to Sam. "I'll be carrying Jamie out. You keep this."

They stood back, waiting to see if anyone responded to the system being down, but no one came. Jimbo figured in a storm like the one they were in, nobody would have even questioned it. And then, it was late in the night and the place was empty. They moved stealthily through the main hall, making their way to Jamie's room as fast as they could.

There was Jamie, white as a corpse, out cold on the bed. Jimbo almost gasped at the sight of her—he thought she was surely dead by the looks of her, but when he put his fingers to her throat, he got a pulse. It was weak, but she was alive. He detached the saline drip, bundled her up as best he could in the blankets, and swept Jamie's limp body into his arms and then over his shoulder. Sam ripped the shower curtain off the hooks to help protect her from getting drenched, and then, just as quickly as they had found their way down the dark corridors, they made their way to the exit, with Jamie in tow.

Everything went without a hitch: nobody dead, nobody hurt, and Jamie was alive.

"You know the way back to the ship from here?" he asked Sam as they ran through the storm to the car.

Sam nodded and got right into the driver's seat. Jimbo laid Jamie in the back, and then got in the backseat with her, holding her in his arms to keep her warm. Sam pulled off the mask and then crawled out the driveway, slowly at first and then, once he hit the main road, he pushed the car as fast as he could risk driving through the flooded streets. The waterfront was taking the worst pounding, and the flooding got worse as they got closer to the port.

"What happens when we get to the ship? Do you have any idea what comes next?" Sam said, watching the road while he talked to Jimbo in the back.

"I'm making this up as I go along, boy, but I know how it plays out for you. You drop us off at the ship, and then you take the car and drive into town. Stay out of the West End—it's going to get the full brunt of the tsunami, if it hits. Get into a place inland and check into the top floor. You got money?"

"I've got a few bucks and plenty of plastic."

"All the better. You need to create a trail for yourself: your cover. Don't park in the hotel garage—leave the car on the street somewhere. All the better if they tow it, so don't worry about that. You go in, looking a little drunk, and make a scene at check-in. You'll be creating a story line, so you want people to remember you coming in. You tell them you're with USOIL and you're looking for another employee—Liz Bartholomew. Ask if she's checked in yet." Jimbo leaned over the seat. "You go into the lobby bar and get a drink—hang out, look drunk, be public about it. Sit at the bar . . . play the bartender, you know what I mean? Talk bullshit—he could be questioned down the road, if it gets to that. Just repeat the story—bad storm, lost your phone, your girl . . . and you tied one on. You think you can pull that off?"

"No sweat, Jimbo. I can do obnoxious real well."

"That's true, Sammy boy. You can."

They managed a laugh in the middle of chaos unfolding.

"No matter who you talk to—and I'm telling you loud and clear—trust no one—you have one story. You left me at the Crow's Nest sometime in the night, you can't remember . . . we drank a lot. Rain was pouring down hard, you wanted to find your girlfriend. You understand?"

"Yeah, I got it."

"One of the guys in the bar was going into town—you got a lift in, because there were no taxis, and you figured it was safest to stay in town, a ways from the harbor—so that's why you went there."

"But the bartender saw us leave together."

"Don't you worry about that—these are my people. They know how to do discreet."

Sam took a right onto a street that was flooded out a few feet ahead of them. In the darkness of that night, they barely caught it in time to avoid plunging the car into the river that was forming.

"Damn! Back this sucker up!" Jimbo cried.

Sam threw the car into reverse and pulled them out, just in time. Close call. "Now what? I don't know any other way to get down to the port."

"Move over—I know these streets," Jimbo said. He got out of the back, resting Jamie's head where he'd been sitting, and got behind the wheel. As Mat had told Jamie, Jimbo could navigate his way around water, all right. Even in a car. He headed back up the road, took a side street, and came back down another way, cutting through town, driving down a one-way street. Nobody was out driving. It was a risk he had to take, and it paid off. It brought them to Harbor Drive, two minutes from where the ship was berthed. The streets were flooded, but the worst was about to happen. The ocean water was almost as high as the pier itself—before long, the streets would be gone.

Jimbo guided the car into the driveway, past the desolate guard station, where, fortunately, no one was to be found.

"What's going to happen to you and Jamie?"

"Huh, that's a question I cannot even think about—don't know how this is gonna go. You just do what I say, boy—and don't look back. Make sure you've got your cover clear in your mind. You lost your phone in the storm, your clothes are on the ship, you tied one on big when you couldn't find your babe last night."

Sam nodded.

"Wait for the latest CNN report in the morning, and then call your old man and tell him *The Deepwater* sailed, to get out far from the coast, in case a tsunami made it in, and you missed it. Let him get you home, safe, and you stay with your daddy for a while. That's where you need to weather this storm. Okay? We're out of time—you go now."

Sam handed Jimbo the medical chart.

"On your way to the hotel, when you've cleared the flooded streets down here, find a pay phone somewhere and call 911. Tell them there's a couple of staff locked up in the admitting office over at the Psychiatric Facility. We can't leave these people locked up with a tsunami coming in."

"I will."

"Make sure it's a pay phone—make the call fast. No more than five seconds tops, and walk right away." Jimbo opened the door and stepped into water up to his calves. Sam started to get out too, but Jimbo stopped him. "You gotta get this car out of here, while you still can."

"Let me at least help you carry her aboard."

"No. I got it. It's safer if nobody sees you. Don't look back—just follow the story and you'll be safe, you understand? You can walk away from this, Sam. You get near that ship, your cover is gone—any one of them could be a witness. I don't know who's who anymore." He opened the back door and as gently as he could, and without saying another word, he lifted Jamie's fragile body out of the car, having first stashed the records under the blankets that enveloped her, and then he carried her, draped in his arms, through the water, up the ramp to *The Deepwater.*

"I'll catch up with you somewhere down the road," Sam called out after him, knowing that, most likely, it would never happen. He watched Jimbo, his hero, walk away, with Jamie in his strong arms, to whatever safety they could find there. He waited until they disappeared from his line of vision: this bigger-than-life man, his hero, and the enigmatic messenger, intertwined in the strangest of destinies ... one that began, and was most likely to end, in the deep.

16

Deliverance

It took all the strength Jimbo possessed to pull the door to the ship's lounge open. The crew was there, confused and annoyed, waiting for an explanation as to why they were being called back to duty. In conditions where no ships could sail, with a tsunami warning out, they needed to be home with their families, not rolling around on the rough water, waiting for Jimbo. He walked in, drenched through, and laid Jamie down on the couch just as he felt she was about to slip out from his arms.

"Good god!" Doc cried. He knew there had to be big trouble coming down, but never could he have imagined anything like this. At the sight of an exhausted Jimbo carrying Jamie's inert body, the crew's attitude shifted immediately.

The captain removed his dripping trench coat and handed it to Alberto. "We need so much help right now, I'm not sure where to start." There was a lake around them from the water he'd carried in. Doc removed the water-soaked blankets and the plastic shower curtain from Jamie. Bobby grabbed some wool scarves and a couple of jackets from the rack and they covered her, as best they could.

Doc started giving orders: "Start by changing out of those clothes, Jim. You're drenched through to the bone. Dom, get me towels and blankets—throw them in the microwave, then bring them to sickbay."

Jimbo was cold and exhausted. For the first time in his life, he felt old—like he was over, somehow—finished. "Take charge for me, Doc. You see her chart's there. I need a hot shower." He headed for his quarters. "Where's Fin?"

"We've got him locked up in the bridge. He tried to run after you—we couldn't manage him."

"Poor boy—you know he hates the rain and he's up there—all alone? Ten minutes . . . work your miracles, Doc."

"Alberto, get me a whole pot of tea for Jamie and make sure there's plenty of coffee. Keep it coming. See what you can do about feeding Jimbo. Phil, Brady . . . let's get her on the examining table," Doc commanded. They carried her to sickbay, still in her wet hospital gown, and laid her down on the table. Doc didn't have time to question why Jimbo had brought her back, but he knew it had to be a life-and-death situation.

He couldn't believe Jimbo had had the foresight to bring her medical records. "Way to go, Jimmy," he said, under his breath. Hopefully he would have enough to go on from the chart to know what medications were racing through her bloodstream, and what would be the best way to treat her.

Dom came with the towels and blankets. Doc dried her, put a clean gown on, and wrapped her in blankets from head to toe. He opened the metal folder of the chart, fearful of what he would find. First question: How did she end up in the Psychiatric Facility? He couldn't believe what he was seeing: the woman was laid out on heavy sedatives. What in the hell? He felt for a pulse. She was there, but so weak. He took a bottle of saline solution from the cabinet and hooked her back up to a drip. "Come on, Jamie. Come out of it."

He turned the thermostat up to ninety degrees, and then sat down next to her, reading her chart—astounded at what it contained. From the admitting report in ER, where she was reported unconscious, to cardiac arrest: three minutes of death before they brought her back. Jamie had been a Code Red hospital emergency. Reading, skimming over the medical reports: "delirium, hallucination," and then his worst fear: "possible hemorrhage, aneurism." He flipped forward hurriedly, bewildered. Why would a patient coming out of coma be immediately sedated? That was completely counterproductive. He kept one eye always on her, waiting for her to wake up, but doing his best to stabilize her and raise her body temperature. He could see eye reflex beneath her lids—a sign she might be coming out of the sedation. As he watched her, he read on. There was a total breakdown in procedure, an unprecedented violation of protocol. From the time she was transferred to intensive care, to being signed into the care of one Dr. Emery Wells, at the separate Psychiatric Facility, a satellite of the hospital—nothing made sense.

He read Dr. Varja's report—carefully chosen words—recommending she not be moved:

"As to the patient's 'psychotic' episodes, the observations posed by Dr. Wells are not consonant; she exhibits severe anxiety, disorientation, and neurological dissonance which, considering the circumstances of her trauma, are not beyond the average range of neurological and emotional response."

What could have happened to cause this intervention? Doc was completely mystified, but it was clear that he wasn't the only one asking the question. Why was Jamie Hastings, a critical patient with possible brain damage, yanked out of the hospital and thrown into a psychiatric facility?

Jimbo came in, looking human again. "What's the verdict, Doc?" he asked, fearful of the reply.

"I can't even begin to guess what this poor girl has been through. She's been injected with heavy sedatives—that's crazy considering her head injury."

"Can you give her something to bring her out of it?"

"I do have the antidote here—flumazenil—it's used to bring people out of anesthesia, and it's indicated for what they've given her in the hospital, but I'm not sure what they gave her in the facility. The chart just says 'sedation.' That's strange," Doc said, scratching his head. "For her to be out like this, they must have given her something powerful. With a head injury, if there's intracranial pressure—flumazenil could cause convulsions. We can't take that risk."

"You have an idea how long it will take her to come out from under the meds naturally?"

"I'm reading she just had a last dose administered a few hours ago. She's showing signs of activity. She sure doesn't need to be on this ship right now—I can tell you that for certain."

Jimbo sighed. "You're wrong, old friend. This is exactly where Jamie needs to be."

"You call it, Jimbo."

"You've trusted me until now, haven't you, Doc?" Jimbo replied.

"I trust you with my life, Jimbo, you know all about that."

"I'm gonna take her back out. You ready to do that?"

Doc glanced over at Jamie, and then back at Jimbo. "If I'm going to die, I'd at least like to know why."

"We're going to outrun death, my friend. Tsunami's coming."

"I've got nobody waiting for me either way, Jimbo."

Jimbo put his hand on the shoulder of the man who had been his friend for so long. They'd been through everything together—Doc was the closest thing to a brother Jimbo had ever known. "I'll gather the crew, and see who's willing."

Doc nodded, and went back to his patient, still waiting for a story that had to be told, knowing Jimbo had the pieces put together. That was all he needed to know, at least for the time being.

Jimbo called everybody back to the lounge. Gone was the laid-back Captain Jimbo, the guy with a story and a beer. Here stood a man who surely knew he was making choices that would put them

236

all in harm's way—life-threatening choices. He was solemn. There would be no humor this night: no storytelling, no running away to the captain's stash.

Everyone gathered around the dining room table.

"Boys, you have surely heard about the quake in San Francisco: 9.3 on the Richter. I am heartbroken to report most of the city is leveled. I haven't had time to hear how far the damage extends up and down the coast. They're telling us the epicenter was five miles out in the ocean, and a tsunami is due to hit the entire West Coast—all the way up as far as Alaska. And as if that isn't bad enough, we're a sitting duck in this killer storm here, the worst I've ever seen in my years out on the Pacific Coast."

Mike, the chief engineer, burst in from the mess hall, apologizing for being late. His hair was glued to his head from the sweat, and his cheeks were crimson red. He looked harrowed and exhausted, and none of his men had come back on board.

"I'm sorry, Captain, I'm afraid it's going to be just me down there."

Jimbo nodded. "You see what's happening out there on the roads—the city is flooding fast. But if a tsunami hits, man, we're talking catastrophe like you never even imagined. I have made my decision to get this ship out as far as we can move her, before this thing comes in. It's going to be a rough ride out, but it's the best bet for saving the ship. It won't be smooth sailing, you know that—it's sure to be rough for a while. But one thing I know how to do is navigate a ship—that's what I grew up doing, and that's what I do best. We'll be without satellite tracking, no radar, no nothing—just Jimbo at the wheel."

The men looked at each other, nothing less than astounded.

"I've got about five minutes to hear your decisions—you're either staying back or sailing out. I can't obligate you, and I wouldn't try—I know the dangers involved. And this isn't the Army. If you decide to stay, take your wives and your kids and get as far away from the shore as you possibly can. If you decide to come with me, I can't guarantee you'll be back. It's a coin toss, either way."

"Captain, it's a killer storm. What makes you think we can even make it out?" asked Bobby.

"I can get her out of port. I know this Lady."

"What about Sam and Liz?" Bobby asked.

Jimbo simply said, "Looks like they're not gonna make it."

Mike was the first to say yes. "Count on me, Captain."

Bobby was next. "In."

"Alberto, Dom, I don't need you—you're welcome to go home," Jimbo said.

Domenico looked around at everyone, feeling ashamed to be the first to bail out—but he had his priorities. "I'm sorry, Captain. My wife ... any day now."

Jimbo put his arm around him and patted him on the back. "You go, son. Get home to your wife—I would do the same. Go into the mountains up high. You hurry now," he said, filled with compassion.

Domenico went out the crew exit, to gather his few things from his quarters and then leave the ship. With no buses running, and no cars on the roads, he didn't know how he was going to get there, but he would get there ... even if he had to wade through the flooded streets all the way home.

Alberto was committed to staying. "You are going to need me, Jim, you are wrong. I will stay." He attempted lightheartedness. "I can't even imagine any of you trying to cook in my galley!"

Brady, on the other hand, was diffident and averse to the whole idea. "I'm sorry—it's crazy to even consider going back out there. You'll run into trouble, and who will answer an SOS? Not even the Coast Guard would be crazy enough to go out in this. I'm sorry— I'm out of here, Captain. Godspeed." He walked out of the room without saying goodbye, too afraid to give power to the words, covering a sense of his own cowardliness with indignation.

Jimbo watched him go. "Godspeed to you, too, boy."

Philippe was the last to come forward. While the others were announcing their decisions, he had studied Jimbo, knowing there was more to his decision to take *The Deepwater* back out. It was as if the whole day had been some other sort of reality, where nothing was what it seemed, and this moment was no different. Jimbo had a strange look in his eyes, as if he saw something the others had missed—as if he could read more of the story. Nobody had mentioned the whales in all this—it was almost as if it had never happened, and yet it wasn't that many hours earlier that they had gone through that utterly bizarre experience: the whales, the accident, Jamie. Philippe knew, instinctively, that Jamie was fighting for her life in there, on the ship—rather than in the hospital, where she needed to be—because of the whales.

As a man, he knew he was needed. And as a marine biologist, he was certain that the most profound experience of his life might very well be waiting out there, back at the Orca sanctuary, where he just knew—in his gut—that Jimbo was heading. "I wouldn't miss this for the world," he said.

Jimbo, a man who always had a story, or a joke, or some words of wisdom to share, found himself struggling to find the words. He was deeply moved, knowing what they might be facing ahead. He took time, reflecting, before he spoke. "I have had cause to question people in my life," he said. "People have come and gone—good people, bad people. People have pulled the wool over on me. People have let me down. Just like everybody else. I don't hold nothin' against nobody—people do what they gotta do. But you're here. I don't know quite what to say. In the old days, they called this kind of dedication 'valor.' I'm grateful to you. And I know you trust me. You have my word: I won't let anything happen to you. I won't let you down." He started to get choked up. As exhausted as he was, he felt like he could break down and cry, but that was not going to happen, especially not in that moment. "Now let's get this Lady out of this raging sea, and take her to the dawn."

They thought he was talking about the ship herself, but it was Jamie he was delivering to the light.

17

Tsunami!

The unmistakable sound of his master's footsteps coming down the hall sent Fin into ecstasy. He thought he'd lost both of them: first Jamie disappeared, without goodbyes, and then Jimbo abandoned him. That is all he could understand. Alberto shut him out in the mess hall when Jamie lay waiting to be taken away, and then Bobby locked him up on the bridge when Jimbo left the ship without him. Since the time he was a pup and wandered aboard, that had never happened. Where Jimbo went, he went. Usually that was only as far as the Crow's Nest, where he would wait, outside the bar, until Jimbo was ready to come home—back to the ship, or over to Lorna's place, where he sometimes spent the night.

"Hey, boy, they locked you up all alone up here?" Jimbo roughed him up a bit, playfully, and they celebrated the bond between them, each in his own way, reconnecting. Fin wanted to climb all over him, he kept jumping up and licking Jimbo's face, but the captain had a ship to sail, and the urgency to get out of harm's way as fast as he could take her out. He got out of his chair and walked with Fin to his bed, where Jimbo stood over him, commanding him to lie down and be still. He knew when Jimbo meant "stay!" and he curled up, knowing this was one of those times, and stayed still—never taking his eyes off his master.

Jimbo went back to his chair, making preparations to start up the engines, running cross-checks with Bobby and with Mike, down in the engine room. "This is the last time we'll be listening to the news, for a while, Bobby—let's see what we can find out."

Bobby tuned in the radio. By now, every station was talking about the weather and the great California quake: the long-dreaded "big one" that had finally toppled San Francisco. They got the local weather-channel report just as it was providing an up-to-the-minute situation report.

The announcer's voice was grave, as he read the staggering news.

A tsunami warning is in effect for the next two hours for the entire West Coast of North America, including the coastal areas of British Columbia and Alaska, from Vancouver Island to Cape Decision, Alaska, due to a severe underwater quake five miles out of San Francisco. Preliminary readings indicate this has been a magnitude 9.3 on the Richter scale, hitting just west of San Francisco Bay. Tsunami with significant widespread flooding is expected. Warnings are particularly alarming due to co-existing storm conditions in British Columbia, with flooding in coastal areas. Exceptionally hard-hit: Vancouver Island. Major cities and populated areas along the California coast have already been inundated, warnings for the entire Northwest Coast now in full alarm. Widespread, dangerous coastal flooding, accompanied by powerful currents, is anticipated and may continue for several hours after the initial wave hits. Residents are warned to evacuate the coastal areas and move to higher ground. This is a public emergency broadcast.

Jimbo told Bobby to turn off the radio. "We're moving out."

In sickbay, Doc prepared for a rough ride out of harbor, locking down everything breakable. He strapped Jamie to the bed—all she needed now was a bad fall to finish her off—and he removed the drip, which he knew would only end up crashing to the floor.

Everyone took the necessary precautions at their own stations. *The Deepwater*'s engines began to rumble as the captain backed out of her berth in the harbor, with nothing to guide him out—no radar, no tracking devices, no radio.

He was defying so many rules and regulations that any number of authorities would easily have had cause to arrest him, but no one was anywhere around to watch him sneak out of harbor. He was well aware of what could happen in the morning, once they discovered that Jamie had been busted out of the facility, but for now no one, not even Mat, could possibly have imagined that Jimbo was crazy enough to take the ship out in such a dramatic storm.

Deftly, Jimbo navigated out of the harbor, squeezing the ship out, past the pier, where smaller boats in the harbor rocked furiously in their moorings, crashing into each other and smashing up against the dock. He knew they wouldn't survive the storm, and he could already imagine what the devastation would look like out there, the day after.

What little information Bobby had managed to get out of the mariners' meteorological service indicated that the wind was not that violent, and that wave swells were high, but still manageable for a ship the size of *The Deepwater*. The storm hugged the coastline, and Jimbo was right—it wasn't as bad farther out. If they could just get through the tide rip, and the current, and move out quickly, they'd be far safer than all the ships in port. If a tsunami were going to hit the coast, the yachts and fishing boats in Vancouver harbor would be torn apart and strewn about the city before the wave was done with them. The best chance for *The Deepwater* was, indeed, to outrun it.

With nothing but his wits and the experience of a lifetime on the sea to guide him, Jimbo drove the ship out of harbor, feeling the full breadth of the tides and currents as *The Deepwater* pushed through the tide rip, rushing through the channel. He steered boldly into the open waters of the mighty Pacific, facing the waves head-on, always holding the bow perpendicular to the waves. The biggest threat to the ship was getting caught broadside—every captain's nightmare. As long as he could hold that forward momentum, and not get caught broadside to a big wave, he was sure he could make it out without incident.

Of concern was the North Pacific Current, which runs into Vancouver Island as it hits up against the continent. It is considered a "transition zone" for ocean currents, and that is no fun for sailors, who have to contend with its unpredictability—and the sheer moods of the Pacific Ocean, which are anything but "pacific" in that part of the world. Without all his navigational equipment to rely on, all Jimbo knew for sure was what he had to go on when they had sailed back in, earlier that evening. Not that it mattered much now. The ocean was alive, constantly changing—always throwing new challenges at those who dared to challenge her. She could lull you to sleep in her gentle waves, or thrust you into your worst nightmare, in an instant.

Jimbo was running on pure instinct and adrenaline. He was well aware that, in the end, no matter how fine a ship you're sailing—no matter how sleek . . . how powerful . . . how sophisticated—it all comes down to that one split-second moment, when your life is in the balance, and how you react behind the wheel. When the sea is ready to spit you up and turn you upside down, bashing you up in her high swells and drowning you in those deep troughs, what matters most is how well a captain commands his vessel, yes, but most of all, how he respects the sea.

And he did. Heart and soul.

In the pitch-blackness of that starless night, with only printed navigational charts to guide him, Jimbo pushed the ship, expertly, through the stormy waters, taking the great waves straight on— never losing direction, never really risking rolling the ship over.

Within an hour of their escape from the harbor, the skies began to clear and the rain stopped. Jimbo's gamble had paid off—they were moving away from the storm and would soon be out of the high-risk zone of the impending tsunami. The farther they headed away from the land, the easier the ocean rode.

Fortunately for Jamie, she was still out cold from the medication, so she managed to miss the very worst of it. No saltines and beer would have put her back together after a ride like they'd just been through, and they were still far from the calm. Some color had returned to her cheeks, thanks to the heat in the room, and Doc was just holding his breath that she would wait to return to full consciousness until they were out of the tempest. With what Jamie had been through, he couldn't see how she could survive being thrown around on a raging ship, laced out on so many medications—and god knows what danger still lurked inside the soft folds of her brain.

Back on land, torrential rains flooded the streets around ports and the harbor with more than a foot of dirty water, filled with garbage and debris, and the sewers were backing up, flooded out below. Parked cars started to slide out freely into the rivers of water washing through the streets, unable to hold ground. Ground-floor shops and offices were inundated, and the electricity was out in several districts of the city. And foolish or simply distracted people, who had neither heeded the warnings nor paid attention to what was happening around them, were trapped in their houses, sitting ducks for the imminent catastrophe that was about to slam into their imperiled lives.

Thanks to her lover, Lorna made it to safety just in time. The taxi drove her to a decent motel up in the mountains, a place to wait out the storm for a few days. When she went to pay the driver, she found a thousand dollars in one-hundred-dollar bills stashed in her wallet.

Jimbo. He never let her down. With nothing but a grocery bag of clean clothes and a few framed memories, she checked in and got a room with a view over the ocean—but all she could see was darkness.

She hung her clothes over the dinette chairs, pushing them up close to the heater to dry, and then jumped into a boiling hot shower. Tired and lonely, afraid of what would come, she slipped into bed and turned on the TV, but the satellite connection was out. She looked for something to read: all she could find in the room was a tourist magazine: *What's On in Vancouver.* With nothing to read and no television to distract her, she turned off the lights and waited for sleep to come, knowing it was anyone's guess what she'd be looking down upon when morning came.

All at once, the sea level at the piers and harbor fronts dropped more than three feet, the tide retreating out, far into the ocean. Within seconds, the sea level dropped again, bringing the boats and ships anchored out in the harbor crashing up against each other, bashing up violently against the pier. Some broke their moorings and went spinning out in the tide, flung out into the ocean like buoys, but with no rope to tether them home.

As the tide receded out into the deep, stretches of the seafloor around the island's beaches revealed old tires, kitchen sinks, and all manner of human debris... everywhere. A great booming sound rumbled, dark and menacing, from the sea, while thunderous explosions from the raging storm echoed nature's fury as they swept over the land.

And then it came.

Rising monstrous from the ocean, a gigantic wall of water slammed unmercifully into Vancouver Island. Almost two thousand feet high, it devoured the waterfront, crushing the harbor in an instant, carrying away everything man had dared place at the very gates of nature's force with so little regard for the unpredictability of the ocean. The pier that Jimbo had escaped was now nothing but a river of sticks; nothing of the structure remained. The Crow's Nest exploded from the force of the wave—gone in an instant. The entire waterfront and the earth beneath it crumbled and broke apart in seconds, leaving nothing behind.

The Psychiatric Facility was completely gone.

The immense mountain of water washed over the entire city, sparing nothing in its path, and then it moved farther inland, topping the trees at higher ground. Had Lorna not left when she had, she would never have lived through it, but from her room at the Blue River Inn, she heard the booming sound of the tsunami before it came in, and realized that the world she knew had disappeared forever into the darkness of the deep. She prayed to god that Jimbo was on the ship, way out far enough from the coast to have escaped the tsunami—and that he would make it back to help her pick up the pieces, and to love her again.

Down at the main harbor, whatever remained of Vancouver's chic tourist district was completely submerged, including the world-famous aquarium, which housed countless sea creatures. Several Orcas, beluga whales, and dolphins had been kidnapped from those very waters, stolen from their pods, and held imprisoned in those cold cement tanks for so long they had all but forgotten the call of the wild.

How remarkable it must have been for them to find themselves instantly submerged in open-ocean water, the walls of their holding tanks buried beneath the waves—free to simply swim over them and back out to sea. It was the world they never hoped or dreamed to see again. Rising with the force of the wave, they rode it back out, letting themselves be carried along with countless other sea creatures, all of them freed by the great mother, Earth, the miracle that had come to return them to the open ocean.

Swept up in the fierce power of the wave, after having been held for so long in containment, they were at first disoriented and terrified, but then they heard the calls. They remembered their own music, songs that had gone forgotten long ago. Guided in streams of ancestral song, the Orcas and dolphins swam away from their human captors, through the turbid waters, and back to join their families, singing once again.

They could hear the cries, the call to action. And through the music, they remembered what they had come to Earth to do.

They headed straight in the direction of the sanctuary.

This same scene had happened at different locations earlier—up and down the coast, where great urban areas had been submerged in the initial wave, and other waves that were still washing their way inland. Wave after wave, the shores were inundated, from San Francisco all the way up the West Coast. All the marine-mammal holding tanks and aquariums along the California coast, Washington, and Oregon were submerged, and the whales and dolphins, and countless other creatures of the sea, were free to go.

They could hear again. They were free. And they were headed home.

18

The Triple Cross

Jamie's mother appeared at the head of the bed, hovering there, like an angel. She was so much younger than Jamie remembered, and never more beautiful. She was showing Jamie a place: was it a palace? A temple? She couldn't tell, so bright was the light that shone around it. She held her mother's hand for the longest time, but she knew the time had come to let go.

"Don't be afraid, Buddha baby. I'll always be here for you, whenever you call. You know where to find me. Wake up, precious, you have work to do."

While Doc had his back to her, checking for damage in the supply cabinet, Jamie's eyes opened at last. "Mama?"

He turned to her, startled to hear her voice.

"My mom's dead," she said, blankly, looking up at the ceiling.

"Take it easy, Jamie. You're coming out of sedation, that's all."

"She's passed over."

Doc held her hand. "Easy does it, Jamie."

"How did I get back here?"

"Jimbo brought you back. We haven't had the possibility to talk yet. We've just been in a race to get out of the harbor."

"It's sweltering in here!" Jamie's mind was overloaded, jumping from one realm to another, wading through the brain fog from more medication than she'd taken in her entire lifetime. She was trying to take everything in, piece by piece, struggling to remember what happened after the accident. She had only a vague recollection of being in the hospital . . . she remembered Liz was with her. Other than that, she had no memory of it, from the time she cracked her head until now. All she knew was that darkness had enveloped her there, and now she was free of it, back in the light. She looked around, feasting on the familiar sight of the ship, aware enough to know that, somehow, she'd been rescued. The shadows had lifted.

"Why have you got me tied down?" she asked.

"I had to keep you from falling. We've been rocking and rolling out here. Let me free up your arms." He lowered the blankets and then removed the protective band from around Jamie's chest, but kept the one that crossed over her lower body still bound. She had to come out slowly—and safely.

She tried to sit up, but could not. "I'm so glad to see you, Doc. Surprised, but glad."

He patted her on the back of the hand. "I wish it was in a little better circumstances, but thank god you made it back, milady."

"What's happened?"

"What hasn't happened?" The ship rocked so hard Doc was having a hard time holding his footing. "I'm missing a lot of pieces, just like you. We wait for Jimbo—he'll be able to tell us that whole story once he's gotten us out of trouble out here."

"What trouble?"

"The 'big one' finally hit San Francisco—in the ocean, off the bay. Last I heard it was a 9.3-magnitude earthquake."

Jamie was incredulous. "My mother lives in the Marina."

Doc looked grave. "We don't have any radio for the time being, but there was a tsunami warning all the way up to Alaska. Jimbo got you and brought you back here. He's running the ship out far enough to outrun a tsunami, if it hits, like they think it's going to."

Jamie thought about how fate had plucked her out of San Francisco in time, but she knew it had not spared her mother. She was
sure of it. It had thrown her together with Jimbo ... and now here
she was again, back in the deep, as if the ocean simply refused to
release her until her work was done.

"You're lucky you missed the last few hours. The flooding on
the waterfront was a foot deep. Jimbo brought you in, soaked
through—the both of you were drenched. It's been rough-going out
here, and we're not really out of danger yet." The ship slipped back
and forth like a skateboard, rolling with the waves, up and down.

"I need to go back to the whales ... back to the sanctuary."

"Whoa, now. We've had enough adventure for the time being.
Right now, we're headed for calmer waters."

"You don't understand."

"Look, Jamie, you need to take it real easy now. Let's concentrate
on getting you to sit up, before you run the marathon, shall we?"
Doc moved the back of the bed up. "How does that feel?"

"I feel dizzy."

He took her blood pressure. 85 over 60. Dangerously low.

She asked him to remove the band that had her bound to the
bed. "I need to talk to Jimbo."

"You try to move, you're going to pass out—if the ship herself
doesn't knock you off your feet first. Don't resist—I'm trying to
help you. You've already got one serious head wound. Don't make
things any worse."

"Can you get him to come here?"

"He's got his hands full at the moment, but he'll sure be glad to
hear you're awake."

"I need to tell him to head back there," Jamie said, insisting.

"Honey, right now we're just working on staying alive—it has
priority."

"Jimbo knows. He knows! I need to talk to him."

After everything that had happened in the last twenty-four hours, Doc was at the end of his tether. Jamie's insistence was exasperating. "Dammit, Jamie! Don't you get it? We're almost out of danger here. You're just going to have to cool your jets."

"There's no time to wait, Doc . . . it's one minute to midnight."

Philippe appeared outside the door unexpectedly. He was breathless. "We've got an injury in the engine room. It's Mike. He was thrown up against a main."

"Is he out?"

"No, but he's hurt."

Doc grabbed his medical bag. "You stay here," he said. "And Phil . . . don't let her move. Her blood pressure's way low. She could pass out before her feet even touch the floor." He rushed past Philippe to tend to Mike.

Jamie, implacable now, seized the opportunity. "I need to go to Jimbo. Can you undo these bands and help me?"

"You heard the Doc. We're still in pretty rough water. Best to stay lying down."

"I'm strong enough. Please take me to Jim." All Jamie was wearing was a flimsy hospital gown, made of lightweight cotton. Outside the stifling sickbay, it was thirty degrees colder.

"Let's wait for Doc. When he gets back, I'll go to your stateroom and get you something to wear, and then we'll go upstairs."

"No time—give me your jacket?"

Against his better judgment, Philippe acquiesced to Jamie's overpowering will. He undid the band holding her, and helped her into his jacket. "It will take two minutes for me to run to your cabin and get some warm clothes for you."

"Later. Help me up to the bridge."

He wrapped her in the blanket and held her up, steadying her, as they headed towards the lounge, to the stairs. Fortunately, at that very moment, Jimbo had just come down to check on her. *The*

Deepwater was almost out of the worst turbulence, calmer waters just ahead, and Bobby was at the helm.

"I don't believe my eyes. Jamie! You're walking. Thank you, god." He hugged her, without reservation. Her body was so fragile, he couldn't feel her energy at all. It was as if she were slowly disappearing. "I'm guessing Doc didn't give you permission to get up, right?" He looked at Philippe sternly.

"Don't look at Philippe. He had no choice—I was coming up to you with or without his help."

Jimbo sent Philippe up to the bridge. "Tell Bobby I'll be a few minutes longer, and then find Alberto for me. We need plenty of coffee up there."

Philippe let go of one arm, and Jimbo grabbed the other. "Damn, Jamie, you are the most stubborn woman I ever did see. Come on, we'll go to your suite and get some clothes on you. I get cold just looking at you."

"There's so much I have to tell you."

"The only way I'm listening to you is if you're lying down, with some warm clothes on your little ice-blue body here. Let's see if you're strong enough to make it down the hall."

With Jimbo holding her up, Jamie made her way to the cabin, but she was far too weak to dress herself. Jimbo sat her down on the bed, propping her up against the pillows, and then he ruffled through the dresser, looking for something warm for her to slip into. He found a fleece jogging suit, and plenty of wool sweaters. As if he were dressing a child, Jimbo got her out of Philippe's jacket and slipped the sweatshirt over her head, feeling how she trembled in his arms. He helped her into the pants, and then sat her up, untied the gown's knot, and pulled it out from under the sweatshirt, taking care to protect the intimacy of her body: showing respect. He rifled around in the dresser again, and found woolen socks, which he slipped over her cold, bare feet.

Jamie lay still, letting him care for her.

Once she was dressed and under the blanket, he pulled up an armchair and said, "I'm all yours." He noticed the crystal skull on the night table. It fascinated him—he had this sense of it prompting something within him, and he found it difficult—almost impossible—not to stare at it.

"I bet you this isn't the first time you saved me, Jim." Filled with gratitude, she reached out and put her hand on his knee.

He'd never really learned how to deal with moments like these, and he was uneasy before her immense capacity to express her feelings. "Well, let's make it the last, shall we? I can't keep up with you, girl."

"You trust me?"

He nodded. "I do, Miss Jamie."

"How high up are you? How much do you really know?" she asked.

Jimbo squirmed, and said nothing. He looked away, evasively.

"How high up, Jim?"

"I can't really talk about that."

"I've seen everything. I know the story. It's all being triggered by the towers—you know about that. I know you do."

"You mean Alaska?"

"I mean Alaska, and the highways of towers lining the ocean floors. The whole system is setting off a series of calamities around the globe. It's almost too late for Planet Earth, Jimbo. Do you hear me? The clock has almost run out." Jamie shivered, deep and violent—to the bone. "I went down to this city. I was there. The whales and these beings down there . . . they've got the resonance frequencies to shut it all down. They can disrupt the system with higher earth resonance patterning—but the sonar and these towers . . . they're killing the whales and dolphins. They're the music weavers. It's drowning out the music, blowing their brains out. It's deliberate. All these 'tests'? They want to block the music."

"What do you mean, 'you were there'?"

"I died in the hospital. I don't know how long, but I was shown the way. I saw them—this beautiful city of lights. I didn't want to come back, but I had to—for them. For the planet. I had to deliver their message. They know you're trying to destroy them, but they don't know why."

"I always thought we were trying to open communication with them . . . I swear. We've had all kinds of remote viewers working on it for so long; they got glimpses, that's all. The government knows they're there. But I never knew the plan was to destroy them." He shook his head in resignation. "Thank god we haven't succeeded."

"They move between dimensions, in and out of time, too—that's why you can't catch them. They're in the love zone, Jimbo. Your radar, the sonar . . . none of that can enter there. It's like trying to hold quicksilver in your fingers."

"What are they doing here?"

"They live here, like we do—they've been here for hundreds of years. But, right now? They're trying to save the planet from being blown apart." She looked despairingly into Jimbo's eyes. "We need to stop the sonar."

"We have nothing running—not even the tracking system."

"I mean, we have to stop the sonar around the globe. I'm talking about the military. Can you get them to stop testing—right now?"

"What military are you talking about? Everybody's working sonar."

"You're not hearing me. Do you have the power to stop all military sonar testing now? Right now? That's why I'm here—that's why I was called. These beings in the colony—they can reverse it, but they need the whales to override those low frequency waves."

"I beg your pardon? You want little Jimbo man to tell the highest powers of the planet to turn off their weapons? Nobody's got that kind of power—the sheer magnitude of it is beyond your imagination. Not even presidents can do that."

"9.3 off San Francisco? There will be another earthquake off Alaska in a few hours. And another, and another after that. They've lost control of their own weapon—it's self-perpetuating now. Look around you, Jimbo. It's your call."

Jimbo leaped to his feet. "I may just have a shot at it. You stay here, though. You have to promise me you will lie down."

Jamie threw the cover off. "I've *been* lying down." She reached for Jimbo's arm, and together they walked back up to the bridge.

He called out to Bobby, from outside the door. "Do me a favor: get a leash on that dog and hold on—he's going to go berserk the minute he sees Jamie. If he jumps up on her, count on it—she's going to fall right over."

"Hold on, Captain, I'm tying him up right now." They waited until Bobby gave the thumbs-up that Fin was secure, and then walked in. "Wow, Jamie, it's hard to believe you're up and running," Bobby said. "We thought we were going to lose you."

Fin, with his heightened canine perception, immediately sensed that Jamie was wounded and weak. He approached Jamie gently, welcoming her back, devoting himself to her. He was careful, protective. He lay at her icy feet, covering her in the warmth of his body.

Everybody was home now.

Jamie was thrilled to see Fin again, too. They were connected to each other, just as they were both connected to the whales and the dolphins.

"Go ahead down to the galley, Bobby. Grab yourself something to eat. Make sure everything's okay downstairs. I need a little private time up here with Miss Jamie."

Bobby took his cue and made a discreet exit.

Jimbo turned on the radio for the first time since he had left harbor, sneaking out under the radar. The news was devastating— far worse than he had predicted. A tsunami estimated at eighteen hundred feet, the largest to ever hit land, had devoured Vancouver Island, completely submerging the most-populated areas, and taking the waterfront with it. All along the northern California coast, up through Oregon and Washington, tsunami waves had moved inland, submerging entire cities, devastating the population— reshaping the world.

Jimbo switched on the tracking system and waited for the communication systems to come back on. He lifted the radio from its hook. "You are not going to say a word, you hear me?" he warned Jamie. "This is my business, not yours."

Jamie promised.

"You just sit there, real quiet. It's your turn to trust me."

He dialed Mat Anderson in Houston, who picked up after only one ring. "Jimbo?"

"Here I am, Mat—alive and kicking. *The Deepwater* is safe."

"Oh my god—I had given up on that possibility. The news is downright overwhelming. Where are you?"

"We're out of trouble, out here . . . a distance from the coast."

"How the hell did you get out? I can't believe you, Jimmy—you are the Ocean King!"

"I decided to outrun the tsunami. Looks like we got out just in time."

"Only you, Captain J . . . only you. What's the damage report?"

"I'm not sure yet, but I think we're still in one piece. We're lightweight out here. Liz disappeared last night—Sam went to find her and I have no clue where he ended up. I hope they made it up into the mountains. Some of the crew didn't come with me." Jimbo took a deep breath. "I have Jamie."

There was a pregnant pause on the other end of the line. "Jamie is with you?"

"Yes, sir."

"How is that possible?"

"Well, you remember last night ... I told you it was too late to visit the hospital? I'm afraid that wasn't the whole truth. I mean, it was too late to visit—that was no lie, but I went out there anyway. I figured I'm still not too old to charm my way past a few nurses and into a hospital ward, right?" Jimbo signaled Jamie to stay absolutely quiet. "I just had this bad feeling about that girl, Liz. She was too good to be true, from the start."

Mat reached for the Rolaids.

"When Jamie was down, lying there going under, she was trying to tell me about the colony. She could hear them—those big ol' whales were the communicators. I was doing my best to keep Jamie from spilling the beans, man. Liz was right there, listening. Doc calls 'Code Red,' and we decide to bring in a copter to get her to the hospital, and before I even know what I'm doing, Liz decides she's the one going with Jamie, without even asking permission. All nice and neat. Now you have to admit, that's a bit of suspicious behavior from a mere intern, wouldn't you agree?"

Mat didn't answer.

"Well, once Jamie was gone, them crazy whales finally moved out and I headed in to port—storm was coming. It's been damn rough out here. I brought the ship in ... had a few beers with Sam ... and the storm was getting crazier by the minute. We put back a couple more beers and, all of a sudden, Sam decides he's in love with this chick, or something. I don't know—I guess we had more than a few beers ... it made sense at the time! Next thing you know, he decides he's going to go looking for her in town—how crazy is that? And I'm sitting there, by myself, and I just had this sixth sense—maybe I been hanging around Jamie too long—but I could just feel something wasn't right."

Jamie gestured, as if she wanted to add something, but Jimbo pointed his finger at her, warning her not to dare open her outspoken mouth.

"So I decide I just have to shoot over to the hospital, and what do you think I find out there? Try to believe this. Just while I'm drivin' up, there's our little Lizzie, watching them lift Jamie into an ambulance and then she gets in with her and they drive her away. Now I know that's not right, so of course I follow not too far behind. The ambulance pulls up outside this psychiatric facility, a few miles from the hospital. And my mind is racing overtime. Why would anybody be locking Jamie up in a place like that? Meanwhile, I'm thinking, 'Who brought this little babe into the operation, anyway?' And then, bam! The light goes on in my head. This is an agent. She's an agent! And now my question for you, boss, is: who is she working for?"

Still no answer came from the other end.

"You there, boss? Who brought this girl, Liz, into the operation?"

"I don't have that information."

"Before Jamie went out unconscious, she told me what she saw. She did what you wanted—she got in touch with the colony, second day out. So, what happened? Why was she dragged from the hospital, unconscious, into a psychiatric prison? What happened in between, with Liz in there, workin' Jamie? I figure Jamie must have been talking."

"What are you tryin' to do here, Jimmy boy?"

"Me, boss? I'm just trying to figure things out."

"What about Jamie? How did you get her out?"

"I guess it's better I don't tell you those details on the phone."

Mat tried to imagine where Emery Wells was, and what he was going to do when he learned, if he hadn't already, that Jimbo had snatched Jamie from his clutches.

"She did what you wanted, all right. Somewhere in between dying on the table and being shot up with god knows what—she's been down there. You hear? She can see it—they're open to her. And she knows how to get us back. We're heading back out there now."

"I'm listening."

"They're moving around out here, all right. Sam saw them—he got two big mother ships on radar, but I shut him down before he could really put things together. They are trying to open communication, Mat, just like we are. Thing is, they're telling her that the sonar is so bad down there, and those ELF waves out of the towers are so powerful, that they can't hold onto their physical forms—they just keep slipping out. They're 'time walkers'; that's how Jamie described them. That's got to be the most ironic thing I've ever heard! We've been blasting the place with sonar, trying to get a fix on them, and we just keep pushing them out!" Jimbo gave a thumbs-up to Jamie.

Mat listened, trying to anticipate where Jimbo was headed.

"Apparently there are several locations in the Pacific. They're willing to come out and show themselves. Five mother ships off the California coast, two up here. But you have got to silence all navy sonar, and all military sonar, if you want contact."

"Are you tellin' me you can see these craft on radar?"

"No, sir, but she can. Jamie can see and hear them. She's ready to serve as a transmitter, man. You just have to get the sonar turned off."

"I want coordinates, not transmissions."

"Boss, are you hearing me? She has got contact. Isn't this why you sent her…why we're out here? She's got the word: silence the sonar, and they will come out of hiding."

"You know what you're asking me to do? We're talking the highest level—that will take time."

"A 9.3-magnitude earthquake has taken San Francisco out. Tsunamis have leveled the whole West Coast. Jamie says another big quake is going to hit Alaska in a few hours. How much time do you think you're gonna need?"

"You have no idea what you're asking me to do, Jimbo," Mat replied.

"I do, sir. You wanted me to deliver this colony—I can do it. I know now there are several installations all around here. They're willing to talk through Jamie—she's their Emissary. But they can't get past these sonar detonations. As long as we're blasting them, we are never going to make contact. It's your call."

Mat said, "I'll get back to y'all," and the line went dead.

"Sure thing," Jimbo said, disconnecting every electronic device on the ship. There would be no further calls. Under his breath, he said to himself, "Sure thing, Mattie, you double-crossin' liar." He knew that was the last time he'd ever be talking to Mat, one way or the other. After forty years of loyal service to the man he trusted, Jimbo knew they'd reached the end of the line. It was not easy turning his back on that loyalty, even knowing that he'd been used all along. It was the end of an ideal, something he believed in—a man for whom he had given his own life and taken others.

"Are you all right, Jim?" Jamie asked.

He looked up at her, knowing how futile it was trying to hide anything from Jamie. "He wants 'coordinates, not transmissions'?" he repeated, incredulously. "Man, Jamie, if Mat is that evil, and I never could see it, well, then, none of my life has made any sense at all."

Jamie was filled with compassion. She could only imagine what he had to work through. "Evil. What drives men to it? People live in so much fear . . . so much ignorance. They're disempowered, distracted by the noise. Very few people can even contemplate the vastness of reality, Jimbo. The unknowable—it's too frightening. When they realize how very small their lives are on this little dot in the infinite universe, they try to hold on to something—anything that gives them a sense of command over their own existence. The dark ones in power—they are afraid of what the light can do. They're afraid of their own lives and even more terrified of immortality."

Fin, who had been quiet all this time, barked.

"Mat is not an evil man. He's just lost." Jamie had the grace to sit quietly, and let Jimbo have the privacy he needed to work through so many suppressed feelings that finally had risen to the surface. Jimbo had been through almost as much as she had, but his was a different trauma—it was a lifetime of karma in the balance.

"I told you about 'Nam. He gave the order, and we took out a whole village of women and children." Jimbo cried, releasing the sadness and guilt he'd buried for so long. "Ling was there. We had to follow orders . . . but I never understood why. We killed so many innocent people. I've never forgiven myself. And now, after all this time, I come to find out he's been waiting to do it again— destroying the innocent, and using me to do it. He's ready to do it all over again."

"Take me to the sanctuary?" Jamie asked, gently, stroking Fin. "They're waiting."

"We're on our way," said Jimbo, wiping the tears from his eyes.

While *The Deepwater* moved steadily forward, bound for the sanctuary, the top management of the world's governments, the Secret One World Order that had taken Planet Earth to the breaking point, called back all military and navy operations—unilaterally, around the globe. All sonar testing, all underwater explosives, were to be ceased immediately, and they were to remain disabled until further notice. Such an order, from so far up that no one, not even presidents, could identify its source, was unprecedented. The enormous war machine that tormented the oceans, and had driven so many whales and dolphins to their death, was momentarily stilled. On hold. Silent.

The admiral of a Japanese submarine, in maneuvers off the coast of Fukushima, stared at his communications officer in utter bewilderment. They both reread the message from headquarters, to be sure they'd gotten it right: the entire fleet was ordered to immediately turn off all radar and sonar equipment, regardless of their position, until "further notice."

In Norway, naval officers at their base in the North Sea went into a preemptive emergency drill after receiving orders to cut all sonar testing across the board.

At the Pentagon, a five-star general stood dumbfounded in the briefing room as he read the top-level security report: cease and desist orders for all military exercises involving sonar anywhere, at all stations around the planet.

No one in any position of military authority was sure whether World War III had just begun, or whether a force from beyond, which they all knew existed, had just taken command.

19

Until We Meet Again

With no equipment running, and only the ship's compass and the stars to guide him, Jimbo headed straight for the sanctuary. He had one crewman minding the engines, one man at the helm, and himself to count on for the safe navigation of the ship. It was almost as if he were sailing out blind and wounded, throwing himself at the mercy of the ocean, and the will of the whales. But he had Jamie's eyes, and he knew she could see for both of them.

Engulfing the coast in its mantle of rage, the storm was behind them now. How much more it would take from the Earth they still could not know. There would be time enough to go back and face the disaster . . . time enough to help rebuild. Up ahead, past the dark clouds that obliterated the light of dawn, the sun would shine again, and it would be clear sailing on through for *The Deepwater.*

Doc stormed in, looking for Jamie. "What am I going to do with you?" he said, like a father scolding a child, knowing there was no containing her. "You are almost the worst patient I have ever had."

"Let me guess," she said, looking at Jimbo.

"That's right—Jimbo takes that prize. But you're a close second. The two of you . . . I tell ya, you're two peas from the same pod."

"Not to worry, Doc. You've done what you can," she replied, cryptically. "I'm stronger than you think."

"I'm not done yet! You're going to lie down, whether I have to knock you out again to put you down."

"Okay, I will agree to that. I'm ready to rest, just don't try to tie me down on the examining table again. That can't happen," Jamie said. "Will you walk me down?" She walked over to Jimbo and put her arms around him. "You're an old soul, Captain James. There's so much I would love to tell you, but I have to lie down now... I have the worst headache."

"Back downstairs," Doc said, worriedly. "Doctor's orders."

Jamie was filled with tenderness. "I'm sure this isn't our first lifetime together, and I know it won't be our last." She kissed Jimbo on the forehead, and went with Doc, who walked her slowly, carefully, back down to the lounge. Fin followed, quietly, in Jamie's footsteps.

Alberto had the galley up again, with hot tea and coffee the first order of the day. How long had it been since Jamie had anything in her stomach? She couldn't even remember. She took her place on the sofa, across from Jimbo's chair, and agreed to lie down there, wrapped up in blankets, under Doc's watchful eye. He took her blood pressure and was relieved to see it had climbed back up to only slightly under normal, a positive sign. Alberto brought her a cup of raspberry tea, which she drank down with gusto, and then she lay down, her head pounding, slipping in and out of sleep, back and forth in her dreams, swimming with the whales.

Fin never left her.

She awoke to the music of whales: not the cries she'd heard from their despairing hour, but a celebration. This was a symphony in Earth sharp; every instrument in the ocean played it: the waves, holding the rhythms; whales and dolphins, singing the opus of the ultimate symphony; a mysterious melody, emanating from the deep. It played to a different Earth vibration—the unfettered pulse of Earth's own heart, beating.

She waited until Doc was out of sight, and went out the door, onto the main deck, wrapping herself up in the blanket. Fin followed, quietly. Up ahead of the ship, she could make out the Orcas, just as she had before—when they had first entered the sanctuary. It was as if she were reliving the same exact scene over again. Only now, the frenzy was over.

She walked over to the railing, hypnotically, and peeked over the edge. Sure enough—there was the whale: the great Humpback, looking up at her—calling out. As Jamie entered deeper into a state of trance, she felt the pull of the colony, calling her home. Mesmerized, she climbed up the first rung of the railing.

Fin went ballistic, barking wildly. He pulled at her pant leg, to take her back down, but she was going to jump, intent upon it. The Humpback was calling her, lifting her great fin, as if to wave her forward.

The door from the lounge burst open. Jimbo and Doc ran out.

"For the love of god, Jamie!" Doc shouted.

Jimbo cried out to her. "Aw, man, Jamie, not this way, please."

Jamie teetered with one leg over the railing. She looked back at Jimbo, smiling, and then threw herself into the waves below.

Fin was up on his hind legs, searching frantically for her. He ran over to Jimbo, his master, his friend, torn between that loyalty and the love he'd known since he was a pup, and the destiny that awaited him. In an instant, before Jimbo could even move, before he could fathom what was about to take place, Fin ran back to the edge, climbed over the buoy, and leaped over the railing, into the ocean. It all happened so fast, neither Jimbo nor Doc could possibly have stopped either one of them.

Doc grabbed the buoy and threw it as far out as possible, but they were long gone. Even if they had somehow surfaced, Jimbo knew they didn't want to be saved. They were going towards something, not away.

Something far greater was waiting for them, in the deep.

Once again, Jamie swam alongside the great whale, bathed in the music, coming home. Fin caught up to her, and the mighty being scooped them both up in her huge fin, propelling them into a tunnel—the same one she'd journeyed through in her death, racing towards the light.

There was no struggle. They passed gracefully through the darkness of the vortex, through the depths of the great ocean, and then into the light, where the illuminated city awaited them. Everywhere around them, formless light beings swirled and swayed in the currents, dancers to the symphonic rhythms of the whales' song.

A gateway opened, they floated through it, and then it disappeared behind them.

Doc and Jimbo stood frozen, unbelieving witnesses to what had just transpired. They ran to the edge, to find a stream of whales swimming into the center of the sanctuary. Dolphins, too. The whales' song was so immense they could hear it from the deck, as Jamie had.

Jimbo looked out on the water and there he saw the humpback whale, dancing around in the moonlight. She kept breaching from the deep waters, leaping over and over again in the waves. In the abstraction of all that had taken place, as surreal as it all had been, Jimbo was convinced she was thanking him.

Or was the mighty whale the embodiment of Jamie's spirit, waving goodbye?

Around the oceans of the world, the great whales were in chorus, singing the primordial sounds of the Earth. Uninterrupted by the numbing, deafening sounds of the great drums, they raised the volume of the ocean song to such an all-encompassing intensity that the network of underwater towers began to disintegrate. One by one, they toppled and fell to the ocean floor.

As the frequencies of the whales' song reverberated across the oceans of this great planet, the Alaskan towers and their sister structures around the world—the "great weapon"—ceased emissions. In one mighty, symphonic crescendo, the entire field of antennae started to vibrate, clashing with the song of Earth's own high-intensity fields, bringing the entire network of destruction crashing to the ground, in pieces.

The light-filled vessels of Earth's underwater colonies emerged from the underwater cities in key positions around the world's oceans, sailing along next to the whales. They were free to come out of hiding at last, materializing form in the new harmonics of Earth's oceans.

In the middle of the sanctuary, with no one at the helm, Jimbo and Doc were swept up in the bittersweet wonder that Jamie had left behind, but the sadness lingered. They were in it, so very much a part of what was transpiring, a very important part of the awakening of the new Earth.

As they stood there, in communion, Jimbo was the first to notice a strange luminescence in the water, just off a ways in front of the bow of the ship, closer in than the Orcas still holding position there. He called Doc's attention to it, and they rushed up to the ship's bow to investigate. The light became brighter and they could see an enormous displacement of water ahead of the ship. As in a dream, they saw a mammoth craft rise to the surface of the water. It was pure light, illuminating the ocean for miles.

While two humble human beings watched in utter awe, it shot like a rocket right out of the waves. It hovered over the ship for what seemed like a moment and felt like forever, and then it flew up into the star-studded sky. In an instant, it was gone, as if it had never been and never happened.

Alberto and Philippe rushed out from the lounge. "Did you see that? Oh my god, something shot right out of the ocean!" shouted Alberto.

Doc looked at Jimbo, bewildered and amazed, and so tired. "Do I get to wake up from this dream soon?"

"This is the most awake I've ever been, my friend."

Jimbo reached into his pocket and pulled out his cigar case, which contained the half of a Cohiba that Jamie had never finished, and lit it up. "I'd like to think that whatever that was, wherever it's headed—she's in it."

"Where else would she be?" Doc replied, looking up in sheer wonder. "You delivered her to her destiny."

"With Fin?" Jimbo asked, hoping.

"With Fin, Jimbo." He patted him on the back.

"Huh?" said Philippe. "Where is Jamie?"

"Jamie?" Alberto said, completely perplexed. "You mean she missed that?"

Bobby ran out. "You saw it?"

Everybody nodded.

"God only knows what we are going to find when we go home," Philippe said.

A bright light flickered in the star-studded sky and went out.

Jimbo took a long hit from Jamie's cigar as he searched the stars. "We *are* home, boy. We're home . . . and we are not alone."

Epilogue

Some perceive Earth, and all the life it sustains, as a great conscious being: one mind, one body and soul. Others are so disconnected, they cannot feel the very heart of her, nor hear the song of Mother Nature, which lives somewhere deep within us all, but which, for them, lies buried in silence.

There are those who realize how infinitely small we are in the great expanse of the universe, and how this universe is just as infinitely small in the vastness of the Cosmos of Soul. And there are others, who live in separation, a sensate, physical experience into which they believe they appeared from nothingness, passing through this earthly plane for just this one, brief journey ... to then disappear back to nowhere.

Whether ours is the only celestial life-bearing station in the Cosmos is yet another conundrum seeking resolution, bouncing us back and forth between the poles that define that ambiguous expanse of possible realities we call "human consciousness." More and more of us embrace the idea that we are far from alone in this universe, yet still others deny with vehemence that life, or at least intelligent life, could possibly spring from the same elements that surely exist on countless other spinning wheels, in the great beyond.

Such is the duality of our earthly experience.

Here, on this little blue dot in space, a great drama is playing out for all humanity: the struggle of darkness and light. We have faced it before, and we will surely pass this way again—for, as long as the Earth is plagued with the misfortune of possessing an over-abundance of mineral resources, there will be those who insist on destroying every living thing to exploit and possess those resources. There will be infinite wars fought for the most insignificant reasons, but always there will be healing—a return to harmony. There will be beings of darkness and beings of light, from the Earth and from beyond, drawn into the drama to help reestablish the balance, and right the scales. As there are now.

This dynamic tension is forever threatening to tilt the world to either side, to the dark side or to the light, and there may never be a time of final resolution but, rather, a perpetual, infinite field of opportunity where each of us will choose to build or to destroy, to love or to hate, to give birth or to kill.

The questions of our existence are endless. The answers—for those who cannot see beyond, those who dare not think outside the confines of limitation—lie waiting to be discovered: *the Hidden.* At the bottom of the great oceans, through the eye of a mighty whale, in one's own subconscious, spinning somewhere out in space—the treasure chest lies waiting to be discovered, unlocked, and revealed.

We hold the keys.

If only we will free our minds, and open our hearts.

And listen . . . to the music of the Earth.

About the Author

Often called a "real-life Indiana Jones" by fans and readers around the world, Patricia Cori is an inspiring icon of truth and a living model of the adventurous spirit within us all. An internationally acclaimed author with several best-selling publications to her credit, she is one of the most well-known and established authorities on the realms of the mystic: views of the world and multidimensional reality that challenge the status quo.

She has been interviewed on hundreds of talk-radio and TV programs, including CNN, Coast to Coast FM syndicated radio, the Urban Journal Radio, KJAC Radio Montreal, and 21st Century Radio.

In 2012, she founded the global nonprofit association Save Earth's Oceans, Inc., dedicated to restoring the balance of our fragile ocean ecosystems and saving the whales and dolphins from whaling, slaughter, and exploitation. As president and CEO of the organization, she is determined to raise the consciousness of human beings around the globe to the potential of the human spirit, in order to alter the course of our destruction of the environment and to reestablish the harmony of Earth in balance.

To learn more about Cori's global workshops, events, and appearances, contact her at patcori@tiscalinet.it or visit her website at www.patriciacori.com.